BENEATH THE STONE

BENEATH THE STONE

Typesetting and cover design by Formatting Experts

ISBN 978-1-8382227-3-4
Published by Volker-Larwin Publishing

BENEATH THE STONE

A NICK FISHER NOVEL

ALEX DUNLEVY

NAMED CHARACTERS

Agamémnon . . . . Restaurant owner, Kendrochóri

Alékos . . . . Owner of the kafenío in Kardánes, with Varvára

Aléxia Katzatákis . . . . Mother with scruffy smallholding in Kardánes

Amalía Vernardákis . . . . Daughter of Anna and Manólis

Andréas Katzatákis . . Eldest son of Aléxia, brother of Theodóris and Grigóris

Anna Vernardákis . . . . Wife of Manólis

Chrístos Manikákis . . . . One of Náni's constables

Cora . . . . Eight-year-old daughter of Nikki, in Kardánes

Crispin . . . . Important client of Ogden, Cranfield

Dimítris Galánis . . . . Lawyer to the Katzatákis families

Dimítris Foteinákis . . Chainsaw owner in Kardánes (with tree surgeon business)

Déspina Karagiánnis . . . . One of Náni's constables

Dieter Krampe . . . . German man living in Kardánes

Eléni Fotákis . . . . Aunt ('Mother') of Pandelís and Roúla

Evangelíne Vókos . . . . Mother of María

Franz Engel . . . . Birth father of Heinrich

Gary James . . . . . . British man, married to Janet, with house in Kardánes

Giorgía Fotákis . . . . Wife of Pandelís

Grigóris Katzatákis . . . Youngest son of Aléxia, brother of Andréas and Theodóris

Heinrich Hedinger . . . . Grandfather of Lukas, husband of Ilse

Ilse Hedinger . . . . Grandmother of Lukas, wife of Heinrich

Janet James . . . . . British woman, married to Gary, with house in Kardánes

Jason Buckingham . . . . Nick's son

Jen Buckingham . . . . Nick's ex-wife

Julia . . . . Roúla's personal assistant at Ogden, Cranfield

Kiki . . . . Eléni's name for her dead sister

Kóstas . . . . Owner of the kafenío in Saktoúria

Krónos . . . . Son of Agamémnon

Lachlan . . . . Roúla's junior at Ogden, Cranfield

Lauren Fisher . . . . Nick's daughter

Lech Borkowski . . . . Polish man living in Kardánes, married to Monika

Leftéris Katzatákis . . . . Brother of Yiánnis

Lena . . . . Swedish artist and sculptor living in Saktoúria

Leonídas Christodoulákis . . . Second Lieutenant in the police, Chaniá Prefecture

iv

Lily . . . . Receptionist at Ogden, Cranfield
Lukas Hedinger . . . . Grandson of Heinrich & Ilse
Manólis Vernardákis . . Chainsaw owner living in Kardánes, married to Anna
María . . . . Sofía's cousin in Kardánes
Márkos Papatónis . . . . Chainsaw owner and farmer in Kardánes
Matéo . . . . Three-year-old son of Nikki (aka Mati)
Michális . . . . One of Náni's older constables
Mísha . . . . Dog belonging to Cora & Matéo
Monika Borkowska . . . . . Polish woman living in Kardánes, married to Lech
Náni Samarákis . . . . Investigations Sergeant, Réthymno Prefecture
Nick Fisher . . . . Former DCI with the Met, now living in Crete
Nikki . . . . Owner of house in Kardánes, mother of Cora and Matéo
Níkos Antoníou . . . . One of Náni's constables
Pandelís Fotákis . . . . Eléni's nephew
Roúla Fotákis . . . . Eléni's niece
Samantha Martin . . . . English girl who died the previous year
Sofía . . . . Nick's housekeeper
Stávros Theodórou . . . . . . Lieutenant in the police, Réthymno Prefecture
Stéfanos Makrís . . . . One of Náni's constables
Stélios . . . . Fisherman based in Plakiás
Theodóris Katzatákis . . . Middle son of Aléxia, brother of Andréas and Grigóris
Tzíka . . . . Malinois police dog (K-9)
Vangélis Theodorákis . . . . Police constable and dog handler
Varvára . . . . Owner of the kafenío in Kardánes, with Alékos
Vasílios Andréou . . . . Owner of house in Kardánes
Werner . . . . German soldier who was kind to Eléni
Xará . . . . Kóstas's teenage daughter in Saktoúria
Yiánnis Katzatákis . . . . Brother of Leftéris
Yiórgos . . . . Fisherman-philosopher from Saktoúria

PROLOGUE

Snorkelling was always a problem for her. There was something odd about her face. Something non-standard – perhaps the knobbly bridge to her nose – because every time she tried, the mask filled with water and she would choke and splutter and tear the damned thing off, exasperated. Every single time. She bought several masks. Once, he even took her to a specialist divers' shop, where a tanned, young Greek with clear, blue eyes persuaded her to part with forty-eight euros for a special, adjustable one. The intensity in those eyes could have persuaded her to do most things, mind you. The mask was reassuringly expensive, but it was no better. In the end, she gave up. He would have to snorkel on his own.

But then, a new type of mask emerged. It resembled the visor from a space helmet, and it covered the whole face. That nose of hers would no longer get in the way. And no more breathing tubes in the mouth. Air came through a valve in a rigid plastic tube which extended backwards from the top of the mask. And that kept the viewing screen clear too, they said. In the run-up to the holiday, he found *Mermaid Aquatics* online and ordered a pair of their *Jusbreathe* masks. When they arrived, he slipped them into the bottom of his rucksack.

*

The temperature reached twenty-eight, the day after they arrived. They drove to a wide beach on the Bay of Messará where a promontory ended in three giant, rock towers. To the west, they could see distant mountains, glistening crystal-white against a deep blue sky, lingering snowcaps melting in the strengthening sun.

The water was colder than expected. They splashed around for a while, then he went to get the new masks. She slipped hers over her head and held it in place as he tightened the straps. It felt strange.

1

Braced for another disappointment, she put her face in the water and started floating, paddling gently with her feet. She tried to rein in her excitement, tested it with more vigorous strokes. It was weird at first, being able to breathe normally. She put her head fully underwater and a tiny bit of water trickled in but then the valve closed and, when she raised her head clear, residual water drained from the base of the mask as it was designed to do.

"I think it might work," she said, in a muffled yell, giving him a thumbs-up.

He hugged her and they jigged around, masks clacking together.

"There's so much I want to show you," he shouted, as they swam off.

They spent the morning in and out of the water. As she grew in confidence, they ventured further out. Even at ten metres, the water was clear, all the way to the bottom. And the new mask gave her one-hundred-and-eighty-degree vision without steaming up. The only disappointment was that there was not a great deal to see. Fish were few and far between.

They found a taverna at the back of the beach for lunch and ordered fresh-grilled kalamária, tzatzíki and Alpha beers.

"I thought there'd be more fish," she said, after a while.

"On the menu?"

"No, in the sea, you idiot."

"You have to go looking in the right places, at the right time. We need to go deeper, get near those rocks. And late afternoon's best. When they come out to feed."

She was not sure he knew what he was talking about. He was so confident, always the ready answer. She liked that about him but knew to add a pinch of salt. Sometimes a whole handful.

"You mean those *big* rocks?"

She was watching waves surge against jagged, sandstone towers. The land must have heaved, centuries ago, thrusting them above the waves, angled and stratified. Geology at its most violent. And they still looked razor-sharp.

"Yes. We'll work our way out there."

"Looks a bit rough."

"Come on! You're a good swimmer. We don't need to get too close and anyway, the wind dies down, later in the day."

"Hmmm."

She remained sceptical, but this time he was right – or perhaps lucky. Later in the afternoon, the wind faded, and some fierceness left the sun, though it was still very warm. The waves subsided.

They snorkelled their way up the side of the promontory, staying close as the water deepened. She saw sea bass, red snapper and smaller, rainbow-coloured fish, the iridescent green predominating. And then a shoal of perhaps twenty pipe fish passed in front of her. *Like tiny swordfish with extra-long noses,* she thought, smiling to herself. *Pinocchio, telling lies.*

By now they were nearing the giant rocks and battling the swell, but she found she could cope. Beyond the third rock, he ventured out further, enthralled by the underwater rock formations, while she sought calmer waters on the far side of the promontory. Some weed was gathered there, and the water was a little foggier, but silver was flashing urgently ahead of her. She realised she was looking at a much larger group of fish in one small area, pushing up against an overhang, near the surface. Her heart beat a little faster as she moved in. As fish left the pack, others swooped in, racing past her head. She drew closer.

He was absorbed in the rock structures when something made him turn around. Had he heard something? And then he saw her. Twenty or thirty metres away, she was in the shadow of the middle rock. Her arms were batting water, legs kicking violently away from the rock. Something was wrong. She was trying to get away from something. Desperate to escape. Without hesitation, he raced through the water to her. He saw her legs still kicking but now she was trying to tear off her mask and, as he got closer, he heard muffled cries. He seized her shoulders and felt her body recoil. She turned then and tried to fight him off in panic. And then he saw. Her mask was spattered with vomit, her eyes wide, pleading. She was choking. Quickly, he loosened the straps from the mask, and she was able to rip it off. Then she vomited again and coughed violently. He held her close. She was shuddering.

"It's all right. I've got you. You're okay now," he said.

But she was shaking her head slowly. And the terror was still in her eyes. She tried to speak but took in a mouthful of seawater. She prised herself free of him. Now, she was pointing across and down, towards the rock, looking terrified and helpless. Then she swam off sideways, trailing her mask. He went to follow, but she waved him back, seemingly unable to speak. He waited while she swam off fifteen metres and began treading water. She looked a little less shaky now. She should be okay for a minute.

He turned back towards the rock and ducked under. He soon saw the gathering of silver fish. As he approached, they scattered. He saw ragged, pink tendrils gathered in a tight cluster, but the background made no sense. It was not growing out of the rock, but out of some dark, amorphous mass caught under the overhang. He swept the remaining fish away, saw some feeding at other points. A larger fish was tussling with something which it finally managed to tear away. Bile rose in his throat. His heart lurched, then raced. And then came the sickening, gagging realisation as his eyes ran over the form before him. He saw what resembled an umbilicus. Then something paler, waving below a darker area.

This was no plant. He was looking at a body. Or part of a body. A human neck from which the head had been brutally severed. The fish were feasting on the flesh of the neck and from each point where all four limbs had been hacked off. It was a torso. Dark, bloated. Some body hair, no breasts. A male torso. Something that used to be human.

CHAPTER 1
NÁNI

Náni was pleased with herself this Monday morning. Proud, even. It felt good to be a proper detective, at last. Investigations Sergeant Samarákis was a mouthful, but with a fine ring to it. The years in Athína paid off in the end but now, as she gazed out over the beach area and the Venetian fort, she felt thrilled to be back in this friendly, vibrant, little city.

She spent half the morning meeting her small team of constables, one-on-one and then as a group, to tell them a little about herself and what she expected of them, which was plenty. Honesty, loyalty, commitment. Working smarter. Working as a team. Keeping her informed, always. Only one female in the group, she noted with irritation. She would need to do something about that in due course. But they seemed a keen bunch; well-meaning and surprisingly respectful. She was just thirty-two herself, with no track record in Réthymno, so she felt no right to their automatic respect. Perhaps the aura of the capital had crossed the Aegean with her. If so, she was happy to benefit from any halo effect.

The alarm on her watch beeped twice. It was time. She crossed the open-plan office, fielding one or two knowing smiles, and knocked briskly on the door before entering.

The Lieutenant looked over his spectacles.

"Come in, Sergeant. Have a seat."

She perched on the office chair, knees together, observing the desk piled high with files, the overflowing ashtray, the dregs of iced coffee in plastic beakers. The man looked unhealthy. He was pale for a Greek, with sunken, black eyes and thinning hair. In his early to mid-forties, she guessed but looking older. Overweight. He pushed the keyboard to one side to make room for his elbows and grinned at her.

"I don't plan on calling you Sergeant for the rest of our lives. It's Anna, isn't it?"

"I'm called Náni, sir." Her eyes were twinkling as she went on: "Am I here for the rest of my life, then?"

"Only if you're *exceptionally* good, Náni. I am Stávros but you can call me Lieutenant."

She said nothing. He looked at her steadily.

"What do you think of them?"

"The team, sir? They seem keen."

"And just out of nappies?"

"I didn't say that, sir."

"You didn't need to. They're young and there's not a great deal to get their teeth into here. Some drug abuse, petty crime, minor sex offences, illegal immigration. Serious violence is rare. They have retained their innocence, you might say."

"No murders, sir?"

"No. Just vendettas. And next month I'll have been here three years."

"Don't they count then, sir?"

"Vendettas? They've been going on for centuries in the wilder areas. There's not much we can do about family feuds. We clear up afterwards, jail the perpetrators but they're fêted as heroes in their villages, martyrs to the cause. And so, it goes on …"

"But there have been other murders in Crete. I'm sure I—"

"There were two in Chaniá, quite recently. The American professor, of course – what a tragic waste that was – and then the young, English girl, down in Síva."

Náni nodded, remembering.

"And in Iráklio, there was the barman who hit the drunken English lad outside the club a while ago and managed to kill him with a single blow. The other English kids who brought gang warfare to Mália and knifed a nineteen-year-old lad over something trivial. In Lasíthi, the crazy farmer who took out his family with a machine gun from the war – and then himself with an ancient Luger. Now, technically, two of those were manslaughter, but people were killed … Not here, though. Not in my prefecture, Náni."

"Apart from the vendettas."

He half-closed his eyes and tilted his head a fraction to acknowledge the point, but he was beaming as if the near-perfect track record were a single-handed achievement. *Like some Wild West marshal who'd cleaned up the town and earned the right to hang up his gun belt,* she thought. Were he to kick out his legs and rest shiny, cowboy boots with jangling spurs on the corner of the desk, maybe light a cheroot, it would not have surprised her.

She thought: *You self-satisfied prick,* but she said: "You've been fortunate, sir."

His face darkened a fraction and he flipped the folksy approach to the back-burner.

"You've been through the outstanding cases with the team, I'm sure. I want you to stay close to those, Sergeant. And put a firecracker up Níko on those burglaries. He's slow at the best of times but he's been weeks on that. Is he getting anywhere? It's on an ex-pat development and I'm getting flak from the Brits in Crete crowd now. They're always a pain, but it's even worse when they have a valid complaint.

"The lad Stéfanos is rather good, by the way. But he loves his desk research and his computer a little too much. Get him out in the field, where you can. I'd like to see what he's made of. But I want your *personal* focus on a case that's just come in."

Náni leaned forward in her seat.

"It seems we've lost a tourist. A Swiss lad, twenty years old. His grandfather, Heinrich Hedinger, reported him missing to the Spíli police at ten thirty this morning, just an hour ago. He was last seen in the village of Kardánes yesterday evening.

"I want you to get down there. Take one of your team with you. Interview Hedinger, ask around in Spíli and Kardánes. See what you can unearth.

"At that age, he's probably sleeping off a skinful of rakí or shacked up with some girl – or boy. You never know, these days. But the tour bus was obliged to leave without them this morning, so he has either been very irresponsible or he could be in real trouble. You need to move on this. It will be a high visibility case with a foreigner involved.

7

The media will pick it up. I'll let you run with it for now, but I may need to get more involved, before long."

"An irresponsible *Swiss* person, sir?"

"I know. Doesn't seem likely, does it, Náni? So, you'd better get down there right after lunch. Stay close. Keep me in touch with every development."

∗

The police station at Spíli was a sleepy outpost. Two burly constables were smoking outside, looking bored. Náni and her constable went inside and found the uniformed Desk Sergeant who, by contrast, looked dapper, slightly built and intelligent. He stood.

"Sergeant Samaráki?"

"Yes – please call me Náni – and this is Constable Manikákis."

"Welcome to Spíli."

"Thank you. What can you tell us, Sergeant?"

"Only what the old man told me."

"Hedinger?"

"Yes. I have him in a room across the hall. He's expecting you."

"Bring us up to speed, then."

"They are here on a coach tour: Hedinger, his wife Ilse and their grandson, Lukas. I didn't know such a thing existed, but it's a history tour of sorts; features places of interest from World War II."

"The Swiss were neutral, weren't they? Why would such a tour interest them?"

"I'm not sure."

"Hmmm. Hardly a twenty-year-old's idea of fun – delving into wartime history on a bus tour with the grandparents."

"That's what I thought, but the trip was Lukas's idea, they told me."

"The very idea of such a tour sounds distasteful. Are they reliving their famous atrocities?"

Her cynicism won a look of reproof.

"It's not like that at all, Náni. It's about understanding and healing. I think it's a good thing. They are mostly Germans, intent on learning

8

what life was like for their relatives here and trying to make sense
of what happened. A thoughtful and respectful group, I would say.
More interested in empathising."

"According to Hedinger."

"Not only him. Over the last two evenings, they left good impressions, here in Spíli."

"They spent a lot of money, I suppose."

A touch of irritation crept into his voice.

"That helps, of course, but it was more than that. They showed humility."

Náni remained sceptical.

"All right, Sergeant. Thank you for that. Let's go and meet Herr
Hedinger."

Their chairs scraped on the wooden floor as they stood and made
their way across the passage to a light-filled room with a table and six
plastic chairs. A deeply tanned, white-haired man looked up and then
stood with some difficulty. He was tall and spare. The Desk Sergeant
made the introductions and they all sat.

Náni was struck by the blue of his eyes. She saw nobility there, but
also warmth. The eyebrows were bushy and sun-bleached.

"I don't speak German and I assume you don't speak Greek, so
would English work?"

Hedinger nodded.

"We are here to find your grandson, Herr Hedinger," Náni said, right
off the bat. "Is Frau Hedinger all right? Wouldn't you like her to join us?"

"Ilse is quite distraught. She is happy for me to tell you everything
we know."

"So, you all arrived in Spíli the day before yesterday, I gather."

"That's right. On the tour bus. We were in the Amári Valley all
day. Beautiful. And then we came here and spent a lovely evening at
Yiánni's taverna."

"And yesterday?"

"Yesterday, most of the group took the Pátsos Gorge trip with the
wine-tasting and the lunch. There is much wartime history in Pátsos
village, I understand."

"But you didn't?"

"No, we decided to do our own thing. Ilse stayed by the pool while Lukas and I set off to walk to Kardánes. As I told this gentleman, my father was stationed here in the war. We know he often visited the village, so Lukas was keen to explore the place. I thought it would be good to spend some time together, just the two of us."

"Kardánes, from Spíli; quite a hike."

"You are correct, Sergeant. It's about seven kilometres and around five hundred metres of uphill climb."

"In thirty degrees heat."

"Indeed. It was a little stupid of me to try. I have always kept myself fit, but I am seventy-six now. In the end, it was too much. I admitted defeat and turned back. I persuaded Lukas to go on alone. We parted company at about four pm."

"And that was the last time you saw him?"

"Yes. It took me two hours to make my way back, then I cooled off in the pool, ate some food and went to bed. I was exhausted. Ilse joined me around nine thirty, she says."

"And Lukas had not returned."

"No, but she wasn't concerned, because he sent a text saying he was joining some new friends for a meal at the kafenío there. She knew he was carrying water and a good torch for the walk back, but obviously, he would be late."

"But he didn't make it back at all?"

"It seems not. When he didn't appear for breakfast, I went to wake him because the tour bus was due to leave at ten. The bed was made up. I called Lukas's mobile right away, but it went straight to voicemail."

"What time was this?"

"About eight fifteen this morning."

"But you didn't file the missing person's report until what, ten thirty?"

"No. My first thought was an accident walking back in the dark, or perhaps he'd stayed in Kardánes somewhere and overslept. I was keen to find him quickly – in time for the bus, with luck. So, I took a taxi up to the village, following our route. I asked the guy to drive slowly while I looked for any sign of him. Nothing. Then, in the village, I spent half an hour asking everyone I saw if they remembered seeing him."

"And did they?"

"Oh, yes. Several people saw him, chatted with him. And they all assumed he left, later that evening."

"What about the people he ate with?"

"I didn't find them."

"Did you go to the kafenío?"

"It's closed in the mornings. I rang the bell, but no-one appeared."

"Did you find anything else?"

"No, so I came back at nine thirty, hoping Lukas had returned in the meantime."

"But he wasn't there."

"No. I spoke to Ilse and then we told the tour manager they would have to leave without us, and then I came straight here."

"Has Lukas ever done anything like this before?"

"Like what? We don't know what he has done, do we?"

"I'm sorry, Herr Hedinger. I meant: is he a reliable, predictable person? Does he do what he says he's going to do?"

"Oh, absolutely. Lukas is not wild like some kids. He's a good boy."

"Do you have a photograph with you?"

He took a phone from the inside pocket of his light safari jacket and started tapping keys and swiping the screen.

"I took a few yesterday, on the way up. They are not good. Lukas is the photographer in the family."

He placed the phone on the table in front of Náni. She saw a fresh-faced young man, blond-haired with sunglasses, standing on a rock above a view of Spíli. He looked young for twenty, she thought.

"Is he tall, like you?" she asked.

"He is *taller* than me. One point nine metres."

"Do you have any photos without the sunglasses?"

"I'm not sure, I can look. Or Ilse may have some. But he has blue eyes, like mine, maybe a little darker, and he wears glasses – ultra-light frames. They don't change his face."

"Okay, you will send this picture to my phone, please. This number is confidential. And send me more without sunglasses, if you can. We will go to the village now."

"Shall I come with you?"

"No, Herr Hedinger. Stay with your wife. Make sure you keep your phone charged and by your side in case Lukas needs to contact you or we have news to give you. In any event, I will give you regular updates."

The police officers sprang to their feet, pleased to be doing something, finally. Hedinger looked a little bewildered at the speed of events.

"Is there nothing I can do?"

"Yes, you can support your family and find those photos for me." Náni looked at him kindly for a moment. "We will do everything we can to find your grandson, Herr Hedinger. I promise you."

CHAPTER 2
NICK

Nick Fisher stood back and admired his work. The paint was a creamy stone colour rather than the ubiquitous white. It looked good, he decided, but he hoped it would dry a little darker.

These finishing touches to the spare bedroom were in readiness for Jason's visit. It was the next stage in their tentative healing process, and everything needed to be right. Since the boy's release, video chats had helped, but this three-week break together would give them time to get to know each other again; to get closer, like a proper father and son.

Nick had paid some rare attention to his appearance. He cut down on the booze, lost a little weight and toned up with swimming and mountain walking. He was browner, leaner and fitter. And he felt good. He felt like a dad it might be *okay* to be seen with, though *cool* might be a bit of a stretch.

He even learned some Greek. He took up Lena's offer of lessons and made steady progress. He could understand the spoken word quite well now. At least he would know more than his son. His efforts won respect from Sofía. Now, she would take the odd break from her housekeeping duties to attempt conversation. This tended to be rather one-sided and often concerned astonishingly morbid topics which seemed quite at odds with her sunny disposition. This morning, she had been bashing around the house, talking to herself for the last hour or so. Now, she appeared at the door and spoke in English:

"You want I do in here, Níko?"

"Not this week, Sofía. No point. But next time, big clean. Okay?"

"For Mister Jason, I know."

"Quite right."

She relaxed and leaned her broom against the door.

"Look nice, this paint."

"Well, thank you. I'm not sure yet. We'll see how it dries."

He started painting again but she was not leaving.

"You know Kardánes?"

"What's that, Sofía?"

"It is village, near Spíli."

"Ah."

"My cousin María. She live there."

Nick braced himself for another harrowing tale of family illness or death.

"I see her yesterday. She say many police in her village, ask questions."

"Oh really?" Nick put down the paintbrush and turned to look at her. "What's happened?"

"They say a young man is missing."

"A local lad? Someone you know, Sofía?"

"No, no. A guy from Switzerland – a tourist. So, I think of you, Níko."

"Now why would you do that?"

"You help the police, maybe. Like before? You find this man."

"Woah, there. You're forgetting a few things, Sofía. I only got involved because my son was arrested for murder, and I worked with the cops at Chaniá, not here. It was all months ago, anyway. They'll have forgotten all about me. And honestly? The last thing I want is to get caught up in some tedious missing person case with Jason about to arrive."

"Is strange village, Kardánes. Communists. Not so friendly. Not like Saktoúria."

"Doesn't sound like they'd have many tourists then."

"No. Why this guy was there? María don't know."

"Well, let's hope he turns up soon. Probably made the mistake of trying the rakí."

"You *joke* with me!"

She punched his arm and grinned, before grabbing her broom and leaving, shaking her head. He picked up the paintbrush and dipped it again. One more wall and he could head down for a swim, followed by a plate of kolokíthokeftédes, a Fix in a frozen beer glass and a chat with Stélios, while gazing at the Libyan Sea from Taverna Apanemía.

CHAPTER 3
KARDÁNES

With Hedinger gone, Náni got straight to it.

"Your constables don't seem to have a lot to do, Sergeant. Shall we get them searching between here and Kardánes?"

"Hedinger already did this."

"A seventy-six-year-old man hangs his head out of a taxi window on *one* of the possible routes. That's not a search where I come from, Sergeant. I want your lads figuring out *all* the possible routes back and walking every damned one of those roads and tracks and checking the undergrowth for at least ten metres each side."

"This will take all day."

"It might take a couple of days, but it has to be done." She was standing over him now, looking hard into his eyes. "I'm not sure you're grasping the urgency of this. A young man is missing. He could be lying injured somewhere. Maybe in pain. Or he could be lost. It's June. It could reach thirty-five degrees today. He will run out of water. He needs our help."

"Tourists disappear all the time, on some whim, and then they roll up again, wondering what all the fuss was about."

"And perhaps he will. Let's hope so. But it worries me that a seemingly responsible, young man goes missing like this. It's out of character for him. And it's messed up their holiday. I don't see him alarming his grandparents like this. I think something's happened."

"Okay, okay." He heaved himself to his feet.

"And you know what it'll be like when the media get hold of this. Frontpage news. Our responses will be scrutinised. We'll need to show we did everything we could."

He raised his voice slightly. "Yeah, yeah. I've got you. Okay?"

"All right. I'll leave you to check the routes, then. We'll go on up to the village. Join us later, if you can."

*

It was a village most people passed by on their way to Lígres beach. You could miss it altogether, as there was only a handful of houses on the main road, but if you glanced left at the right moment, you would glimpse what passed for its main street and a scattering of buildings which looked across to Mount Kédros or down the hill to Spíli. A few had been restored by foreigners with money, but most were dilapidated, stone dwellings cheered by bougainvillea in purple, white or glorious red. Náni noticed a pleasant, stone-paved sitting area under a pair of large plane trees. There was a shrine with a small fountain, right next to the kafenío.

"Pull up here, Manikáki. I'm sorry. I've forgotten your first name."

"It's Chrístos, ma'am."

"Right. Let's go and introduce ourselves."

They saw a group of three older men huddled around an outside table under the trees. They were drinking Greek coffees with water on the side and clacking their kombolói as they talked. A backgammon board lay on an adjacent table. One of them looked up in disinterested fashion but did not speak. Another cleared his throat in a rather disgusting way and spat.

Inside, an energetic-looking woman of about forty was wiping Formica tabletops. Behind the bar, a painfully thin, unkempt man who looked to be in his late sixties gave them a wan and toothless smile.

"Kalimérasas," said the woman brightly, "what can I get you?"

Náni noticed the tiny red spots in her cheeks and the stained apron.

"Nothing for the moment, thank you. We're here on police business." She looked at the tables, hesitating for a second.

"Please, sit. I have finished now." She jerked her head at the man. "My husband, Alékos." He smiled again and tilted his head in acknowledgement. "And I am Varvára."

"Thank you. I am Sergeant Samarákis and this is Constable Manikákis. We are looking for the young man from Switzerland, Lukas Hedinger. I understand he was here last night."

Varvára wiped her chubby red hands on her apron and sat down. Someone must have told her the man was missing as she registered no surprise. Alékos brought a chipped carafe of iced water and three opaque

16

glasses and placed them on the table, before padding back. From the tremulous hands and the rheumy eyes, Náni took the bar to be his natural home. He would be a good deal younger than he looked.

"He was here, yes. He came late afternoon, perhaps five thirty, and sat outside with a Mýthos beer. Alékos talked with him a little. And then he came back with the Polish couple – at seven, maybe? I cook them dinner."

"They live here, in the village?"

Varvára nodded.

"And, how did they get on, do you think?"

"They were serious at first but then, with the wine and the rakí, they were laughing all the time."

"No arguments?"

"No!"

"And what time did they leave?"

"Before nine, but not much before."

"And did you see anyone else with them?"

"A few people came over to say: *Yeiá sas*. Everyone likes the Poles. They are very friendly, and they try hard to speak Greek. But I don't remember anyone else *sitting* with them."

"All right, Varvára. Thank you. Now, I'd like to use this as my base for the day. Would that be all right with you?" She glanced back at Alékos, but it was Varvára who spoke, without reference to him:

"We would be honoured to help the police. You must tell me when you want something to eat or drink."

"Thank you. But now …"

Varvára got the message, smiled hesitantly, and left them to it.

"How well do you know this village, Christó?" Náni asked.

"Not well, ma'am."

"Well, that's about to change. I want you knocking on every door, showing the picture of this young man, which I'll send to your phone. It was taken yesterday so the clothing is the same. Find everyone who spent time with him during the afternoon and evening and ask them to come here to speak with me. I want to make a jigsaw of his time in Kardánes, do you understand?"

17

"Yes, ma'am."

"According to the town hall, there are one hundred and forty-eight residents in sixty-three houses, so it will take you four or five hours, I guess. Text the names of those you are sending me as you go along. I'm particularly interested in anyone who saw him or spoke to him after he left here, so after eight thirty, say. Got it?"

The constable was scribbling furiously in his notebook, but he managed a nod.

"Start by making yourself a checklist of questions and show me before you go. It's so you ask everyone the same thing and don't forget to ask *all* the questions *every* time. That's important. Boring, but important. Right?"

"Right, boss."

"And, if anyone can't make it here in person, have them call my mobile today. Without fail. Got it?"

"Yes ma'am."

"And don't forget the kids. They have sharp eyes and good memories. Try to speak to them, where you can. Not just through their mums and dads."

The constable looked a little overwhelmed, but he moved to another table and compiled his checklist. Twenty minutes later, he was on his way, armed with notebook, phone, some spanakópita from Varvára and a bottle of Fanta. It was ten minutes to two.

Náni spotted a pile of incoming mail waiting to be collected and started looking through it. She was surprised to find several non-Greek names, including a Borkowski. She waved the letter at Varvára.

"This would be the Poles, right? Borkowski?"

"He is Borkowski, she is Borkowska."

"And there are other foreign names."

"Yes. We have English, Irish, one Portuguese and one German now."

"That surprises me."

"It's not expensive here, but we are near the south coast beaches, so it does not surprise me so much. Except for the German. *He* surprises me."

"Why do you say that?"

"There is still bad feeling here. Germans are not popular. If you know about the war, then you know why."

"Surely, anyone who cared must be long gone by now."

"People have long memories here, Sergeant. We keep grudges like others keep family photographs; safely stored away. That way they don't fade."

Náni looked for the humour behind her quip but found none. Varvára was sifting through the letters herself now.

"Here. This is him. Krampe."

"Do you have a phone number for the Borkowskis?" Náni asked.

"No, but that letter you were waving? It's from Cosmoté; the bill for the phone. And the kettle has almost boiled."

"Varvára! I'm shocked. Do you read everyone's mail?"

"Not at all, Sergeant, but this is special case: urgent police business, no?"

"Well, I won't arrest you for it, and it would save a little time."

Varvára winked and disappeared into the kitchen. In a couple of minutes, she was back, returning the letter to the pile of mail and handing Náni a scrap of paper.

"This their number. And I make tea, but you can have coffee if you want."

"Tea would be lovely. Then, I will call them."

*

Lech and Monika Borkowski arrived at the kafenío at two forty-five. They looked to be in their mid-forties or so; an attractive, fit-looking couple. They smiled and waved at Varvára and Alékos.

"Here we are again. We just can't stay away!" they called, in accented English.

They ordered a tea for her and a beer for him and sat down with Náni, still chuckling gently.

"Thank you both for walking down. I appreciate it. Shall we talk in English?"

"Really – it's no problem. We want to help. And English is probably best, though we understand Greek quite well now."

"I understand you ate dinner with Lukas Hedinger last night?"

"We know him only as Lukas."

Náni took out her phone.

"But this is him, yes?"

"Yes."

"What time did you leave here?"

They looked at each other, pondering.

"Was it eight thirty? No, a little later. Remember, we got back just in time for your programme."

"But that was after the sunset."

"Ah, yes."

Náni saw Monika place her hand on his arm.

Lech turned back to Náni:

"The sunset was spectacular last night. We just stood and stared for five minutes, so maybe it was around eight forty we left here."

"Did Lukas go back with you?"

"No. He was facing a long walk, so we parted in the street here, just outside."

"You didn't offer to drive him back?"

"No, Sergeant. We enjoyed plenty of Alékos's wonderful wine and then some rakí. It would not have been a good idea. And he's a fit, young man. It's downhill from here, and he had water and an excellent torch."

"Was the young man drunk, would you say?"

"We were all tipsy, for sure, but we were not falling-down drunk." He leaned forward and lowered his voice. "Don't tell anybody, but the rakí here is not as strong as Alékos would have you believe."

"It doesn't seem to have done *him* much good."

"No, but this is years of dedication, believe me."

"So, did you see which way Lukas went?"

"Up the hill here, then he would have turned right, past the church, to head down towards Spíli."

"Did you see him take the turning?"

"No. We'd walked away ourselves by then, up our own hill. You can't see around the corner."

20

"So, he could have carried on, past the turning?"

"Up the hill? Why would he do that?" asked Monika.

"I've no idea, Ms Borkowska, but perhaps I shouldn't rule it out."

"He didn't say he would do that."

"But he could have."

"Yes," they chorused, looking doubtful.

Náni went on to question them about their evening and their impressions of the young man.

"He is a serious, rather intense fellow," said Lech. "Don't get me wrong. He's a nice enough guy, but he lost his parents already and I think this has made him more serious than most young men of his age."

"Until the rakí, at least," said Monika.

"Sure. He loosened up then, but earlier he was asking about the history of the village. He asked a lot of questions about things we don't know. We are from Warsaw. We lived here just four years. We don't know stuff from way back.

"I think he latched onto us because we speak German and English and now a little Greek. His English was good, but not his Greek. And most of the villagers speak only Greek. He took many photographs, but he found very few people he could talk to."

"Luckily for him, perhaps," said Monika.

"Why say that?" asked Náni.

"They don't much like Germans here. It's not like down at the coast. There is still bitterness from the war. I don't think they'd appreciate this guy – who *looks* very German – asking questions about the war in that intense way of his. Maybe it was better that the language defeated him."

"What was he asking about the war?"

"His grandfather—"

"*Great*-grandfather," corrected Lech.

"Sorry. Yes. His great-grandfather was a corporal with the occupying German army. They were stationed near here. Lukas has been digging into his family history. What did he call him, Lech?"

"Er …" Lech blew out his cheeks and widened his eyes.

"Ah, wait," said Monika. "I remember now. It was Franz. He called him Franz."

Náni noticed a small group waiting at the entrance to the kafenío. She thanked Monika and Lech and checked her phone. Sure enough, a text from Chrístos listed five names. It looked like four of them were already outside.

CHAPTER 4
EARLY PRESSURE

The rest of the day in Kardánes was frustrating. Chrístos found a total of six people who admitted to speaking with Lukas and all dutifully turned up at the kafenío for a brief interview with Náni. The trouble was, all of them met him between five thirty and seven. No-one was able to shed any light on his movements after he left the kafenío. None of them took exception to him. In fact, they found him charming and were flattered by his interest in their village. Two of them mentioned photographs, Náni noticed. It seems he took a lot.

By eight fifteen, Náni was ready to call it a day. Chrístos had returned over an hour earlier and all the short interviews were now complete. She checked with the Sergeant in Spíli, but he was long gone. A constable confirmed what she already suspected. No trace of Lukas was found on any of the routes down and yes, it was a thorough search, he assured her.

They thanked Varvára, waved to Alékos at the bar and made their way back to the car. Birds were fighting for roosting places and the sky was turning pink. There was wood smoke in the air.

"Have we learned nothing useful, Christó?" she asked. "Has it been a complete waste of time?"

"There are days like this, boss. Days when you might rule a few things out, but you don't learn anything new."

"I know. Shitty days. And I prefer ma'am to boss."

She slammed the car door.

"If we could at least determine whether Lukas went down the hill as he was expected to or up the hill for some reason, we could focus our search."

"There's not much up the hill. Perhaps another ten buildings on that lane, a handful on the other side. The village is mostly below the kafenío."

They were just coming into Spíli now. Náni slapped her hand on her leg.

"Stop the car, Christó," she said. "Look."

The street faced west. Crimson, magenta and yellow streaks covered half the sky now. The sun was a fiery ball, suspended above the horizon.

"It's beautiful, Sergeant, I know."

"No, look at the tourists, Christó."

"The ones taking photographs, ma'am?"

"Exactly. What time is it now?"

"Eight thirty-nine."

"About the time Lukas left the kafenío. The man Borkowski commented on the extraordinary sunset. Perhaps Lukas went up the hill to catch it. You know – that moment when the sun slips below the horizon? Like these people, everyone loves to take that."

"Why not take it from where he was?"

"Because the kafenío is surrounded by village houses and trees. He wants an uninterrupted view. Remember, he's downed a few drinks. These are his last few minutes in the village his great-grandfather knew so well. He's twenty years old. He's romanticised this guy's life. Hero worships him a little, in all probability. It's a powerful moment for Lukas. It's worth walking a few metres in the wrong direction to capture such a moment, wouldn't you say?"

"Maybe." Christos did not sound convinced.

"It would explain why the Spíli guys found nothing on the routes down. He didn't go down. He went up," she said.

"He wouldn't have gone far, just for a snap."

"How far is the top of the village – the last house?"

"Maybe a hundred and fifty, two hundred metres. There's a small farm beyond that, then nothing till you get to Drimískos."

"Did any of the people you sent me come from that part of the village?"

"No. Nobody around there saw him, they said."

"All right. Tomorrow, first thing, I want you to make a list and draw me a map. Go to the town hall if you need to. I want to know who lives in every one of those houses between the kafenío and the farm."

*

The atmosphere in the Réthymno station the next morning was not the same. Náni felt it as soon as she walked through the door. There was danger in the air, a new urgency. She could smell perspiration along with the coffee. She sensed pressure, too, maybe stress. As if a major bollocking had been handed out. The Lieutenant's office was empty.

"He's with the boss, ma'am," said Déspina, the female constable.

"The Captain?"

"No, ma'am, The Brigadier-General."

"Wow. What's happening?"

"I don't know, but he's been running around, looking stressed out. There must be something going down."

At that moment, the Lieutenant barged through the swing doors.

"Náni – my office, now."

She followed him in. He threw his jacket onto a chair and sat on the edge of his desk, drumming his fingers. She remained standing.

"We have a problem. The Captain's going to be out of action for some time. Months. He's been diagnosed with a serious lung condition. I've been asked to deputise for him."

"Congratulations, sir."

"I'm not sure they're in order, Náni. It means a lot more stress and no more money, at least for now. And I'm going to have some major cases dumped on me."

"Sounds exciting."

"I'm sorry to spring this on your second day here."

"Well, it's not your fault, is it, sir?"

"No, but I'll need to lean on you, Náni. A lot. You'll have to handle the Lukas Hedinger case. And, the way things are in this country, you know better than to ask for more resources, I hope?"

"I can cope, for now, sir."

"Let me know if you hit problems."

"Sir."

"And good luck, Náni."

"Thank you, sir. You too."

*

She had wanted to reassure the Lieutenant, but she felt apprehensive, to say the least. This was a lot to take in on day two. The first thing must be to brief the team. Let them know that she, in turn, would need to rely on them through this period. They would need to take responsibility, manage their cases like grown-ups. Cope.

Their reactions were a window to their souls, or at least their attitudes. Most relished the challenge, happy to be their own boss for a while. But two of the older ones took it as another blow to the punch-drunk; one more wound inflicted by a poorly run, under-resourced service that did not give a damn how hard their jobs were becoming. This kind of attitude irritated the shit out of her, but she kept that to herself. She understood things were tough, but she needed them to step up, for her. It would not be for ever. She promised to be available for them as much as she could.

Next, she called Hedinger.

"Have you found him?" he asked, in a tremulous voice.

"No, Herr Hedinger. Not yet, I'm afraid. I just wanted to update you with what we've been doing."

She went on to explain about the searches of the tracks, the door-knocking in the village and the interviewing of those who admitted meeting Lukas.

"I am getting frightened, Sergeant. It's been almost two days."

"We'll be back in the village today, asking more questions."

"What about hospitals? Have you checked? Maybe he hurt himself and someone took him in."

"We are checking that, but surely any rescuer or hospital would have made contact somehow? He's carrying plenty of ID, I believe."

"Yes, he is."

"And you've been trying his phone, Herr Hedinger?"

"Still voicemail."

"Tell me, I remember you saying Lukas is *the photographer in the family*. Would you describe him as keen?"

"Oh, have I not mentioned that? How stupid of me. Yes, he is very keen. And rather good."

"Just on his phone, like the rest of us?"

"Oh, no. He has a phone, but he also carries a camera with him. A rather good one. We helped him buy it last year."

"Do you recall the make?"

"It is a Nikon. I think an SLR? Digital, of course. I can't remember the model number, but it was over five hundred euros. Why do you ask? You haven't found it, have you?"

She could feel his desperation. He was clutching at any straw.

"No, Herr Hedinger. We found nothing, as I said. I'm just exploring an idea. I'll let you know if it comes to anything. It's a long shot, no more. One other thing. I assume his toilet things are still in his room?"

"I imagine so."

"Please use a pair of tweezers and pop his toothbrush and a hairbrush or comb, into separate, clean, plastic bags for me, without touching them, then take them around to the Spíli police station along with a piece of Lukas's clothing. Make it something he has worn recently which has not been washed, perhaps a tee shirt or a vest, also in its own clean, plastic bag. Ask the Desk Sergeant to keep the bags there for me. Would that be okay?"

"This is for DNA?"

"Yes, or if we decide to use a dog to help with the search."

"A dog? I see. Yes, I'm sure I can manage that."

Hedinger was silent. She sensed his hopelessness. Imagined him picturing the dog unearthing his grandson's body. When he spoke, his voice was heavy with weariness.

"Ilse and I are grateful for your efforts, Sergeant. We will remain in Spíli. Please keep us informed and let us know if there is anything else we can do."

She ended the call, stood and looked out of the window. *He was being kind to her, but she was getting nowhere. Letting them down. Letting everyone down. Perhaps she would never find him.*

"Déspina! Where the *hell* is Chrístos?"

"He's out, ma'am."

"I can see that, Constable. Where is he?"

"I think he said the Records Office?"

"Ah, yes."

She got herself some coffee and tried to calm down, remember the method. Then she walked around her team, sitting with each of them for a few minutes, talking through their workload, giving a nudge here, a kick there, but her eyes were flitting between the clock and the door. She needed to get back to Kardánes.

CHAPTER 5

THE DEEP END

Christos finally appeared at ten past eleven. He dumped his notes on the desk along with several paper bags and two beakers.

"I thought I'd grab something from the bakery. We might not have time later," he said.

To small cheers, he lobbed bags with pastries at the three who were still in the office. Náni walked over and sat down.

"You'll go far with that attitude, Constable. Now, what have you got?"

"Tirópita or spanakópita. Usual thing, ma'am."

"I'll take one of each, if I may, but I meant: what have you got on Kardánes?"

He poked the straws through the lids of the iced coffee beakers and handed her one before laying a sheet of paper in front of her.

"This is my attempt at a map."

She saw a square with a *K* and dotted lines forming a *U* shape leading off in two directions. The one on the left said, *up to Borkowski's house etc.* whereas the one on the right swept past a box with a cross on top, after which an arrow to the right said: *down to Spíli 6 km.* Beyond the turning were several more boxes, some shading and some annotation.

"So, here, with the *K,* is the kafenío and, just past the church, this is where Lukas was expected to turn right, yes?"

Náni nodded, her mouth full of spinach and filo pastry.

"If he went *up* from there, as you suggested, he would find just seven more houses and then the farm, way up here."

His finger circled six boxes beyond the church, then jabbed at a larger box almost at the top of the page.

"This building is two houses," he said, pointing to the first square on the left, after the church. "And the next one here is a ruin. Nobody lives there. The last one on the left-hand side is a modern house, set back from the road. It has a garden full of vegetables and a kazáni for making rakí. I know this man. It is Manólis. He lives there with his wife and daughter. They take in grapes from all around."

He paused for a bite of tirópita, then swirled his coffee so the ice cubes rattled and sucked some liquid through the straw before turning back to the sketch map.

"On the other side of the road, the right-hand side, the first house is quite large. One hundred and ninety square metres. It is a restoration of an old Turkish house, I think. Old stones with new concrete. A British couple owns it: Gary and Janet James. I don't know if they are in town. They are not permanent residents. Then, opposite the ruined house, there is a little alley. Here, do you see? If you walk down, you come to a small stone house. This is the house of Eléni Fotákis, a very old lady."

"A widow?"

"I assume so. She lives there alone."

"And this one?"

"The last one on the right is a smallholding belonging to the Katzatákis family. There are four in the house. The father died three years ago, so it is now the widow, Aléxia, and her three sons. There is also a daughter, but she married and moved to Kissós village."

"So, this is not the farm."

"No. They have a few sheep and chickens and olive trees, but it is just a smallholding. The farm up here is bigger. They grow grapes, olives and prickly pears, keep many sheep and a few goats and turkeys."

"And who lives there?"

"A Márkos Papatónis."

"Just him?"

"I think so. He must have help, though. It's a fair-sized place."

"Good work, Constable. Shall we go and knock on a few doors?" She nodded at the last two pies. "Let's take those with us, eh? And we can check out my sunset photo theory while we're at it. Did I tell you he has a serious camera, a Nikon?"

*

They parked outside the church at twelve twenty-five. Swallows and house martins were darting about, chattering. A nut-brown old man

30

was watching a younger man sawing through a plank on trestles, the blue door to a house open behind him.

"Kalimérasas," Náni offered, but he just stared back at them. Perhaps he was deaf. *But even the deaf can lipread a greeting,* she thought. *Even the dumb can wave.*

They walked past the front of the church and what must be the Spíli turning and found the first house on their left. It was a dilapidated, old, stone house, divided in two. An overweight woman in her thirties was hanging out washing, some of which was children's clothes, Náni saw. She consulted her notes.

"Kaliméra. You must be Nikki?"

"I told him already. I didn't see a thing."

"I know you did, but I wanted to speak to you myself. The young man has been missing for almost two days now. His family are very concerned."

"I'm sure they are."

"This is a twenty-year-old man, rather tall, with blond hair and carrying a camera, we think."

"I saw what he looks like; the constable showed me a photo. I'm not going to miss a tall, blond guy around here, am I?"

"What about your husband?"

"He wasn't even here, Sunday evening. Not till late, anyway. He was taking his mother back to Arméni."

"What do you mean by *late*?"

"After ten, for sure, when he got back."

"And the children?"

"Oh, they're in bed by eight."

"What have you got?"

"One of each. Cora is eight and Matéo is nearly four."

"Can I speak to them?"

"They're out playing right now, with the dog. Up the hill somewhere. You might see them if you're going up there."

"All right. Thank you. Is your neighbour home, Nikki?"

"Dunno. Sorry. You'll have to knock."

Náni turned to Chrístos, raising her eyebrows.

"It's a Vasílios Andréou, ma'am. An older gentleman, a widower."

They crossed the scrappy bit of garden and rang the bell. A solitary young goat started bleating, to the side of the house, but no sound came from inside. They rang again.

"He might be in the kafenío. He spends most of his time there, these days," called Nikki.

They waved thanks and moved on up the lane.

The large house on the right was incongruous. It looked prosperous and smart, unlike the rest of the village. There was a new-looking, green Suzuki Vitara in the drive.

A voice called down from the roof terrace, in English: "Hello there. Can I help you?"

"Police. May we speak with you, Mr – er – James?"

"Hang on. I'll come down."

He let them in and guided them up an external staircase to a tiled roof terrace where a tubby, middle-aged woman stood to greet them.

"Hi. I'm Janet James. Can I get you something to drink?"

"No, thank you."

"Well, at least sit down for a minute."

"Thank you. We're investigating the disappearance of a Swiss man, Lukas Hedinger."

"We spoke to this gentleman yesterday."

"I know you did. I was just hoping I could jog your memories."

"I did see the lad earlier in the day," said Gary James. "I don't think I said, before. I popped across to the kafenío for a beer and he was there, but we didn't speak. He was sitting outside, talking to Alékos, around five, five thirty."

"But you don't recall seeing him later."

"It's not a matter of *don't recall*, Sergeant. We *didn't see him*. I think he went up the other hill, started chatting to people up there."

"And then came back to the kafenío."

"Did he? I didn't know."

"And you didn't see him later, after eight thirty?"

"No, definitely not. We would have been inside by then, eating dinner and watching television."

There was no answer at Eléni's neat little house but Manólis told them she was often at her son's, near Réthymno. Manólis himself, a big, red-faced man, saw nothing. Neither did his long-suffering wife or their charmless, overweight daughter. Just as they were leaving his place, Chrístos grabbed Náni's arm. She followed his eyes and saw two children peering from their hiding place behind a wall of the ruined house.

Slowly, the girl stood up, then the boy. They were looking shamefaced and hanging their heads as if caught in some terrible naughtiness. Then the dog appeared. It was a Jack Russell of sorts and started snapping around the heels of the police officers, barking furiously. The girl rushed over to calm him.

"Stop that, Mísha! For goodness' sake. Heel!"

"You must be Cora," said Náni, "and Matéo? And this is obviously Mísha."

The dog was whimpering now, *longing to sink its teeth into my leg*, thought Náni.

"Who are *you*?" said the girl.

"I am Náni, and this is Chrístos."

"You don't live here, do you?"

"No. We've come to find our friend, Lukas."

"Is he lost?"

"We think he must be. Have you seen him?"

Chrístos held out the phone with Lukas's picture.

"Mister Beaney," said Matéo.

"Why do you call him that?" asked Náni. The girl answered for him.

"He has a bendy toy with very long arms and legs."

Náni crouched to bring her eyes into line with Matéo's.

"Did you see our friend? And did you think he looked like Mr Beaney?"

"Mister Beaney, Mister Beaney, Mister Beaney," he chanted, joyously.

She glanced up at Cora for help.

"What are you talking about, Mati? Was it Sunday night when you kept looking out of the window?" She turned to Náni. "I remember him singing Mister Beaney then when I was in bed and *he* was supposed to be asleep."

"You share a room?"

Cora nodded, making a face.

"Was it Sunday night, Mati?" she asked him again.

This time the boy did a huge nod, first lifting his chin and then bringing it right down, almost touching his chest, hair flopping forward. Then he paused for a second before doing it again, to make sure. Cora grabbed Náni's phone and clicked to re-activate the picture.

"And was it this man? Was *he* Mr Beaney?"

Another huge nod.

"What was he doing, Mati?" asked Náni.

This time Matéo mimed an exaggerated walk, throwing out his arms and legs. Chrístos snorted with laughter.

"Was he walking past your house?"

Nodding and grinning now. *What a great game. What a responsive audience.*

"That way?" Náni held out her left arm, pointing, "Or this way." She did the same thing with her right arm. But he looked confused. Cora rolled her eyes.

"Doh!" She used her forearms like ramps. "Was he going up the road or down the road, dummy?"

The boy held his right arm like a ramp, copying his sister, and traced his left forefinger along it, moving up. He looked very pleased with himself.

Náni spoke again: "So you saw our friend, Lukas, who looked just like Mr Beaney, and he was walking uphill, past your house. Is that right, Mati?"

He was nodding and grinning, his riddle solved. Náni wanted to shout *Hooray* in relief. Instead, she turned to Cora.

"What time would this have been, Cora? Try to be as accurate as you can."

"We were sent to bed at eight, as usual. Then we're allowed half an hour to get into bed and play or read. Mummy came to tuck us in and put out the lights and it was after that."

34

"How much after?"

"Not too much."

"As much as another half hour?"

"No, but it felt like forever because Mati was being a total pest."

"No, I wasn't!"

"You were, too. No wonder I'm getting bags under my eyes!"

"Hey! Truce, guys. Come on." said Chrístos.

After leaving the kids, they climbed further up the hill to a tatty bungalow to the right of the lane. A dark blue Isuzu pick-up faced out of the drive. Every panel was dented, the right wing crushed and rusted, the front bumper hanging off. It might have been in a Destruction Derby. Stacks of firewood were crammed into the fibreglass carport. The woman who answered the door could not have been more than fifty-five, but she had very few teeth. And she looked like she needed a good shower. Her hair was matted to her head and her skin seemed to be covered in sores and mini eruptions of the flesh. Aléxia Katzatákis saw nothing of any blond man, she said. Her three boys were napping after the morning's work, but she woke them and dragged them, blinking, into the sunlight. All were a head taller than her with dark, curly hair, two with bushy beards, one clean-shaven. The three of them looked strong and quite attractive, in a gipsy way. Náni thought it would be a bad mistake for anyone to get on the wrong side of them and remembered Stávros and his vendettas. Despite their fearsome appearance, they seemed pleasant enough, but they could add nothing to their mother's blank looks. None of them saw a thing, they said.

As they trailed up the steepest bit yet, towards the farm, Náni felt her energy and self-confidence sapping. Apart from the kids confirming that Lukas walked up the first bit of this lane, there was nothing to show for their efforts but a growing collection of head shakes and blank looks. Where on earth did the man go?

No-one answered the door to the farmhouse, but then a tractor swung into the drive and a good-looking man of about forty smiled faintly at them and stepped down.

"Yeiá sas," they said.

"Yeiáaa."

"O kýrie Papatóni?"

He raised his eyebrows and tilted his head, by way of confirmation. Then he narrowed his eyes and peered at Náni, or perhaps he was just squinting in the sun.

"How can I help you?"

Chrístos reeled off his usual questions and Papatónis was all exaggerated courtesy and charm. He seemed genuinely sorry he was unable to help.

"Do you have a card perhaps, Sergeant? I will keep my eyes open and call you if I see anything."

"I don't have one yet, but I can give you the number of the police station." She scribbled the number on a sheet from her notebook and handed it to him.

"Náni, is it? Okay, I will watch out for this poor man, Náni, and help in any way I can."

"Perhaps you could look in any outbuildings for me? Just in case he is hurt and took refuge there?"

"First thing I did when I heard he was missing. He's not on my land, I assure you."

As they made their way back down the hill, Chrístos said:

"He seems like an okay guy."

"Does he have a wife?"

"Are you interested then, Sarge?"

"I already have someone thank you, Constable, and, by the way, that was a completely inappropriate remark."

"Sorry, ma'am. His wife left him; I believe. No kids."

They lapsed into silence for a few moments. Now they were passing the Katzatákis house again. Then Náni spoke:

"The view from here is impressive."

"Hmmm."

"Nothing in the way."

"But there was no need to come this far up."

"Not quite this far, no."

Mísha barked at them again but thought better of attacking. And the louder the dog barked, the more it edged its quivering, little body backwards, in fear. They ignored it. Náni looked for the kids, but they were out of sight somewhere.

Towards the bottom of the hill, they saw Nikki again. Náni pointed at the house next door with a question on her face and Nikki jerked her head at the kafenío with a resigned look on hers. They exchanged tight smiles.

At the kafenío they found five men playing cards. Varvára pointed out Andréou, a small, white-haired man with a moustache. He did not appreciate being separated from his comrades.

"What's this all about?" he demanded, and Chrístos explained again.

"You interrupt my game because some bloody Nazi's disappeared? So what? Good riddance, I say."

"The man is a Swiss national, kýrie Andréou," said Náni.

"Don't give me that. We know a German when we see one," he said with venom and spat. His four friends were staring back, unsmiling. Only the rattling of their kombolói and the hissing of the cicadas relieved the stony silence.

Chrístos moved his eyes to indicate they should leave, but Náni was not finished.

"Herr Hedinger *happens* to be Swiss, but his nationality makes no difference under Greek law. Nor to me. Nor in the way the law is enforced, here in Crete. Be in no doubt, gentlemen, if this young man has come to harm, the culprits will be found and punished to the *full* extent of that law. I promise you."

She made eye contact with each of the men, then turned on her heel and strode away. The constable followed. After a few metres, they heard dark laughter behind them.

CHAPTER 6
A CRY FOR HELP

Náni was fuming all the way down the hill, but somehow, she remembered to pick up the plastic bags Hedinger left at the police station. They stopped for a quick snack in the garden at María-Kóstas taverna and she checked her phone while they waited. It was almost seven thirty. There were two messages. One from Hedinger with two more photos of Lukas, who looked even younger without sunglasses. The other was from the Lieutenant: *Call me as soon as you get this.*

Chrístos was about to order some food when Náni touched his arm. "Just a minute, Christó."

She waited while the waitress went away, then punched the keys.

"I need you to get over to the morgue," said Stávros without ceremony. "A body has been found at Triópetra. The ME is bringing it back. It's young, white male – could be your missing lad."

"Drowned, sir?"

"Hardly. Mutilated and dumped at sea, poor bastard. So, it's going to be a murder, damn it."

"Ah, tough luck, sir."

"How strong is your stomach, Náni?"

"I'll cope, sir," she said, but she could feel dread building inside, and not just of seeing a mutilated corpse. Everything seemed to be spiralling out of control, already.

"Are you still in Spíli? Can you pick up something, for DNA?"

"Already bagged up sir, just in case."

"Good thinking, Sergeant."

"We'll be on our way then, sir."

She ended the call. Chrístos was waiting expectantly.

"We have a body. It could be our young man." She was conscious of a shrillness creeping into her voice.

"Do we have time to eat something, Sarge?"

"Sorry, no. But I think you might thank me for that."

*

It was after eleven that night when Nick's phone rang.

"Nick? It's Leo. Leo Christodoulákis."

The sound of his voice took Nick right back to the smoke-filled office in Chaniá, seven months before.

"Whoa! Long time no hear, Leo. What brings you to call?"

"I'll come straight to the point. When I worked in Athína, there was a bright, young, Cretan woman in my team: Náni Samarákis. I could see potential there. I suppose I took her under my wing. She just got made up to Investigations Sergeant, based in Réthymno."

"So, you were right."

"I just got off the phone with her. She's a tough cookie but she's landed a monster, right at the start of her new assignment. What started as a missing person case has morphed into a gruesome killing with all the hallmarks of a gangland slaying. The body has been dismembered and so far, only the torso has been found. They're waiting for DNA results but worried it might be this missing Swiss lad. Whoever it is, it's going to be a murder."

"Sounds like an exciting break for an ambitious young cop. Anyway, someone more senior will get involved soon."

"Not going to happen, Nick. Not unless they send someone from Athína. Resources here are hopelessly stretched. Have been for a while. And now the Captain at Réthymno has gone down with cancer and the Lieutenant is out of his depth. It wouldn't take much to overwhelm that idiot, mind you. So, yes, Náni is excited, but she's also shit-scared. She wants to take it on, but she doesn't want to screw up and wreck her career just as it's getting started. I guess that's why she got in touch."

"So, you called me."

"It just seems ideal, Nick, if you're interested. She needs close support from someone with seniority and experience and she could get

39

that from you without having to give up the case. I might even be able to get you on the payroll this time. I think they might stretch to a hundred a day, plus expenses?"

"Wowee. And what does Náni think of that idea?"

"I wanted to speak to you, first."

"So, you haven't told her. Or her boss."

"Not yet, but it's a perfect solution for everyone, don't you see?"

"It's not perfect for me. My son's coming to visit."

"Jason? Oh, that's great, Nick. I'm happy for you. When's he coming?"

"In less than two weeks."

"You could have it wrapped up by then."

"Fat chance of that and you know it."

"I thought you were keen to get involved again if an opportunity arose."

"What's she like, this Náni woman?"

"Bright, dedicated, impatient. Like we used to be, Nick. Early thirties. Bit of a ballbreaker. Doesn't suffer fools gladly."

"Oh, joy! Does she have a sense of humour, by any chance?"

"I'm sure you'll find it, Nick."

"All right. This is the deal. If – and only if – you get her and her boss *thoroughly* on side with this, I will make myself available at the irresistible daily rate offered, but I'm *not* going to let my son down again. No way, Leo. When his visit starts, I'll need to be with him. That's not for negotiation. You know the history. You know I can never let him down again."

"Understood, Nick. Thank you. I'll get back to you tomorrow."

Nick put the phone down and stared out at Jupiter, the newish moon and the countless stars of the Milky Way. *I should have said No*, he thought. But that irresistible excitement was burning bright, outshining the guilt. His pulse was already beating faster.

Leo was back in touch late morning Wednesday. It was all agreed. Nick was to report to the police station in Réthymno at five pm and ask for Sergeant Samarákis.

CHAPTER 7
ROUGH CUT

The Medical Examiner called Náni just after noon on Wednesday.

"Thank you for the hair samples, Sergeant. We must wait for DNA test results to confirm the identity, but what I can tell you now is that the body is a young male, eighteen to twenty-five years old, in good health. The skin on the torso is dark because most of the blood has pooled there, but there are still patches of unaffected skin, enough to show the natural complexion was pale. Along with the blond hairs, this makes me think he was Northern European."

"So, he could be Swiss."

"Swiss, Austrian, German, Dutch, maybe Scandinavian. Any of those. Do you have any more bits for me to play with?"

Náni was taken aback. The woman's gravelly voice sounded ghoulish almost; inappropriate.

"We found nothing more in the immediate area."

"No, well they would have removed the head and limbs to hinder identification so they would be damned stupid to dump everything in the same place."

"They were stupid enough to let the torso float to the surface."

"True."

"How long ago did he die, Doctor?"

"A few days, no more. The immersion makes it difficult to be more precise. What I can tell you is: all the body parts were probably cut away with the same tool."

Náni was on full alert, now. "What would that be, Doctor?"

She heard a Zippo lighter flipped back, the flint wheel flicked and then closed, then a pause as the ME sucked in smoke before responding.

"It's the striations they leave on the bone. You are fortunate, Sergeant. Not many of my colleagues would recognise these. But they are quite distinctive when you know."

"What was it, then?"

"A chainsaw, used post-mortem."

"Oh, God. There must have been blood all over the place."

"There are ways to minimise that."

"How?"

"Time helps. After the heart stops pumping, it doesn't take long for the blood to thicken. But also, the bulk of the blood may have been directed into the torso. That would explain why the skin has darkened so much."

"Directed? Sounds rather pragmatic. Could a murderer be so cool and logical through such a grisly process?"

"Pragmatic, or possibly *psychopathic* behaviour. It's hard for *us* to imagine killing someone and then cutting them to pieces but, for a psychopath, it would barely raise their heartbeat. It might even be an amusing diversion … Or, if not a psychopath, perhaps the person concerned is familiar with cutting up animals. That would have made it easier to get through the job, I imagine. Perhaps a surgeon, a vet or a butcher? Maybe a livestock farmer?"

"But none of those would use a chainsaw."

"Normally, of course not. But who knows the circumstances?"

"All right, thank you, Doctor."

"You are welcome."

"Can you tell me when we'll get the DNA result?"

"Within forty-eight hours, officially. I'll try for late tomorrow."

"Great. Please call me as soon as you have something."

As soon as she ended the call, she walked round to Stéfanos's desk.

"I have a job for you, Constable. It's urgent and important. I want to know everyone in or near Kardánes who owns a chainsaw. Name, address, type and make of saw and when and where bought."

"There's no licensing requirement, ma'am."

"I'm aware of that. You'll need to contact all the local stockists from Réthymno to Agía Galíni, get them digging into their records. Go and see them where you can, rather than phoning. Impress on them the need for confidentiality. Use that research brain of yours. Get me the best list you can by tomorrow night."

"I'll do the best I can, ma'am, but if they paid cash we'll get nowhere."

"These things can be three or four hundred euros, so cash is less likely, but even then, the vendor may recall the buyer. These are small communities, Constable. Ask, ask and ask again. Do your best for me. But don't go asking in Kardánes. Not yet."

*

The Lieutenant's remark caught Náni off guard.

"I'm sorry, sir, who is this guy?"

"He's a retired British police officer who lives in Crete, Náni. He was a Detective Chief Inspector in London and comes, strongly recommended, from your old boss, Christodoulákis. He helped him solve that case in Chaniá last year – the English girl, Samantha Martin."

"Leo didn't tell me he was doing this. I thought this was *my* case, sir."

"That's just it, Náni. This is a way of *keeping* it yours. Fisher will work *with* you, alongside you, but we will retain control. He is not to act independently; he is part of *your* team. And I think he could make a huge difference. You know we're stretched here. With him on board, there's a chance we can keep the case rather than having someone from Athína foisted on us. If all goes well, we – and specifically *you* – will get the credit for solving a murder of international significance."

"Sir, if it's my case, then surely I get to decide who works on it with me? I'm struggling to see how some ageing Brit is going to help me solve a case in the mountains involving a village full of duplicitous Cretan characters and a dismembered body."

"He's an experienced detective, Sergeant. He can think outside the box. A wily, old dog, by all accounts."

"Well, sir, I have a lot of respect for Leo, so I'll meet the guy, hear what he has to say. But I refuse to be saddled with some incompetent dinosaur just to fix the politics of the situation. With respect, it's my job to solve the crime, not to appease the bosses and their mates."

"Well, if you're not happy to work with this man, I think we'd have to go cap in hand to Athína and ask for someone to come over and take charge. I appointed you to investigate a missing person, not to head up a murder investigation, Náni. It's too much to expect of you, too much weight to put on those young shoulders. I don't want you to crash and burn."

"So, accept him or lose the case, you're saying, sir."

"We might lose the case anyway, in due course, but this looks like the only way I could keep you in charge, at least for now. Just meet the man, Náni. See what you think."

*

When the Desk Sergeant called through, Náni made her way down to reception. She saw a quite powerfully built man in his early fifties, tanned and with thinning, grey-blond hair, a little too long. He was wearing a denim shirt with stone-coloured chinos and boat shoes.

"Mr Fisher?"

He turned and smiled faintly.

"Sergeant Samaráki?"

"I thought we'd get out of the office for an hour, find a quiet café if that's all right with you?"

"Sounds much better, less formal."

"Yes, and, to be honest, I'd prefer to keep you out of sight until we have a firm arrangement."

"Fair enough – and thanks for speaking English with me. You do it very well."

"No problem."

She led them a short distance down, behind the beach, to one of the large cafés which, at this time of day, was almost empty. They sat opposite each other at a red plastic table and ordered frappés, iced coffees.

"So, tell me, Mr Fisher. What do you think you can do for me?"

"Are you *interviewing* me?"

"I need to understand how you can help."

"I was *asked* to help by Lieutenant Christodoulákis, and he said you and your boss were happy with the idea. If that's not the case, I can go back home."

"You're retired, aren't you? Why would you want to get involved in this?"

"I'm not sure I need to explain myself to you, Sergeant. I'm a senior police officer who retired early, only three years ago, with almost thirty years' experience. A few months ago, I helped the Chaniá prefecture solve the Martin case. I've offered my services at a bargain-basement rate and I'm ready and willing to help you solve this case. Take it or leave it. It's all the same to me."

"I need to be sure we can work together."

"I've worked with all kinds of characters over the years. I'm sure we'll get along."

"What is your attitude to women, Mr Fisher?"

"I rather like them. Even married one, a while ago."

"I'm talking about working alongside women."

"I treat women the same as men. If they're good at their jobs – or at least try to be – they will have my respect."

"Sounds a little patronising."

Nick showed the palms of his hands and shrugged.

"I don't know what you want me to say, Sergeant."

"What have you done to help women achieve equality, Mr Fisher?"

Nick sighed inwardly but decided to play the curved ball with a straight bat.

"The only thing required of me, as I saw it. To level the playing field. I truly don't give a damn whether a person is male or female, black or white, disabled or able-bodied, gay or straight or somewhere in-between, I care about how they perform on the job and, to a lesser extent, whether they can work as part of a team."

"What about redressing the balance?"

"Are you serious? If you're asking, *have I given preference to women*, then the answer would be *No*. I'd view that as a strategic decision which wouldn't make much sense at the tactical level."

"Meaning you wouldn't do it?"

"Meaning I'd do it if I were told to, as part of a strategic directive. Otherwise, I'd choose the best person as I saw it. As I always have. Simple as that."

"How is your Greek?"

"Lamentable but improving."

"What about technology?"

"I can use a mobile phone, do an Internet search, drive a car …"

She looked at him steadily as she sucked her iced coffee through a straw.

"What do you know about chainsaws?"

Náni went on to brief him on the case and Nick assumed he must have passed the interview or whatever it was. Either she thought she could work with him now or, more likely, she had no real choice in the matter and the charade was a little face-saving exercise, nothing more. After perhaps twenty minutes, she stopped talking and looked at him expectantly.

"So, we don't know for sure this body is Lukas," said Nick.

"Not yet, but I think it's him."

"Okay. Let's assume it is. Have you told the Hedingers?"

"Not yet."

"I think you should. Otherwise, if they call, you'll have to lie about it. Or they'll think you failed to communicate a highly significant development. Both are undesirable outcomes. You'll lose their confidence."

"I didn't want to upset them if it proves to be someone else."

"I know. But, with respect, that's the wrong decision, Náni. You're a policewoman, not a social worker. They have a right to know what we know."

"You're right. I'll deal with it."

"Okay. So, thinking things through, we have a young Swiss man who has been murdered. No question. People don't dismember the bodies of those who die by accident. Agreed?"

Náni nodded.

"The young man was last seen in Kardánes and we have found no trace of him leaving the village. So, our first premise must be that he was murdered somewhere in the village, sometime after the boy Matéo – Mati – saw him, which was around sunset last Sunday evening. Correct?"

"Correct."

"We don't know *how* he was murdered, so there may or may not be

46

blood at the scene of the murder. We don't know *where* in the village it happened. And we don't know *who* did it or *why*. We do know the body was then carved up using a chainsaw, but we don't know *where* that happened or *who* did it. And, if it wasn't done at the scene of the crime, we don't know *how* the body was taken from the murder scene to the place of dismemberment. Nor do we know *how* the bits of body were then taken to the coast and dumped in the sea."

"We're trying to trace chainsaw owners in and around Kardánes."

"Those things are loud. If they used it in the village, late at night, people would know. Have you asked the question?"

"Not yet."

"Or it wasn't used in the village at all, in which case Lukas was killed in the village and then moved to where his body was cut up, or abducted first, then killed and cut up elsewhere."

"We have so many unanswered questions."

"We do. But don't let that get to you. I think we keep our powder dry on the chainsaw and follow the blood."

"Excuse me?"

"We know a chainsaw was used. They – whoever they are – don't know that we know. They won't even know the torso has surfaced or that it's now a murder inquiry. Let's keep it that way for now. It may give the perpetrators a false sense of security. We keep our focus on the blood. There must be quite a lot, somewhere."

"I thought maybe a K-9?"

"A police dog? Good idea. Can you get one?"

"I'll find out."

*

Náni took Nick back to the office and introduced him to Stávros and those of her team who were still there.

"By late tomorrow we should get a bit more to go on," she said, as they were leaving. "The DNA results, hopefully, Stéfanos will have researched the chainsaws and I will know about the dog. I suggest we meet back here first thing Friday."

47

"And you will speak to Hedinger."

She looked at her watch and saw it was ten past eight.

"Yes. I'd better do it now."

Nick recovered the Jeep from the car park near the beach, fought his way through the sluggish traffic in the city centre and picked up the Spíli road, heading south. It sounded like tomorrow would be the calm before the storm. He could finish painting the spare room in a couple of hours while it was cooler, then use the rest of the day to familiarise himself with Kardánes. He would give Sofía a call first. It would be interesting to see if they could make sense of each other on a phone.

CHAPTER 8
NICK EXPLORES

María was a teacher and spoke English well, according to Sofía. She would expect him at eleven thirty if he could find the house. He parked the Jeep by the church, walked past the kafenío and up the hill. After a hundred and fifty metres, there was an offshoot to the left with four houses. As promised, María's was the modern, yellow one.

An impish-looking woman of about fifty opened the door and grinned. She was even smaller than Sofía and of a slighter build.

"Mr Fisher?" she said, in English. "Please come in."

It was a house devoid of character, a concrete box with aluminium windows, but the rich colours of fabrics gave it some life. An old lady was crocheting in an armchair by the sitting-room window. She looked up without smiling.

"My mother," explained María. "Sofía's Aunt Evangelíne."

The old lady half-closed her eyes and nodded, by way of greeting, but she said nothing.

"We will go onto the terrace, Mr Fisher. Will you have some coffee with me?"

"I'm sorry, I don't like Greek coffee, María."

"I have Nescafé."

"That would be lovely, thank you."

The terrace was very neat. Terracotta tiling was shaded by a giant trellis supporting a mature vine and a flowering passionfruit. Concrete steps painted a gleaming white led from the corner to a roof area where washing was fluttering. On each step stood a pot with a different coloured geranium. There were two saggy-cushioned armchairs with wooden arms and a shiny green, metal table with four upright chairs. Nick took one of these and sat, admiring the view of Mount Kédros and the lush valley to the left which led back to Spíli.

María returned with a tray of coffees and simnel cakes.

49

"You've made a nice home here, María," he said. "And what a view!"

"Thank you, Mr Fisher," she said with due modesty but obvious pleasure as she poured the coffee. "Please help yourself to cake. I make."

"I will, thank you. They look delicious."

"We've been here for six years, so now we are organised and comfortable."

"Just you and your mum?"

"And my husband. He works at Dímos – the council office – in Spíli. I am a teacher at the school there. I teach history and English. Part-time now. We have two daughters, but they live with their husbands."

"Thank you for seeing me, María, and for your excellent English."

"No, it is good to meet you. Sofía tells me about you, so now I see."

"Oh, dear."

"No. It is good. She likes you."

"It's hard to tell, sometimes."

"Ha! This is Sofía. I know."

"I am here because of the Swiss man. The police have asked me to help – as Sofía predicted."

María gave him a knowing look.

"I was hoping you could give me some background on the village: what it's like, its history, the personalities. I'm particularly interested in the people who live above the kafenío, up the other hill."

"You mean like the Katzatákis family?"

"Exactly."

She pushed the plate of cakes a little nearer to Nick before continuing. *Generosity or self-denial?* he wondered, as he popped another into his mouth.

"The village is okay. Most people are friendly, but there is resentment here, among the older people. There was a civil war here in Greece – *O Emfýlios Pólemos* – between the forces of the left and the right. Kardánes people supported the communists under General Márkos. Some in the village even fought with Márkos. They were guerrillas, fighting from bases in Bulgaria or Albania. They did okay, even put a provisional government together at one point, but the world turned against them. Tito in Yugoslavia was supportive, but then Stalin did a deal with Churchill towards the end of the war. They drew a line through Eastern Europe. As part of that, Stalin agreed to withdraw his support for the Greek communists and Churchill switched his support to those that wanted the old order back in Greece. The fascists and royalists, some of whom were also collaborators."

"Churchill did that?"

"Yes. I think late 1944. He must have decided Greece could not be communist if it was to be on the western side of that arbitrary line. The partisans felt betrayed. There were demonstrations in Athína, fighting in the streets between British troops and left-wing sympathisers – civilians. Some had been friends. Now many were killed."

"I had no idea."

"It's not something they teach you in school, in England."

"I thought the civil war started later, in 1946."

"No. That was just the third phase. It all started under German occupation. It was a difficult time. Complicated. The communists were doomed to failure, like in the Spanish war. Many were imprisoned, some executed. A few made it back to the village."

"So, who in the village would remember any of this, María? Surely, they'd have to be incredibly old?"

"People live a long time in Kardánes. The village is known for it. There are five or six who are over ninety. But the bitterness gets passed down, too. Sons and daughters resent what happened to their parents, and so it goes on."

"Are we talking about disgruntled leftists or is there anti-German feeling, as well?"

"I think both. Maybe it has become the same thing. Some say about the Germans: *How do they have the gall to use Crete as their playground after what they did here during the war?* or *How dare they take over our beautiful beaches and offend us with their nudity?* More recently, others were angered by the deal forced on us after the financial crisis, when they all seem to have so much more money than us."

"You mean by the EU?"

"Yes, but Greeks think the EU is run by the Germans."

"So, how do they show this anger? Is there violence?"

"No violence, no. Not in Crete. They just make it clear Germans are unwelcome, here in the mountains. Greetings go unacknowledged. Directions are refused or poorly given. Vehicles in the way are not moved. Orders are forgotten, or Germans are made to wait longer for food and drink. That sort of thing. It's all rather pathetic. And it's isolated patches of bitterness, no more. Most of us just get on with life, accept the new realities. We have more holidaymakers from Germany than anywhere else, and we need their money. And the Germans are, for the most part, well-behaved tourists who respect our country and are often sympathetic, well-educated people – but I never said this!"

"Or you would get into trouble?"

"With a few people, yes."

"Who would be on the list?"

"I don't want to be accusing people, Mr Fisher."

"I know you don't. And you wouldn't be. But the racist angle is something I need to explore. If you know the names of people who are known to have strong, anti-German feelings, I think it would be important to talk to them, don't you?"

She looked at him steadily for a few seconds. He noticed she was fingering the silver crucifix which hung from her neck.

"I'm sorry, Mr Fisher. I don't think I can help. I am a relative new-comer here. It would not be right for me to pass judgment."

"We won't reveal our sources. I promise."

"I am sorry. I cannot."

They went on to talk about the people who lived on the other hill. María had no time for the Katzatákis family, believing them to be inveterate scroungers and gipsies. The old lady, Eléni, might suffer from Alzheimer's now, which would be a shame because she was a fine woman. Anyway, she seemed to spend more and more of her time with her son in Réthymno these days. She thought the farmer, Papatónis, would be a good catch for some lucky woman, although his wife ran off, so maybe there was something not quite right about

52

him. She hardly knew the James's, but she admired their efforts restoring the house and they always waved and smiled. Manólis kept himself to himself but seemed okay. Nikki, she liked, and she thought the children were sweet and well-behaved, in the main. Andréou she didn't care for:

"He's an angry, disappointed man," she said, "and he drinks too much these days. They say his father was a partisan and the Germans found him hiding in a village church in the Amári Valley. They shot him, along with his friends, then burned down the church. Vasílios was a baby so he won't remember a thing, but *he never forgets this*, all the same, if you know what I mean."

"So, he would have been on your list."

"There is no list, Mr Fisher."

*

It was after one when he left María. She offered him lunch, but he did not want to impose further and also, he wanted to check out the kafenío. He found a shady table on the terrace at the back. Just two other outside tables were occupied. Near the entrance, two older men were playing backgammon, watched by a third. Nearer to him, a woman was eating lunch alone. She would be about the same age as him, maybe a little younger. As he waited for his fried aubergines with tomato sauce, he chewed some fresh bread and sipped his beer. He found himself looking at her again and again. Understated was the word that came to mind. Elegant, maybe. Attractive, certainly. Not the kind of woman he expected to come across in Kardánes.

As she finished her meal, she dabbed her mouth with a paper napkin and her eyes sparkled and crinkled as she returned his smile.

"You are from England, I think?"

"Is it so obvious?"

"Not so much, no. But I heard you speak with Alékos. You are on holiday?"

"No. I live in Crete now."

"Where in England are you from?"

"London."

"How funny."

"What?"

"You are from London, but you live here. I am from here but living in London."

She gave a pretty, little laugh. Like a tinkling bell or a skylark twittering, the girl in her revealed. To Nick's astonishment, he found himself wanting to kiss her on the lips, right there and then.

"Won't you join me for a moment?" he found himself saying.

"Why not. You can help me with this rakí."

She walked over and placed the small carafe and a single glass on the table. Nick took in her trim figure, the light but stylish clothes.

"We need another glass. Aléko!" she called, waving the glass and getting a smiling nod.

Shortly after, Nick's food, a jug of water and the rakí glass all arrived at once.

"Oh dear," she said. "I should leave you to eat your lunch in peace."

"Please don't," said Nick, pouring rakí into two glasses. "If you can bear watching my appalling table manners, I'd be glad of the company. Shall I get another plate for you? There's plenty here."

"Oh, no. Please don't. I ate too much already."

He handed her a full glass.

"Cheers, then."

"Yeiá mas."

"I am Nick."

"Hi Nick. And I am Roúla."

This would have to be a quick hello, she said, because she was due to fly back to England early that evening to resume her work as a lawyer. She chatted a little about her work, but Nick was savouring his aubergines and looking at her face.

"I'm not a high-flying, big-earning lawyer, Nick. I decided a while ago to help those who need me. Sometimes pro bono. I fight cases for immigrants, mostly. I fight injustice. And, I'm afraid there has been a lot of injustice in your country."

It was a rather beautiful face, he decided, quite serious but soft, too. She asked him why he was in Kardánes.

"Oh, I'm just working my way around the local villages. I wanted to see what they were like. This is my first time here. I live in Saktoúria."

"Ah. Clinging to the side of the mountain, then."

"It did take a bit of getting used to, but I'm fine with it now. And you, Roúla, what brings you back to Kardánes? Do you still have family here?"

She hesitated, and for a moment it looked as if Nick's question embarrassed her, trapped her almost. Then she smiled bravely.

"Now, the only family here is my mother."

"What's her name?"

A flash of something akin to anger crossed her face. Then she looked at her watch.

"Oh, my God. I am so sorry, Nick but I have to go. Right now."

He tried to hide his disappointment and played it cool.

"Shame." He grabbed a serviette and scribbled his mobile number on it. "Maybe give me a call, next time you're in town? I think it could be fun getting to know each other."

She took it and put it in her handbag. He saw she was not wearing a ring, and his heart allowed itself a small leap of optimism.

"I will, Nick. I'd like that, too. I'm here every few weeks, these days. Now, I'm sorry to be so rude, but I must run."

And then she was calling out "Yeiá sas" to Alékos and clattering her heels towards her small, red car. She drove off without a wave and that stung him quite unreasonably. *Bloody fool*, he growled inwardly, downed the last of the rakí in one, threw fifteen euros on the table and left to a chorus of *Yeiáaas*, the clacking of the old men's kombolói and the sound of dice rolling.

CHAPTER 9
CHAINSAWS

Náni was arguing on the phone in Greek when Nick arrived, at eight o'clock sharp, Friday morning. He found her accent relatively easy to follow.

"You have *got* to be kidding me! There must be a million damned dogs on this island, and we don't have a single PDTI accredited animal available?"

She nodded at the chair for Nick to take a seat and slid a piece of paper across the desk.

"How long? No, no, that won't do at all."

His written Greek was still extremely limited, and there was a great deal of dense print, but he saw the name Lukas Hedinger printed above a signature and several impressions from rubber stamps.

"All right, do you have a number for them?"

Náni scribbled a number on her blotter.

"No. Well, it's not your fault, is it? Yes, yes okay. Thanks."

She disconnected and looked up.

"Good morning, Mr Fisher, though there's nothing good about it so far. Perhaps you'll bring me a change of luck."

"Nick, please. Call me Nick."

"That's the DNA result. It's Lukas, as we thought. So now, I have to tell the Hedingers, and I think I must do this in person."

"You told them about the torso, I assume?"

"I spoke to Hedinger, Wednesday night."

"How was it?"

"How do you think? The news destroyed him. I don't think he's fooling himself that it's anyone else, but there's always a strand of hope, isn't there? And now it's my job to take that away from him. Leave the poor man bereft. Without answers. I remember, he kept on saying: 'Who the hell could do that, Sergeant? Who could do such a terrible thing to our boy?'"

"Poor sod. At least he has his wife. He's lost everyone else now. I'm happy to come with you if it helps. I'd like to meet them. And it might be useful for me."

"I'm not sure that's a great idea, Mr Fisher. Anyway, before I go, I want to try and sort this bloody dog out. As you probably heard, there isn't one available in Crete for at least a week, but they gave me a number to call in Athína. Why don't you get yourself a coffee while I'm doing that and then we'll pick up with Stéfanos?"

"I'm sorry. What about?"

"Chainsaws, Mr Fisher. Try to keep up."

Nick fumed his way to the kitchen and back. She was upset, he reasoned, and having to tell Hedinger must be weighing on her. But she was not going to be a mate and she was not going to call him Nick. She was going to compete with him and resent his presence all the way. Well, so be it. He would have to prove his worth again. Try to stay civil, professional.

When he got back, Náni was at the table in the Lieutenant's office and Stéfanos was already in situ, looking nervous. Nick managed to dredge up an encouraging smile for him.

"They're calling me back," Náni snapped, presumably referring to the dog people. "Right, Constable. Let's have a summary of what you've found, in English, please."

Nick hurried into his seat, spilling a few drops of coffee on the table. Náni sighed with impatience and handed him a couple of tissues.

"Are you familiar with chainsaws?" asked Stéfanos.

"No," said Náni.

"Just the row they make in my village," said Nick.

"Basic principles then. A chain, not unlike a bicycle chain, is driven by a motor at high speed. There are variations, but, with most saws now, every other link of the chain has cutting teeth. The motors are powered by petrol or electricity. The electric ones can be corded or cordless. They are used for cutting down trees, pruning and logging. There are cheap chainsaws for domestic use and more expensive ones for agricultural use. The prices range from a little as one hundred euros to over seven hundred. You get what you pay for. If you need a powerful workhorse for daily use on the farm, you'd better choose from the top end, something like the Husqvarna Rancher, but for the home, you can pick up a basic one from Lidl."

"So, anyone can buy one and start using it the same day. No controls at all?" asked Náni.

"Well, I don't think the stores would sell to a minor, ma'am, and they do encourage you to follow the instructions, buy safety clothing and watch an online safety video, but that's all. It's up to you to keep yourself safe."

"And these are dangerous beasts," said Nick.

"They are, Mr Fisher. A little less so, these days, with automatic cut-off and better safety equipment."

"But you have to buy the equipment and use it. I've seen guys in my village. They use nothing. Not even gloves or goggles. I've seen them halfway up trees passing an idling saw between them – even when it's getting dark or starting to rain."

"Well, that's not good practice, to say the least. But the real dangers come if you get kickback, trip or slip or drop the saw. The chain will run on for a second or two and that can cause horrible injuries. Anyway, they're out there, and they're in common use. When buying one, the things to consider are: power source, blade length, weight – and, of course, price and the reliability of the manu—"

"But they can all cut up a human body, right?" Nick cut in.

"No question."

"Let's skip to the *results* of what you found, Constable," said Náni.

Stéfanos laid two sheets of paper on the table and placed two fingers on one of them.

"These are the stores I've identified where you can buy some sort of chainsaw. As you can see, they range from stores that sell agricultural power tools to farm equipment suppliers to supermarkets and DIY stores."

Nick saw thirty to forty names listed. About a third were highlighted.

"The list covers the whole of Crete. The highlighted ones are within fifty kilometres of Kardánes."

He moved on to the second sheet.

"And these are the makes and models stocked by the highlighted suppliers."

Nick saw the names Husqvarna, Stihl, WORX and Makita followed by numbers and codes. In all, there were nine different models.

"I have contacted them all by phone and visited those I've asterisked. The others are all east of here, around Míres and Tymbáki. I didn't have time to get over there, but I got the information out of them by phone and email."

"What kind of a reception did you get, generally?" asked Nick.

"Mixed. Quite a few grumbles, people saying I was asking for the impossible. But, when I told them the thing was used in a serious crime, most were keen to help, if they could. And the reality is, these businesses, even the smaller ones, have accounting systems or spreadsheets and they have debit and credit card records. Sorting for transactions between a hundred euros and a thousand euros is not so difficult. And the bigger stores were able to search by product type which made things a lot easier. I made a list of everyone who made a purchase in that price range in the last five years, and I knew some were chainsaws. Then I went to the card companies for their contact details."

He produced a third piece of paper from his file and laid it on the table.

"These are the names I found. People with addresses within two kilometres of Kardánes who used debit or credit cards to make a purchase between one hundred and one thousand euros at any of these stores over the last five years. The ones I know to be chainsaws are marked, along with the make and model."

"Only five?"

"That's all I've found, ma'am. It won't be included if the purchase was more than five years ago or if they paid cash or if they bought it farther afield."

"And only two of the five purchases are *known* to have been chainsaws."

"Yes, ma'am. I'd suggest we ask the others what they bought."

Nick examined the list. The headings showed *Date, Amount, Name, Card Type, Card Number and Saw Type*. There were five names, only one of which he recognised. Three of the entries showed a question mark in the final column.

"So, to focus on what we *do* know, Dimítris Foteinákis bought a Husqvarna 536 in October, almost three years ago, and Márkos Papatónis bought a WORX WG303 just ten months ago. And the other three characters bought something significant on these dates, which may or may not have been a chainsaw."

"That's it, Mr Fisher."

"Did you ask about cash sales of chainsaws?"

"I did. No-one I spoke to recalled selling a chainsaw for cash. Some were kind enough to reconcile their stock records to the sales records and could confirm that all sales of chainsaws were accounted for by debit and credit cards."

"Some …"

"Yes. Others were unable or unwilling to do so. It's not perfect, Mr Fisher, but it's the best I've been able to do in the time."

"You've done very well, Constable," said Náni. "For the moment, thank you."

After Stéfanos left, Nick said:

"Can I suggest another route?" She gave him a hostile glance. "A complementary approach, I mean."

She put her elbows on the table, chin on hands and raised an eyebrow.

"Let's just go and ask. People in a village know who has a chainsaw. They hear them running. We can start with the two we know, then ask the three who might have bought one, but also, just ask around. Chainsaw owners will know other chainsaw owners. The people who run the kafenío may know, too."

"The reason we did it this way, if you remember, was that we didn't want the murderer to know we'd found the body. If we blunder around the village asking who owns a chainsaw, it's a bit of a giveaway, wouldn't you say?"

"I guess I'm questioning that strategy now. Why don't we leak news of the body to the press and then move in on the village?"

"The murderer will run. That's why."

"Well, if that happens, we'll find them and bring them back. But I'm guessing, in a close village situation like this, they'll have no choice but to keep their heads down, be careful and hope they can get away with it. If they run, all their friends and neighbours will know. And so will we. The other thing is the press. Much better to let them know now, and keep them on our side, than to have them discover the murder later."

"It's a big story. A foreigner chopped to bits on his holidays. Many people would want such a story suppressed."

"I see that Náni, but I'm not sure it's in *our* interests."

"The press will get in the way."

"They will, but I'm sure you have a press officer somewhere in this building. Get him briefed. Let *him* be the spokesperson, at least to begin with. When we have some answers, you can grab the microphone."

"We could lose the case to Athína."

"It's a risk, for sure. But they must know already. Your senior officers would have to keep them informed. They won't be discovering it from reading some newspaper. No, we'll lose the case if they don't think we can solve it, simple as that. Or if they cave in to political pressure from the Swiss Foreign Secretary or something. All that goes away if we're seen to be on the road to nailing the bastards."

Náni was reconsidering, looking at Nick with a new tolerance, maybe even the first, faint glimmer of respect.

"All right, Mr Fisher. I'll talk to the Lieutenant."

"Didn't he ask you to run with it?"

"Yes, but the implications of the international press—"

"What if he says, *No* for some political reason?" Nick interrupted. She was tapping her pen on the desk again.

"So, what? We just leak it?"

"One confidential phone call. Unattributed sources. The press will do the rest."

"I would be fired."

"If it were traced to you, perhaps. But it won't be. Maybe it was the ME's office? Someone on the beach at Triópetra? The snorkellers who found the body? One of your junior cops. Who the hell knows?"

She was up now, staring out of the window with her back to him. Then the phone rang.

"Samarákis … Yes, I did. It's for a murder inquiry involving a foreign national … You don't?"

She rolled her eyes and shook her head at Nick.

"… But surely … How many are there? … What, all more important than this one?"

Then she listened for more than a minute, tapping her pen.

"… Are you quite sure? This will delay a crucial part of our investigation."

She was scrunching up the phone cable in her free hand, perhaps imagining it was around the caller's neck.

"… Well, if that's the best you can do, I'm going to have to live with it, aren't I? … Yes, please do. Thank you."

She banged the receiver down. "Useless bastards!"

"Tail wagging the dog?" asked Nick, helpfully, a faint grin playing on his lips.

"I don't know what that's supposed to mean, Mr Fisher, but they tell me we have to wait a week for the damned K-9. There are very few and they're all tied up."

"As they should be."

She stared at him angrily but the mild inanity in his expression caused the tight line of her mouth to soften. Then the twitch of a smile appeared at the corner of her mouth.

"Very amusing, Mr Fisher. They will call me if one frees up. Now, I must go to the Hedingers. You can come along, but no questions, please. Not today. They'll need to grieve. After that, we can try talking to the names on Stéfi's list. But first, I need to make the phone call that never happened."

"Then you might want to do it from my mobile rather than your desk phone," he said, handing it to her. "Come on, Náni, you can do it on the way."

They decided to take both vehicles, for flexibility. Nick hammered the Jeep south in his efforts to keep up with the sleek, blue and white Skoda with the blue light on top.

CHAPTER 10
LEARNING

When Hedinger saw them, he came out and closed the door quietly.

He looks all of his seventy-six years today, thought Nick.

"Could we walk this way a little?" he said. Náni and Nick followed him to the empty bar area where he sat down heavily at a table. They joined him.

"You have come to tell me it was Lukas," he said.

"I am so sorry, Herr Hedinger. DNA tests confirmed it was your grandson's body."

He raised his head a little as if watching Lukas ascending to the heavens, or perhaps to keep brimming tears from falling from his eyes. A house martin swooped down and raced across the surface of the swimming pool.

"He loved the birds here. The swallows and the house martins. All of nature. Such a gentle boy ... and now this."

They were silent. Náni laid a hand on the old man's arm.

"Would you like me to tell Ilse?"

"No, no. I must do that. You see, I didn't tell her when the body was found. I needed to be sure it was him. Perhaps that was wrong of me, but I wanted to protect her."

"Must have been difficult for you."

His watery eyes narrowed as he stared back at them.

"When you've loved someone for fifty years, Sergeant, it's not so difficult to shield them from harm for a few days. Especially when it is something as dreadful as this."

"No, I see that. Now, if I may, I'd like to introduce Nick Fisher. He was a senior police officer in England, but he lives in Crete now. He has worked with the Greek police before and he will help us find out who did this. We are on our way to the village to resume our questioning."

"I am sorry for your loss, sir," said Nick. "I will do everything I can to help."

"I am sure you mean well, Mr Fisher. But I don't think you *can* help. Our only grandson has been taken and you can't bring him back. And now, the Hedinger name will die with me. I cannot imagine who did this dreadful thing to Lukas, or why. If you find out, it may bring *closure*. I think this is the word they use these days. Will that help us? I doubt it."

*

"You need to brief your press officer, remember," said Nick, at the car. "The journalist could be calling him any minute."

"Her, actually. I know I have to call, I'm just not sure how to handle it."

"It's easy. You told the journalist *unattributed sources*, right? Then tell your Press Officer the journalist called *you* – rather than the other way around – fishing for information. They knew the Swiss man was missing, they heard some body parts were found, and they put two and two together … connected the events. You have no idea how they got their information, but you thought it best to say nothing and refer them to the Press Office. Then ask her if she needs more information on the case, which she will."

"As simple as that."

"Yes. And if she presses you on the source of the leak, you point out all the other places it could have come from, say you doubt very much that it came from the police, but you'll be interviewing your team members, just to be certain."

"Helpful and co-operative."

"Exactly. Then you'll hear nothing more. She'll be up to her arse in alligators by then and won't have time to worry about how it all got started."

"Up to what?"

"Busy. She'll be extremely busy."

He left her to make the call and walked over to the Jeep.

*

They decided to tackle the three names with the unidentified purchases first, rather than alerting the known chainsaw owners any earlier than necessary. One was not quite in Kardánes, but several

65

hundred metres down the Spíli road, so they called there first. It took the old man several minutes to go back through his records but then his face lit up.

"I should have remembered," he said in Greek, as he led them to his shed and pointed out a long, green metal pruner. "There you are," he said, with obvious pride. "It was expensive. I think I paid one hundred and twenty-five euros, but the plastic ones kept breaking whereas this is good and solid. Well made, works well. I use it for the olive trees."

The second candidate was in the heart of the village. This time it was a woman who answered the door. Her husband was out, she said. She blinked a few times at the list.

"Two hundred and ten euros, March last year? Wait, yes. I remember the name of this shop. Come, I show you."

They followed her into a courtyard, and, behind the front door, she pointed to a fibreboard box, painted white. They looked baffled, as they were supposed to, until she lifted the lid. Inside the soundproof box was a shiny, metallic blue machine with pipes coming out of it. It looked like a pump of some kind.

"My husband buy this. It is for the water."

"It boosts the water pressure," said Nick.

"The pressure, yes." And, by way of confirmation, she ran the outside shower and the noisy machine kicked in.

The address for the last one on the list, they realised, was Manólis's place, next to the ruined house.

"That's odd," said Náni, "The card is not in the name Vernardákis."

They waited while his wife called him in from his allotment. He took a cloth and wiped the sweat from his red face and the mud from his gigantic hands. He looked at the list.

"Yes, this is us," he said. "It's my wife's card. She uses her maiden name. Perhaps I'd forgotten mine or it didn't work for some reason."

"And what did you buy?"

"Let's see, that's almost five years ago. But we don't pay out three hundred and forty-five euros very often …"

"Could it be the saw?" offered the wife.

"Was it so long ago? Hmmm. I guess it might be."

"Are we talking about a chainsaw?" asked Náni, getting nods. "Perhaps you could check your bank records for me?" Náni said to the wife. "And perhaps you could show us the saw, kýrie Vernardáki?"

They followed him across a large, front garden where giant sunflowers and artichokes featured alongside more mundane crops. It was in a shed next to the lane.

"There you are. It's a Stihl MSA 120." He reached it down for them to inspect. "Good machine. German. Makes a hell of a row, but less than some, and it works well."

"When did you last use it?"

"I'm not sure. Early spring? March, maybe?"

"And what do you use it for?"

"Pruning, logging for the winter fires. We're six hundred metres up here – it gets pretty cold at times."

"Do you keep animals here?" asked Nick.

"Just the dogs. Why do you ask?"

"I'm wondering if you'd have used the saw to cut animal flesh, at any time?"

"God, no."

And then he caught on.

"What is it you're saying?" He looked aghast.

"Someone used a chainsaw to cut up the body of the Swiss lad. Maybe someone in this village," said Nick.

"Christ."

"And we need to take your saw for a forensic inspection."

"You don't think I did it?" said Manólis, panic rising in his voice.

"Just one moment, sir," said Náni, taking Nick to one side.

"What's going on, Mr Fisher? We didn't say anything about confiscating saws."

"Look at it, Náni. Three months in a dusty shed and it's clean as a whistle. No sawdust, no bits of twig or leaf, not even any dust. Doesn't that strike you as odd?"

"You think it's been cleaned."

"Probably. Anyway, unless we find one covered in blood, we should take them all in, get them checked out."

She stared for a moment, then nodded.

"We're taking all chainsaws in the area for a forensic check, Vernardáki. If there are no traces of human blood or tissue, it will be returned to you in due course. It's a procedure we must follow to eliminate you from our enquiries. Do you understand? At this stage, you are guilty of living in Kardánes and owning a chainsaw; nothing more. If it's clean, you have nothing to fear."

He looked somewhat reassured and they thanked him and walked away with his saw, which Nick carried by the shoulder strap, in case of fingerprints.

*

It was hardly worth driving up the hill to the farm, but they did so anyway. It would save carrying the saw too far. Papatónis showed genuine concern when he heard their reasons for asking. His English was impeccable.

"They used a chainsaw? Oh, how disgusting! How upsetting for his family. It's a brutal tool. I don't enjoy using it, but, as you can see, I have many trees. It is necessary."

They came to a large, concrete outbuilding to the rear of the farm-house and followed him inside.

"This is mine. You're welcome to take it away, but I'll need it back before long."

He reached up and handed the orange and black power tool to Nick.

"We'll be as quick as we can, kýrie Papatóni. Thank you."

"Also, remarkably clean," said Nick, as they left.

"Well, it is quite new," said Náni, consulting the list.

The same could not be said of the last one on the list. Foteinákis was a younger man with a beard and a van.

"I'm happy to show you, Sergeant," he said, "but please don't take it away. I use it every day in my business, sometimes all day. I am cutting olive trees, everywhere around here."

The Husqvarna was a workhorse. It was three years old but looked fifteen. Leaves and small twigs were caught up in the chain. The machine was streaked with orange mud and shrouded in sawdust.

"I'm sorry, kýrie Foteináki, but we need it for a few days. If you need to hire a replacement, you can claim at the police station."

"I don't have time to mess around with that!"

"I'm sorry, sir, but you don't have a choice. This is a murder inquiry and we have to take your saw in for forensic tests to eliminate it – and you – from our investigation."

Nick gave him a sympathetic look as he took the machine from him, but the man was still shaking his head angrily as they moved away.

*

Náni decided to drive the three saws straight to the forensics team in Réthymno, but Nick wanted to stay behind in the village. Náni warned him not to ruffle too many feathers and he gave her the withering *I've been doing this for thirty years* look and almost won a smile.

Nick's eyes roamed around the kafenío, just in case, but she would be in London by now. Friday afternoon and the place was deserted.

"Am I too late for lunch?" he called to Alékos.

"What means *too late*?" he replied. "You are in Greece and you are hungry. I have food. You will sit, please."

Nick did as he was told and ordered some rabbit stifádo.

"Good to see you again. You here yesterday, with Roúla, no?"

"Briefly, yes. You must know her well."

"All my life. We are in the school together."

"Seems like a nice woman."

"She big brain, work hard. She live in England now."

"Yes, she told me. I guess her husband's British, then," he floated.

Alékos stared at him, puzzled, then threw him a sideways grin.

"She has no husband. No man at all, I think."

Then, seeing Nick's reaction, he punched Nick's upper arm as he went off chuckling, to cook. The food, when it arrived, was rustic but very tasty. Later, when Alékos brought out a saucer of cherries with

69

yoghurt and a small carafe of rakí, Nick introduced himself properly and asked Alékos to join him. The place was still deserted.

"So, does Roúla come back often, from England?" he asked.

"Yes. More now, because of her mother."

"Ah. She must be getting old."

"She is over ninety and a little …"

He rolled his eyes to suggest that her mental faculties were failing her.

"Ah, I see. Must be difficult for Roúla."

"Her brother, Pandelís, is in Réthymno. He takes Eléni back there quite often, I think. His wife is kind to her."

"Would this be the lady who has the little stone house up past the church, on the right?"

"There is only one Eléni in Kardánes, Nick."

"Is she there now, do you think?"

"I don't know. Why you ask?"

Nick decided to come clean and explained he was working with the police.

"If I can speak to you in confidence, Aléko, we have found the body of the missing Swiss man and he was murdered, perhaps in this village."

Nick was touched to see a genuine wince of compassion sweep across Alékos's troubled face.

"His poor family," he said. "Who does this?"

"We are investigating."

"But what has this to do with Eléni?"

"We just want to know if she saw or heard anything."

Nick topped up their rakí glasses, the faint clink of glass the only sound apart from the rhythmic throb of the cicadas.

"Would you be able to help me with something, Aléko?"

"What you want?"

"Do you know who, in the village, owns a chainsaw?"

"Oh, my God. They use this on the boy?"

"After death. They cut up the body."

"Here, in Kardánes?"

"We don't know yet. Maybe."

"Okay, I know of only two. Dimítris the tree surgeon has one for his work and Manólis has one he uses from time to time."

"What about the Katzatákis family?"

"They have no money, these people."

"And I thought Márkos Papatónis owned one?"

"Does he, now? I know he used to borrow Manólis's."

"And would the Katzatákis boys borrow it too, sometimes?"

"They borrow anything they can, then keep it. But Manólis would not lend anything to them, least of all a chainsaw. I'm sure of this. Those boys are crazy stupid."

"So, just the three saws in the village?"

"I think so."

Nick stood and stretched, thanked Alékos, rounded the bill up to fifteen euros and left. He decided to head back to Saktoúria and let this all distil over the weekend. He felt like stretching out on the sofa with some Miles Davis, perhaps *Sketches of Spain,* and an ice-cold beer. Things were sure to ramp up next week.

CHAPTER 11
FOLLOW THE BLOOD

It was not until Monday afternoon that Náni called.

"We have blood traces on one of the saws, Mr Fisher."

"Excellent. Which one?"

"The one you said was too clean. You were right. It was cleaned well, but not well enough. No prints, but they found residual blood traces on two of the chain sprockets."

"Human blood?"

"Yes. That's confirmed. They are trying to determine the blood group and test for DNA, but these are tiny traces, so it's a challenge."

"We're talking about Manólis's saw?"

"Yes, and I'm on my way to question him. Do you want to join me, at Kardánes?"

*

They saw Manólis from the lane. He was wearing a protective boiler suit and spraying his sunflowers. When he saw them, he stopped and removed the canvas helmet to reveal a puce face and damp strands of hair. They met at the front door to his smart, modern house.

"Is there somewhere we can talk in private?" said Náni without preamble.

Manólis narrowed his eyes but then jerked his head and led them to a smaller, sheltered, rear garden area. The overweight daughter was sitting at a garden table, playing with a cat, but Manólis told her to go inside.

"We can use this. Just give me a minute to get this damned suit off."

Two minutes later, his mousy wife delivered a jug of water and three glasses. Manólis returned, his face recovered to its usual red. He sat down and poured himself a glass.

"So, what's all this about, Sergeant?"

"It's about your chainsaw."

"Have you brought it back?"

"No. And I'm afraid you're in trouble, Vernardáki. The saw has been cleaned recently but the forensics team still found small traces of human blood on the chain. How do you explain that?"

"*My* saw? There must be some mistake. I haven't used it for several weeks, as I told you, and certainly not for cutting up a body."

"Well, it looks like somebody did," said Nick.

"You saw where I keep it. The shed is padlocked and there have been no break-ins."

"Have you lent it to anyone?"

"No. Not for ages."

"So, you *have* lent it to someone in the past."

"Márkos used to borrow it, once in a while, but he bought himself one about a year ago. I never lent it to anyone else."

"Márkos Papatónis?" asked Náni.

He nodded.

"Where do you keep the key?" asked Nick.

"I'll show you," he said, and they rose and walked around the side of the house and past the sunflowers to the very front of the garden, by the lane.

"It's behind the shed, on a hook, tucked under the roofline."

"On the shed itself, you mean?"

"Yes, but on the hedge side. It's quite difficult to spot, see."

"Who else knows it's there?"

"Just my wife and daughter and me, as far as I know."

"And the thief," added Nick. "Is there another key?"

"I suppose there must have been, originally, but it's got to be ten years since I bought the padlock. I've no idea what happened to it."

Nick was looking at the padlock. It seemed solid enough, showed no signs of tampering.

"And this is the same padlock as always?"

"Looks the same."

Náni slipped on forensic gloves and took down the key.

"Let's just make sure it works," she said, undoing the padlock without difficulty. "So, Vernardáki, the saw was taken by someone who knew where to find the key. And, outside the family, the only one is Papatónis, you think?"

"He might have seen me get the key one time. Who knows? But why the hell would he want it now?"

Náni was placing the padlock and its key in an evidence bag.

"We'll borrow these, just in case our thief was foolish enough to leave fingerprints."

"That's okay. I've another I can use. Without the chainsaw, there's not much of value anyway."

Náni asked if he would show them around his land and any outbuildings.

"It's what you see, Sergeant. I have land enough for a big garden but no more. There is a double carport attached to the house, this shed and another in the back garden you might have seen. No outbuildings."

And nowhere to dismember a body, thought Nick.

*

When they were back in the road, Náni said:

"I don't think it was him, do you?"

"Not from the way he reacted, no," said Nick.

"And I can't imagine his wife or daughter carving up corpses."

"No. So we are left with Papatónis."

"Assuming he saw where the key was kept *and* remembered. But why take it when he has one of his own?"

"It seems odd, but it makes for perfect cover, doesn't it? The best way to ensure no blood traces were found on *his* chainsaw was to use someone else's. And no-one would suspect him of doing such a thing *precisely* because he already owns one."

"Sounds a bit clever, Nick."

"Maybe, but he's not stupid, this man."

"And throwing suspicion on Manólis like that? Not a nice thing to do to a friendly neighbour."

"I'm sorry. You're expecting our killer to be nice?"

Nick joined Náni in the police car for the short drive up to the farm.

She drove through the gates with the blue light flashing and flipped the siren so it miaowed briefly.

Papatónis was standing there, arms folded, the open door behind him. He was wearing a blood-stained, leather apron.

"Please forgive my attire, Sergeant. I've been slaughtering sheep."

"You do that *here*?"

"Not in the house, obviously. I use the barn over there if there are just one or two. For larger numbers, a truck comes from the slaughterhouse."

"Would you show us?" asked Nick.

"I've finished now."

"I meant the *place* where you do it."

"You might explain why you're here, first."

"We have more questions for you, Papatóni," said Náni.

"You do? Really? Well, all right. I can show you, but it's not pretty."

"I didn't imagine it would be," said Nick. "Tell me, how do you do it, exactly?"

As the three of them walked across to the large, concrete shed, he explained.

"First, I must choose which are to die; the God moment, I call it. Farmers can't afford to be sentimental, but I struggle with that. I pick them out the evening before and separate them from the flock. You must harden your heart against the pathetic bleating. Earplugs help." He grinned, ruefully.

"Why separate them, then?"

"Sheep have short memories, Mr Fisher. By the morning, they are no longer missed. Life continues as normal. The flock is not distressed."

They were at the shed now. He held the door for a moment.

"I've not cleaned up yet. It's a gory mess, I'm afraid."

He looked at each of them in turn, as if checking for signs of squeamishness, then led them inside. It was a large shed and smelled of fresh meat and sweet, sickly death. Out of the sunlight, it was black-dark until their eyes adjusted. Then they saw the bodies of the lambs, hanging upside down from hooks, yawning necks draining blood into a large, rectangular, plastic tub. The floor was covered in blood-soaked straw.

"I have a bolt-gun which I use to stun them and then I slit their throats. It's all very quick. I don't know of a better way. Later, I will skin them and butcher the one I'm keeping."

He waved at a rack of butchering tools. Nick saw a cleaver, two large knives and what must be a bone saw.

"And you do the butchering where exactly?" asked Náni.

He pointed to a large table, topped with a marble slab. The slab looked clean but the wood to each side was discoloured and crusted with dried blood.

"Seen enough?" he asked.

Nick cast his eyes around the shed. There was plenty of space and the thick, concrete walls would provide soundproofing. With a chain-saw and all these butchering tools, everything he needed was here. And they were at least two hundred metres from the nearest house. It was the perfect place to dismember a body.

"I think so. Thank you."

"Then we will go to the house and I will change. Then you can ask all the questions you want, Sergeant."

*

They gathered in the farmhouse kitchen. The house was older than it looked at first glance. There was character here: a large fireplace, a deep sink, heavy, dark wood furniture. Nick was impressed with the neatness of the place. The man was organised. And he smelled better without the hideous apron. In fact, he was now fresh-faced and good-looking.

"You live alone, Papatóni?" asked Náni as he handed out water glasses.

"I do."

"But you seem well organised."

"Well, thank you. I have a woman who helps me with cleaning and laundry. And there are always between two and four lads working on the farm with me."

"But they live elsewhere?"

"They do."

"I'm told you were married, at some point."

"Still am, on paper. Separated. I brought my wife here from Iráklio. She wanted to come. Said she loved the country, but farm life was too basic, too brutal – and too lonely for her, in the end."

"So, where is she now?"

"Back in the city, I imagine."

"You don't know?"

"No, I don't know, Sergeant. I'm sure she'll be in touch when she wants a divorce."

"How long ago did she leave?"

"Almost three years."

"And you'd been together how long?"

"Ten years. Married for eight of those."

"There were no kids?" asked Nick.

"No kids."

"I hope there was a fair settlement when you split," said Náni.

Papatónis arched an eyebrow at the question and left a second or two before answering:

"She didn't want anything. Just left with a few bits and pieces. I assumed she'd found someone else to live off."

"You mean live *with*," said Náni, pointedly.

"I know what I mean, Sergeant," said Papatónis.

The words sounded bitter, but he looked open-faced and pragmatic, rather than emotional.

"When did you last hear from her?" asked Nick.

"I have never heard from her. Not since the day she left."

There was a pause. Náni and Nick exchanged glances, then Náni spoke.

"If we might return to the subject of chainsaws?"

"Have you brought it back already?"

"Not yet, I'm afraid. Now, we know you bought yours ten months ago, but you've owned this farm for many years. How did you manage before?"

"I didn't use chainsaws at all until four or five years ago. Evil things. But, in the end, I got weary of being robbed by Foteinákis. So, I started hiring them or borrowing them, here and there."

"I believe you borrowed Vernardákis's sometimes."

"That's right. When he got the Stihl, he let me borrow it here and there."

"Did he lend it to anyone else?"

"I doubt it. You wouldn't lend it to anyone who wouldn't treat it with the utmost respect. Even then, things can happen if you're not extremely careful."

"But he knew you'd be okay."

"We've known each other a long time, Sergeant."

"Do you remember where he kept it?"

"Just in the shed, at the front of the garden, in those days."

"And, when you went there, to borrow it, would he get it out of the shed for you?"

"If it was there at the time, yes."

"So, you would see him open the shed?"

"Sometimes. What of it?"

"It's kept padlocked. Did you see him retrieve the key and open the padlock?"

"I may have done. I really don't know, Sergeant."

"Well, did he have the key in a pocket? Did he go to the house to retrieve it? Was it under a stone?"

"Where are you going with this?"

"I'm wondering if you borrowed his chainsaw one more time."

"I've got a perfectly good one of my own, as you know. Why on earth would I?"

"You're an intelligent man. You know how difficult they are to clean, especially if blood and tissue get into the recesses of the chain mechanism."

"What? Hold on. So, I killed this man and then stole Manólis's machine to cut him up. Is that what you think?"

"I don't know what to think, Papatóni, but there were human blood traces on Manólis's saw. You knew where it was and where the key was kept. You have the perfect barn for dismembering a body. And I'm also concerned about your disappearing wife. I'd like you to accompany us to Réthymno for further questioning and I'd like your permission to search your premises and take blood samples from the barn."

"Hang on. Presumably, there was no blood found on *my* chainsaw, and yet you arrest *me*, rather than Manólis though there is blood on *his* saw. And now you think I butchered my wife, too? What the hell is going on?"

"We have questioned Vernardáki and I'm satisfied he knows nothing about this. Also, I am not arresting you, Papatóni. You will come of your own free will and grant your permissions. If not, however, I *will* be obliged to arrest you and seek a search warrant."

"You give me little choice, then. But you have this completely wrong, Sergeant, and you'll be wasting our time. When that becomes clear, I'll be seeking compensation from the police."

Good luck with that, Nick chuckled to himself, but he was yet to be convinced the man was guilty of anything.

CHAPTER 12
YOUNG LOVE

Something was wrong. The Jeep looked odd, somehow. And then he saw. It had been trashed. All four tyres slashed, and wet concrete poured onto the driver's seat, where it set solid in the sun, a grey mound, sixty centimetres wide and thirty centimetres high. Across the bonnet, some Greek words were daubed, in red paint.

"Bastards!" shouted Nick, looking up and down the deserted lane. "You cowardly, fucking bastards. I'll have you!"

"Looks like you ruffled some feathers," said Náni, from the police car window.

"What does it say?" asked Nick.

"It's just a warning to keep away."

"What does it say, exactly, Náni?"

"I think the British equivalent would be: *Fuck off, English pig*. Sorry, Nick. You'd better get in. We have to go to Réthymno. We can sort something out from there."

"Who would do this? Concrete, for fuck's sake. Jesus!"

"It wasn't me," Papatónis piped up from the back seat. "None of this was me."

"For your sake, you'd better be right," said Nick, fuming.

He was so angry he could not think straight. If this was supposed to frighten him off, they did not know him very well. Now, more than ever, he wanted to catch this killer and anyone else who was implicated. And then he wanted to throttle the bastards, one by one.

After fifteen kilometres, his anger cooled enough for him to remember. Náni had called him Nick. He glanced at her then and registered a faint *Hooray* inside. Maybe the attack on the Jeep helped form a bond there; fellow sufferers at the mercy of life's pillocks.

*

Back at the police station, Papatónis was taken to one of the interview rooms. Náni's team were passing around the local paper. The journalist had not held back. The front-page headline was *Tourist Dismembered* above a shot of Lukas's face. Nick was scanning the article when Náni emerged from the office.

"I've organised a forensics team to get over to Papatónis's farm. They can be there by mid-morning tomorrow. We can search the premises at the same time."

"Are you sure you're not jumping the gun, Náni?"

"I don't understand you."

"Aren't we getting ahead of ourselves? We haven't even questioned the guy properly."

"I have a bad feeling about him, Nick, don't you? Did you believe the story about his wife? Why was there no contact whatsoever since she left? It's weird. And why did she take nothing and seek no settlement from him after ten years together? And didn't you think it was rather convenient that there were two sheep to slaughter so he could splash sheep's blood all over his shed to disguise any traces of human blood?"

"Those questions need to be answered, for sure ..."

"We're headline news now – *your* idea, remember? That means I can get resources. But it also means we must move things forward or we'll lose the case. Papatónis has given us permission to search. I'm using it; simple as that."

"Fair enough."

"Now, before we question him, let's get Níkos to organise a tow truck for your Jeep."

The formal interview lasted an hour and a half. Náni led the questioning from the outset. They covered much the same questions as before but in more depth. Papatónis was irritated by the whole process but calm and consistent with his responses. He did not *borrow* the saw. He knew nothing about Lukas's murder, and he assumed his ex-wife was alive and well but had no wish to contact her and stir up the past. Nick said less and less as the interview progressed. Eventually, he excused himself and went to catch Constable Níkos Antoníou before he went home.

"It's all sorted for you, Mr Fisher," said Níkos. "The Jeep has been taken to a repair shop in Kissós. You can call them tomorrow and discuss what can be done. Here is their number. I am sorry but there were no unmarked police cars available. However, there is a rental car waiting for you in the car park. Here are the keys. It's a white Suzuki. The registration number is on the tab."

"Brilliant. How much do I owe you, Níko?"

"Sergeant Samarákis said the police would take care of it, Mr Fisher."

*

The next morning, Nick drove the Suzuki to Kardánes early. He wanted to be present at the search and thought he might grab some breakfast at the kafenío first.

There was no sign of Alékos, but a busy little woman was bustling about, tidying up.

"Kaliméra," called Nick, heading for an outside table in the shade.

"We are closed, sir. I am sorry."

"Oh dear, I was hoping for a little breakfast."

"The kafenío doesn't open till noon but okay, I have to be here anyway, for supplies, so today I can help you. I am Varvára. Welcome."

"You're very kind, Varvára. Thank you. I'm Nick."

He ordered eggs and peppers with some filter coffee.

As he waited, he observed the comings-and-goings. *This must be the day for taking in stock,* he thought, as he witnessed a delivery of bottled water and then a small man, who arrived in a pick-up truck piled high with vegetables, unloading potatoes, onions, aubergines and courgettes. Next came the post van and then, lastly, a noisy, old, white van with a leaking exhaust and gears that graunched painfully. Lyra music was booming from the roof-mounted speakers. It sounded emotional, tragic. A thick-set, unsmiling man with a moustache got out and opened the rear doors to reveal several white, plastic tubs. Nick thought he recognised him as the guy who delivered fish to Saktoúria. Varvára was giving the postman a rakí inside – at nine forty am, Nick noted – while the fish man waited, drumming his fingers on the roof of the van. Finally, the postman left and Varvára emerged, wiping her hands on her apron. The man showed her the fish and Nick saw her lean inside the van as he lifted specimens out of the ice for her to see. She looked unimpressed and started haggling with him until a grudging acceptance was reached and he started hauling fish into the kafenío for her. She came over.

"I am sorry you must wait, Nick, but everyone comes at the same time today!"

"Don't worry. I have a little time. Tell me, is he the same man who delivers fish to my village, Saktoúria?"

"Yiánnis? Yes, it would be. He covers all the villages from here to the coast."

"I thought I'd seen him – or heard him. His van wakes me up sometimes."

"Ha! Yes, it will do that, for sure."

She went back to cook, and Nick noticed the van was still there, but the man was not. And then he spotted him. He was on the other side of the road with a younger, bearded man and they were arguing. They were keeping their voices low but there was no mistaking the fury in the younger man's demeanour. He was raising his arms, questioning, and then striking down for emphasis. His eyes were boring into Yiánnis's. At one point he shoved him hard, on the shoulder. He glanced around then and seemed to hiss instructions at the older man. At this point, Varvára came out with money in her hand and the younger man stood back, greeted her in a rather formal, stilted manner, then turned and walked back up the hill. When Yiánnis turned, Nick glimpsed both fear and indignation in his eyes before he climbed into the van and crunched the gears, leaving a plume of blue smoke behind him.

A few minutes later, Varvára arrived with a tray.

"What was that all about?" he asked.

"I have no idea," she said, "but families argue all the time here. It means nothing."

"They are related, then?"

"They are cousins."

"I thought I recognised the younger man, too," Nick lied.

"This is Grigóris."

Nick looked blank.

"Grigóris Katzatákis?"

"Ah, yes. One of the three brothers."

"Grigóris is the youngest." She leaned closer to him as she placed his coffee on the table, "but he is no better than the rest."

"How do you mean?"

"This is not a good family, Nick. I fear for Amalía."

"You've lost me."

"I'm sorry. I talk too much."

"No. Go on, Varvára. I'm curious now."

"Amalía Vernardákis. She is the daughter of Anna and Manólis."

Nick remembered the plump girl with the cat Manólis shooed from the garden.

"What, Grigóris is pursuing Amalía?"

"I think she has fallen for him, stupid girl."

"Does Manólis know?"

"I doubt it, or he would have stopped it. There is no love lost between the Vernardákis and Katzatákis families."

"You make it sound like Romeo and Juliet, Varvára."

"A little." She leaned her head to one side and a sceptical smile played on her lips. "But Romeo was a nice guy, wasn't he?"

She left him to enjoy his breakfast. Nick was astonished at how readily she shared these confidences with a stranger to the village. She and her husband could be a good source of information for him, at this rate. The eggs were more of a loose omelette, but they were rich,

84

almost orange in colour, and full of flavour with the added piquancy of the peppers. He tucked in, using the fresh, crusty bread to scoop up the runnier parts.

*

By the time Nick arrived at the Papatónis farm, the search was well underway, and the forensics boys were suited up and working in the concrete barn.

"How's it going?" he asked Náni.

"Not much yet, but those are quite interesting." She jerked her head at a small pile of books and magazines. Nick leafed through the material. It was war stuff: cheap novels set in wartime, militaria and gaming magazines. Amongst it was some soft porn.

"What do you make of it, then?" he asked.

"There's more on his computer. A whole lot more. The guy's obsessed with war."

"War generally or WWII in particular?"

"Any kind of war. He has war games on the computer, war poetry books. Even a big tray filled with sand and toy soldiers, model tanks and things."

"Have you spoken to him about it?"

"I have. He says it's his interest, his hobby and it doesn't mean he goes around killing people and cutting up their bodies."

"Sounds like a wargamer. Does he refight historic battles, that sort of thing?"

"I have no idea, Nick. It just struck me as odd, maybe dangerously odd."

"Perhaps. But, in England, it would be no more than eccentric."

Náni looked up from the box she was riffling through.

"And the porn?"

"For a man of his age, on his own? Pretty mild stuff. Listen, Náni. I was thinking. While you're doing this, I might follow up with Vernardákis."

"What for?"

"I want to find out what he thinks of Papatónis and perhaps also ask his wife and daughter about the chainsaw, fill in any gaps."

"Sounds like a waste of time, Nick."

"Well, I don't think I'm needed here, and I learned something this morning. I'd like to follow it up."

"What was that?"

"I'd rather be sure of my facts before I share it with you, Náni, if you don't mind."

"Go on, then. We'll be here for a couple of hours, at least."

*

"My husband is not here," said Anna Vernardákis, in English.

"Will he be long?"

"He has gone to the garden centre at Arméni."

"Could I come in and wait?"

She lowered her head and swung the door back. Nick entered.

"Go on through," she called from behind him.

In the kitchen, the overweight girl with the pretty face was sitting at the kitchen table.

"Kaliméra," said Nick, but she mumbled "Yeiá" at her mobile phone and did not look up.

"I'm Nick Fisher."

"We know who you are, Mr Fisher," said Anna. "Can I get you something to drink?"

"Just water, please."

She took a large, plastic bottle from the fridge, filled a tall glass and handed it to him.

"Shall we sit in the garden?"

Nick followed Anna to the same garden table as before. She raised the parasol and they sat.

"Did Manólis tell you what we were discussing the other day?" asked Nick.

"About the young Swiss man?"

86

"Yes."

"You think *our* chainsaw was used to cut up his body, Mr Fisher?"

"It looks that way."

"And you think Manólis may have done this?"

"Do you?"

"Of course, not. He is a gentle man, Mr Fisher. The saw frightens him. He only uses it when he must."

"Maybe he was given no choice."

"No. I would know. Believe me, Mr Fisher, my husband could not do such a thing without me knowing. There would be a change in him I would see."

"Then you must help me find out who took it, Anna."

"Márkos Papatónis used to borrow it sometimes. Did you know?"

"Yes, and we are questioning him. Do you think *he* could do this?"

"Maybe. I don't know. He's a cold fish, that one, but Manólis seems to get on okay with him."

"Have you or Amalía ever used the saw?"

"God, no. We wouldn't go near the thing."

"Can you think of anyone else, if not Papatónis?"

"Manólis never lent it to anyone else, Mr Fisher. But, if it was stolen, anyone could have done it."

"Anyone who knew there was a chainsaw in the shed and where the key was kept. There was no forced entry, Anna. Someone used the key, opened the padlock and took the chainsaw. Later, they cleaned and returned it."

"Oh, I didn't realise."

"There was insider knowledge. If it wasn't Papatónis, it seems likely one of you told someone where the key was kept, perhaps without realising."

"Do you *know* it wasn't him, then?"

"Just gut feel at this stage, Anna. I was a policeman for thirty years."

"I see."

"What about Amalía?" said Nick.

"What about her?"

"Could she have told anyone? A boyfriend perhaps?"

"She doesn't have a boyfriend, Mr Fisher. She's fifteen years old."

"Are you quite sure?"

"We would not allow it."

"No, and she will know that, so it would have to be a covert relationship; a secret. Shall we ask her?"

"I don't want to drag her into this."

"Would you rather see Manólis arrested?"

Anna looked at him angrily. But she was torn. Nick pressed further:

"If she's involved, Anna, it would be better to know *now*, don't you think?"

Reluctantly, she got to her feet and disappeared inside. A few moments later, she ran back, looking fearful.

"She's gone. She must have run off while we were talking."

"Is that the sort of thing she does, sometimes?"

"No. At least, not until the last few weeks."

"Did you ask yourselves what changed?"

"She's a teenager, Mr Fisher. Odd behaviour comes with the territory."

At that moment they heard tyres on gravel, car doors slamming and the front door opening. Then a tearful Amalía appeared, pursued by Manólis. He looked even redder in the face than usual.

"What the hell is going on?" he demanded, glaring at Nick. "I find my daughter in tears, running up the lane and you here, alone with my wife."

"I came to see *you*, Vernardáki, and your wife has been kind enough to chat with me over a glass of water. Nothing more. I can't explain your daughter's behaviour but perhaps we could all sit down calmly together for a few minutes? I wanted to talk to Amalía, anyhow."

"Next time, you will make an appointment."

"You're right. I was too informal. I apologise."

"Anyway, I thought you'd got your man. The police are all over Papatónis's farm."

"I know. But it's not conclusive. Now, might I have five minutes with Amalía, alone?"

"No, you may not, Mr Fisher. I don't want her upset even more."

Nick looked helplessly at Anna.

"I'll stay with her, Manóli. It's all right. You get on with your potting," she said.

He looked from her to Amalía and back, then went off, shaking his head.

"Thanks," said Nick, and then softly, to Amalía, "Are you okay?"

She looked red in the face, like her dad, but no more tears, for now. She nodded.

"And can we talk in English?"

"Hers is better than mine," said Anna.

"Now, this is just between us, okay? You're not in trouble with me or the police but you must tell me the truth, Amalía. Do you understand?"

More nods and several blinks.

"Now, I may look old to you, but I remember being your age. It's when I started doing things my parents didn't like. Challenging them, making my own decisions. I started seeing all their failings and realising they didn't have any right to tell me what was right or wrong, what I could or couldn't do. Sound familiar?"

"You're *not* me, though."

"No, I'm not, but I think I was feeling much the same at your age. Suddenly, my parents were holding me back. They seemed petty, small-minded. My head was filling with bigger, more important ideas, like freedom, revolution … and love."

This time he won a tear and a pursing of the lips.

"Your mum says you don't have a boyfriend, but I'm not so sure. I think you've been seeing someone. A boy you're keen on. But you have to see each other secretly because you're young and you think your dad would kill you if he knew. Maybe the boy, too."

She rested her chin on her hand and stared off into the middle distance where a pair of crows were fighting on the chimney of the ruined house next door. A dog started yapping, excitedly.

"I love him, Mr Fisher."

"Oh, don't be so stu—" cut in Anna but Nick raised his hand to silence her.

"I wouldn't expect *you* to understand," she said to her mother in a vindictive tone. "What do *you* know about love?"

Anna looked shocked but said nothing.

"Is it Grigóris?" asked Nick, gently.

A light came into her eyes at the mention of his name, and she nodded, colour suffusing her cheeks.

"How long have you been seeing each other?"

"Almost two months."

"And why did he ask to borrow the chainsaw?"

She clammed up, then.

"You didn't, did you? You can't have. Even you're not that stu—"

"Anna, please!" said Nick. "She'll tell us in her own good time."

They watched as Amalía fiddled with the hem of her blouse. Then one of the dogs arrived and jumped onto her lap and it seemed to give her the confidence to speak:

"His mother has to cut wood for the stove. But the sawdust affects her lungs and it exhausts her, too. She's not well and it was breaking his heart seeing this, he said. If he could borrow the saw, he and his brother could cut the wood they would need for the stove and next winter's fires, all in one day. He said he knew how to use one and he'd clean it up afterwards. Dad would never know."

"And you wanted to please him, help him do some good."

"Right."

"So, you fetched it for him."

"No. Too risky. I told him where to find the key and left it to him. I think he took it pretty much straight away."

Anna's head was in her hands, Nick saw.

"Do you remember when this was, Amalía?" he asked.

"Yes. He called me on a Sunday evening. We talked for ages earlier in the day and then he called me again, much later. I was in my room."

"So, it was all arranged by phone?"

"Yes. It was well after dark, but I wasn't in bed yet, so I guess it was around ten, ten thirty."

"The Sunday nine days ago?"

"Er … yes. That's right."

"Didn't it strike you as odd, him calling back about that, so late at night?"

"Not really. We often chat or text quite late into the evening, and he was upset about his mum. Wanted to share with me."

"Have you seen him since?"

"Not so much. He's been busy with family stuff and work."

"Have you seen him at all?"

"Just around, you know …"

"But not for a date."

"Not yet, no."

"All right. Thank you, Amalía."

She gave a little smile of relief and stood up.

"Go to your room, Amalía, and stay there," said Anna. "And leave your phone on the table. We'll see later if you get to keep it or not."

With Amalía out of the way, Anna shared what happened with Manólis and then had to restrain him from rushing upstairs to beat some sense into the girl. When he was a little calmer, he assured Nick that Amalía was going nowhere and would not be allowed access to a phone.

"Don't be too hard on her, Manóli," Nick said. "She's been naïve and foolish but she's in love – or at least she thinks she is. Sadly, she's been played by an evil, young bastard by the look of it."

CHAPTER 13
THE BOAT TRIP

As he walked back up the hill, Nick felt eyes on him. It was one of the Katzatákis brothers, he saw, but not Grigóris. It was the one without a beard. The man looked away, then disappeared inside. Nick noticed a mammoth stack of freshly cut logs crammed into the carport.

Náni spotted him as soon as he arrived back at the farm.

"We're just packing up," she said. "Forensics have gone, armed with dried blood samples from all over the barn."

"How's Papatónis reacting?"

"He's just ignoring us, catching up on farm accounts or something."

"No more anger, frustration?"

"Not really."

"I don't think it was him, Náni."

"What?"

"I don't think he took Manólis's saw. I think it was Grigóris Katzatákis."

He took her through his interview with the Vernardákis family before continuing:

"I think we need to finish up here, and then I suggest you see the Investigating Judge and get a search warrant for the Katzatákis place. I can't imagine they would volunteer permission and I don't want them knowing we're on to them before we're in a position to start the search."

"Is it them – or just him?"

"Who knows? But Grigóris is involved. No question."

"All right. I can do that. But I'm not finished with Papatónis. Something's not right here. We'll see what the blood tells us."

"Agreed."

"And what will you be doing, Nick?"

"Sorry, but I have to head home. My son's arriving in less than a week and there are things I must sort out. Let me know when you have the warrant and I'll be back."

Náni looked a little surprised but said:

"All right, Nick. And well done – quite a breakthrough this morning."

He grinned as he jumped into the Suzuki. He should be getting ready for Jason, and his conscience was nagging away at him. He should be calling the garage about the Jeep, too, but there was something he was desperate to investigate first.

*

He drove home to Saktoúria. It was lunchtime now, so he went straight to the kafenío. Kóstas and his daughter Xará were doing well today; the place was almost half full. Yiórgos the fisherman was at his usual table.

"Níko! Tí káneis?" he roared, his face lighting up behind the bushy brown beard. He half stood and extended his hand.

"May I join you, Yiórgo?"

His right arm threw an extravagant arc of welcome.

"It would be a great honour, Níko." And, when Nick sat, he leaned forward in a conspiratorial manner and said, "I hear you have a new case."

"How did you hear that, Yiórgo?"

"You know Sofía, Níko. She know, everybody know. She proud of her boy."

"Right … Well, it's true. I'm helping find the killer of the Swiss lad."

"I know this. And you must find these bastards, my friend. Anyone who can do this should be cut into pieces himself, while he is still alive."

Xará was at their table now, smiling shyly.

"What you want, Níko?"

He ordered grilled sardines and a Greek salad, with an Alpha beer.

"I think you might be able to help me, Yiórgo."

Yiórgos pushed his plate to one side and put his elbows on the table. His face shone with eagerness.

"Tell me," he said.

"I'm looking for a boat owner, a fisherman. Someone who knows the waters around Triópetra. His fish are sold from an old, white van by a man named Yiánnis to people in the villages between Kardánes and the coast. Yiánnis might also be the fisherman, I'm not sure. I know he's related to the Katzatákis family in Kardánes."

"I know this Yiánnis. He delivers the fish here in Saktoúria, no?"

"That's him, yes."

"Miserable bastard."

"He is rather."

"But he is not fisherman. He has business with his brother. Leftéris catches the fish with his boat. Yiánnis sells the fish from his van."

"You know this Leftéris?"

"Sure. He is okay guy. He has blue and yellow fishing boat, maybe eight metres, with a small cabin, inboard diesel. He keeps her at Plakiás mostly – the new harbour."

"Do you remember the name of the boat?"

"There is a thing painted on the side. Half woman, half fish?"

"A mermaid, you mean?"

"Mermaid, yes. Maybe the boat is called *Gorgóna*? I am not sure."

"Would he know Triópetra?"

"We all do, Níko. It's not far."

Nick thanked him and then his lunch arrived, and the conversation turned to family. Yiórgos knew Jason was about to arrive. When Kóstas joined them for a rakí, they talked of little else.

"You fought for this boy, Níko," Kóstas reminded him, prodding him in the chest. "This visit is your prize – you get one shot to win him back, make everything okay." He stood up heavily, then leaned forward, wagging a fat finger. "Don't fuck it up, my friend."

*

Plakiás was a low-key resort now, since the withdrawal of the package tour operators. For them, it was just too far from the airports. Not many tourists would sign up for a long coach ride after a four-hour flight. And so, mass tourism blighted the *north* coast instead – places like Mália and Hersónissos. The town still got crowded in peak season, mid-July to the end of August, when Italians and mainland Greeks

94

came on the ferries, but now, in mid-June, it was less than half full; still largely undiscovered on the hottest day of the year so far.

Nick wound the Suzuki slowly through the town, recognising several locals, but also some of the tourists, too. Many fell for the place and returned, year after year. Taverna owners called out to him and the bar manager at Ostráko gave him a cheery wave.

The new harbour was on the road leading west to Soúda. Nick remembered the cranes, dropping moulded concrete shapes into the sea for weeks. In time, they would form a natural-looking wall. Or so the sales pitch went. But to Nick, fifteen years later, they still looked surreal; grey, formless torsos, piled face-down on top of one another. A jumble of concentration camp victims. Or a thousand replicas of poor Lukas's limbless corpse.

He pulled off the road onto the concrete apron in front of the small harbour. There were only one or two people about and less than ten boats, ranging from a small motorboat to a ten-metre day-cruiser. Several were fishing boats in bright colours, workhorses with winches and nets, some with cabins, others with awnings for sun protection. And one was bright blue and yellow. On the side, a beautiful girl was painted. Golden ringlets covered her breasts and the lower half of her body was a scaly, silver-green fishtail. Nick's pulse rate ticked up as he neared the boat. It was not *Gorgóna* though. The name scrolled on either side of the bow in Greek script was *Seirín*. Siren, Nick assumed. Close enough. It must be the boat.

"What you want, mister?"

A man was mending nets on the adjacent boat.

"This is Leftéris's boat, isn't it?"

"Who want to know?"

"My name's Nick. I was told he might take me out for a day's fishing."

"Who say this?"

"Some guy in a bar in Plakiás."

"Leftéris is fisherman. He don't do no day trips for tourists."

"Well, he might, surely. I'm offering a good rate. Do you know where I can find him?"

"He sleep now."

"Ah."

"He fishes in the night. You want night trip?"

"Maybe. Or perhaps he would do an afternoon. Is there a number I can reach him on?"

Another man was ambling up to join them.

"I don't have no number for Leftéris. Do you, Stélio?"

The other man shook his head.

"No, but I know where he eats, most days."

"Go on," said Nick.

"It's off the main street in Plakiás, by the river. Taverna Galátea. It's good food and cheap. That's why he likes it, I guess. He's there most weeknights around seven."

Nick checked his watch. It was ten to five and his beach kit was in the boot of the car. He could grab a swim at nearby Soúda before catching Leftéris at the taverna, hopefully. He thanked them both and returned to the car.

*

By six thirty, Nick was ensconced in the open-air bar across from Taverna Galátea. He felt refreshed from swimming across the bay and now there was a cold beer in front of him. And he was thinking. *He knew he needed to tread carefully. This man could be completely innocent. But the brothers were cousins of Grigóri. Yiánnis was arguing violently with Grigóri, and his brother Leftéris owned a boat which habitually went out at night. Thus far it seemed to fit. And yet Leftéris was an okay guy, according to Yiórgos. Could he have been duped by his brother?*

Nick sipped his beer. *The Doors* performed a medley of hits in the background. *Love Her Madly* was playing. *Don't you love her ways?* he heard, and it made him think of Jen. *Don't you love her as she's walking out the door …?*

And then he found himself staring at a man, but it took a second for the message to get to his brain. Was that him? A man of about

96

forty who looked Greek, just below medium-height, stocky and wiry, tanned, powerful arms. He ignored the tourist tables outside and went to the counter, where he chatted for a few moments with one of the owners before sitting alone at a table inside, by the window. He was known here. He was the only man sitting alone, he looked Greek and it was ten past seven. It was Leftéris. Nick stayed where he was. He would let the man finish his meal and then invite himself over for a rakí.

Half an hour later, *Supertramp* had superseded *The Doors*, Nick was replete from a rather dry burger and needed all his beer to wash it down. He could see the man wiping his mouth with a large, white napkin. He moved in. It was a fifty-fifty shot. He hoped they were cousins on the father's side.

"Signómi, kýrie Katzatáki?"

The man looked up lazily and, seeing Nick's fair hair and style of dress, spoke in English.

"I am Leftéris Katzatákis. Who are you?"

"My name is Nick Fisher. May I talk to you about your boat?"

"What is it you want with her?"

"I just want to ask you a few questions, sir. May I sit down?"

Nick sat down without being invited and the man poured himself a rakí.

"People who ask questions are usually from the police, the tax or the press in my experience, Mr Fisher. Which are you?"

"I'm *not* a policeman, but I am trying to help the police."

"Is this official, then? Do they know you're here?"

"No. I wanted to keep it informal, at this stage. Just me. And just a chat."

"A chat about my boat."

"The Seirín is your boat, isn't it?"

"Mine and the bank's. Yes."

"And you're a night fisherman, I understand. Are you going out tonight?"

"In an hour or two, yes."

"Do you fish every night?"

"Every weekday night, sometimes Saturdays."

"But not Sundays."

"No."

"And yet, I believe you took the boat out at night on Sunday, the week before last."

"What makes you think so?"

Nick took a flier.

"You were seen, returning to the harbour."

"I didn't say I never take the boat out on a Sunday. I just don't *work* Sundays."

"So, a pleasure trip, then."

"Something like that."

"Listen, Leftéri. I'm here to help you. Tell me the truth and maybe the police won't have to be involved. You can avoid all that. Get on with your life. But you need to be open with me."

"What is it you think I've done, Mr Fisher?"

"I'm looking for the boat that took the remains of a murder victim out to sea and disposed of them."

"Oh, my God! All right, Mr Fisher. Give me one minute and then I will explain what happened." He leaned forward as if sharing a confidence and patted Nick's arm. "Don't worry."

He got to his feet and went to use the toilet. After four minutes, he was still not back and Nick was about to go in after him when he spotted him at the counter. When Leftéris returned to the table, it was with a fresh mini carafe of rakí and two small glasses.

"We will drink to openness, Mr Fisher."

He poured and they clinked glasses.

"I will be frank with you, but this must be between the two of us. You and me. You will not share this with the Greek tax authorities."

"I'm not interested in tax."

"And you will not tell the police either."

"All right. Just between us."

"You see, it was not a pleasure trip. My brother, Yiánnis, he keeps the books for our business. He always does this. And he is good at it, or so I thought. Clever. Even in the best years, we never seemed to pay any tax."

"Like many Greeks, I believe."

"The culture here is that only a fool would pay it if he can avoid it. But times are changing now, in Greece. There's a huge crackdown. The EU makes them do it, I think, after borrowing all that money. Anyway, on the Sunday, Yiánnis calls my mobile in a panic, late at night. He's just heard a whisper that an investigations team from Réthymno is targeting our business and a few others in Plakiás and they're arriving Monday morning. He says we could face a bill of eighty-five thousand euros plus a huge amount of interest – maybe jail, too. Well, I couldn't believe it. We don't have that kind of money, nothing like. And then I was ready to kill him. He's kept two sets of accounts for seventeen years, the real one and one for the taxman. We have been *evading* tax all those years. Completely illegal. And now he has to destroy all the real records by morning, leave no audit trail."

"Time for a large bonfire, surely, or a shredder?"

"There was too much for a shredder. It would take days. And Yiánnis has a small garden surrounded by other houses. A late-night bonfire would be obvious. People would know, maybe tell. This is what happens here now. People snitch on one another. So, he asks me if we can take the boat out, dump it all at sea."

"Sounds a little crazy. Couldn't he just drive to a gorge and chuck it over the side?"

"But how long would this be safe? Our names are all over this stuff, it would get back. We could never rest. Anyway, eventually he convinces me this makes sense, so I tell him to wrap everything up good, weigh it down and drive it over."

"What time did he get to you?"

"Oh, it was very late. It must have taken him ages to pack it because it was getting towards dawn when we met at the boat."

"He brought packages; I assume. What did they look like?"

"Just black refuse bags, five or six, I think."

"Did you handle them?"

"No, he did this. I was getting the boat ready."

"And did you look in the bags, at any point?"

"What for?"

"Did you?"

"No."

"And then what happened?"

"We took the boat out. To be safe, we went about five hundred metres offshore and about three kilometres down the coast, away from Plakiás."

"And you dumped the bags there?"

"Yiánnis did, while I held the boat steady."

"Would you be able to find this place again, Leftéri?"

"What for? You want to go diving for a load of old books and papers?"

"Might do, just to be sure they are what you think they are."

"I could get close, maybe. Obviously, we didn't leave a marker buoy."

Leftéris glanced at his watch. It was almost nine.

"I need to get down to Seirín now, Mr Fisher. You can follow me down if you wish. I have nothing to hide from you. Take a look over the boat. I'll take you out to the spot if you want; it's not far. We can be there and back in an hour."

Nick was impressed with his openness and eagerness to clear things up.

"Why not?" he said. "I'd like to check out the boat."

Leftéris even paid for the rakí, refusing Nick's proffered note, and then he was jumping into a large, blue, Nissan pick-up which Nick followed down to the harbour. The place seemed deserted now, just the metallic sound of halyards whipping masts and the slap of seawater against the harbour wall. Nick saw Leftéris was already aboard Seirín and he hesitated for a moment.

"What are you waiting for?" he called, smiling broadly and beckoning with his arm. "Come aboard, Mr Fisher."

Nick stepped gingerly off the quayside and onto a plank that led down to the boat's wooden deck.

"Now, you can look anywhere you like. Where would you like to start?"

"Wherever those bags were put."

100

"All right. Well, as I recall, Yiánnis put them on the deck, towards the rear, and then I told him to drop them into the rear hold. It can be livelier than it looks here when the wind is up."

"And you didn't want the bags to fall into the water ..."

"Haha. Well, not just anyplace, you know?"

"So, do you mean back here?"

Nick was behind the small wheelhouse now, where he found a hatch cover adjacent to the stern.

"Yes, that's it, but it's easier to see from inside. Come. I will show you."

He lifted an opaque hatch cover in the centre of the craft and they descended a short, wooden staircase to the lower level, Nick had to duck his head a little as they made their way aft, past the living and sleeping area to a large, white cupboard.

"So, this cupboard door accesses the same area. Yiánnis dropped the bags in from the top and they sat in here until we arrived at the dropping point."

Nick opened the door and found the hatch empty apart from a couple of lifebuoys. It was dark, though. He would need light to see any dried blood.

"Do you have a torch I could borrow, Leftéri?"

"I can bring one. Give me a minute."

Nick felt around in the hatch cupboard but there was nothing to be found. The wood seemed dry enough. He could feel no encrustation. There was nothing more he could do without the torch. He heard water slapping gently against the hull. And then a different sound. Like the central hatch cover slamming shut. *Perhaps the wind caught it,* he thought. He hesitated a moment, then tried to squeeze himself into the cupboard and up, but then that hatch cover too was slammed down and clamped. A moment later, the weight of the boat shifted as someone jumped aboard the bow and then the knocking rumble of the inboard diesel engine kicked in, a gear was engaged, and he felt them reversing sharply away from the quay.

Oh, you bloody fool, Nick Fisher, he thought. Just like one of Leftéris's fish, he'd fallen for it; hook, line and sinker. There were no tax inspectors. Leftéris was not duped by his brother into thinking he was dumping business books. He knew perfectly well what was in those bags. Because he was in on it. There would be body parts, dumped on the seabed, five hundred metres out, at a probable depth of twenty or thirty metres. *And that's exactly where you're going, my son, if you don't get yourself out of this, and sharpish.*

A heavy clunk signalled a change of gear to forward drive and the engine surged from angry grumble to urgent roar as the Seirín pitched forward through the harbour entrance. Between the waves, Nick could still glimpse land through the row of small portholes. Under the harbour lights, he saw the white Suzuki and the dark blue Nissan and, over by the harbour wall, a scruffy white van. *So, he phoned his bloody brother from the toilet. Terrific.*

Then, he patted his pockets to confirm what he already knew. His phone was in the car. He felt his mouth go dry and his heart thump. He was in a strange boat heading out into the darkening Libyan Sea, outnumbered and locked below and no-one in the world knew he was there. Worse still, he remembered. They knew no-one knew. *Because you told Leftéris precisely that, you numbskull!*

He prowled around, tested the heavy hatches, looked for weak spots in the construction of the boat and found none. All that strength designed to keep the sea out was just as effective at keeping him in. And the portholes were tiny. He was trapped. Negotiate, fight, swim? But there was nothing to negotiate with. Fight and die then, or fight and drown – unless he could overpower them both and manage to pilot the boat back. Those were his options. The odds were long, the straws short.

The change beyond the harbour entrance was immediate and profound. The boat was pitching and yawing now in force three, gusting five, Nick reckoned. The engine revolutions were steady now, but the sound of the engine rose and fell with the waves. He could only move around by staggering, sitting down involuntarily or holding onto things. Waves of nausea were not far away.

He thought of Jason, arriving in just four days to be with his dad but, instead, learning of his disappearance or death. It would weigh heavily on the boy, after last year's ordeal.

He thought of Lauren. The bright girl halfway through her degree. The girl with the sparkling sense of humour. The daughter who, alone, stood by him after the break-up.

He thought of Jen and the little acts of kindness they still shared. She loved Stephen now, but she still loved him, too. He was sure of it, though he knew nothing would bring them back together. Maybe his death would simplify her life, deepen her bond with Stephen. The guy was a jerk, but he seemed a kind man; he would look after her. She would be okay.

And lastly, he thought about his new friends. The Cretan friends who welcomed him so warmly into their village, into their lives. Maybe Roúla could be a part of that. Maybe more than that. These were the fragile foundations of his new life. His short, new life.

His bitter self-pity turned slowly to anger. Cold anger. The kind where you know you have nothing to lose. Where you move swiftly, where your heightened senses find resourcefulness, lucidity. In a few minutes, they would arrive at their destination and they would come for him. He needed a plan. If it came to a fight, he was sure he could take Yiánnis, but Leftéris was a different matter. And they could be armed.

He thought about sabotage. There could well be matches in the tiny galley area, perhaps fuel or cooking oil, but any fire would be hard to control, and the most likely victim would be Nick himself. Not a great idea. No, he needed weapons.

He rummaged through the cutlery drawer in the galley, but the knives were all cheap plastic rubbish. There was not even a decent bread knife. He opened all the cupboards then, until his eyes lit on a familiar-looking bottle, under the tiny sink. It looked like bleach. Maybe only a quarter full, but enough. He took off the cap and checked for the unmistakable smell, then found a small, washing-up liquid bottle on the shelf above, removed the cap and emptied the plastic, squeezable container. He swilled it with water. The sink was not draining for some reason, but no matter. Then he filled the container with the bleach and gave it a test squeeze. Weapon number one.

He left the galley then and tried to get into the engine compartment. A hammer, a large screwdriver or a heavy spanner would be a great addition to the armoury. He could get close, heard the mega horse-power diesel throbbing and grinding away, but it was all sealed off. There was no access from below decks, dammit. There must be a hatch on deck.

Then he started rummaging through the cupboards under the sleeping area. He found oilskins, thick, greasy jumpers and boots, a stack of charts, a larder full of canned food and clear, plastic bottles full of rakí. He grabbed a couple of small cans and put them in his shorts, hesitated, then took a slug of rakí, too. Then he heard the engine note change. The revolutions dropped a notch. They were slowing down.

His search became more frantic. He found an electrics box, a tangle of wire, fuses, plugs and bulbs, and spotted a small, electrical screwdriver which he grabbed and tucked into his belt. The engine note dropped again, and the waves started slapping the sides of the boat. Nick gathered his pathetic array of weaponry: baked bean cans in the pockets, a squeezable bottle, half-filled with bleach, and an electrical screwdriver jammed into his belt, at the back.

And then he saw it. Of course, there would have to be one. He must have seen it so many times, it ceased to register, but there it was, bright red, mounted at the exit to the galley. It was only a small one, but it would help. He undid the metal band and lifted it out of its cradle. He was holding the table as he tried to read the instructions when the engine note dropped to idle, and the boat started wallowing. He loosened his belt a couple of notches, moved the screwdriver to his pocket and tucked the fire extinguisher in the back of the belt, alongside the bleach.

He heard the clamps released from the central hatch and then a gust of wind and the sight of the first few stars as the hatch opened.

"It's a beautiful night, Mr Fisher. Won't you join us on deck?"

Nick stayed silent and did not move. Leftéris moved forward and Nick saw the dull sheen of a machete in the moonlight.

"I am afraid I must insist, Mr Fisher. My brother would like to meet you, and we have a very fair proposal for you."

Nick pulled his tee-shirt down over his belt and came into the light as he made his way forward to the ladder.

"That's better. Up you come."

Nick climbed the ladder and stepped out onto the deck, staggering for a moment as the boat lurched.

Leftéris took a step back and levelled the machete at Nick's neck. "Now search him, Yiánni."

The moustachioed fish vendor quickly found his car keys and his entire collection of improvised weapons and placed them, one by one, on the deck. Nick's heart sank.

"A curious survival kit, Mr Fisher," said Leftéris. "I assume the screwdriver is to open the cans of beans and the Fairy Liquid to wash up afterwards? How domesticated you British men are. The fire extinguisher is a mystery, though. I doubt you'll need one where you're going."

Nick said nothing. He was sizing up Yiánnis, as he lobbed Nick's weapons through the hatch to the lower deck. He might be unarmed.

"As you will have realised, Mr Fisher, we have no issues with the Greek tax inspectors. Not yet, at any rate. Our only problem is you."

"And the escaping body part, I'd suggest."

"Yes. That was regrettable." He shot a disparaging look at Yiánnis. "I think you have a saying in England: *the cat is out of the bag*, no?"

"We do, indeed."

"And so, we must be extra careful, now."

"Killing me is not being careful, Leftéri."

"You told me yourself that you are acting alone. I would say no-one else is aware of our involvement."

"That's not the case, but, even if it were, it would only be a matter of time. The police know your cousin Grigóris took the chainsaw. How long before he gives you up?"

"The man's lying," said Yiánnis. "The cops think it's Papatónis."

"Not anymore," said Nick. "But the police don't know who killed Lukas Hedinger. If it *wasn't* you, then killing me would be downright stupid. Why put yourselves on a murder charge if all you did was dispose of the body? Why turn two or three years' jail into fifteen or more?"

"We don't see ourselves on any murder charge, though, do we Yiánni?"

"Murder? No. Not the word we had in mind. We were thinking more of *accident*. Just another foreigner drowns off Crete. No big deal."

"Which is why we are here, five or so kilometres from the beach. It's a long swim, Mr Fisher. I don't think you're going to make it. But I would like to give you a sporting chance. You will remove your clothes and your watch."

"Why?"

"So, when we drive your car round to Triópetra, we can leave them in a neat pile on the beach where you started your swim. It will help the police conclude it was an accident – or perhaps suicide. Have you felt depressed recently, Mr Fisher?"

"A little, but only *very* recently."

"The great British sense of humour, is it? The stiff upper lip? You will undress now, please."

"And, if I refuse?"

"Then things will get rather messy, I'm afraid. Not good for either of us. You will be in pieces, joining the boy at the bottom of the sea, and we will have committed a murder we'd prefer to avoid."

He moved forward, raising the machete, and Yiánnis drew back his windcheater to reveal a large hunting knife, attached to his belt, which he now slipped from its sheath. The lethal blade caught the moonlight.

Nick raised his hands and backed away until he bumped the side.

"All right, gentlemen. Take it easy. I'll do as you ask."

He removed his top and his shorts and then put his feet on the bench, one by one, to unlace his espadrilles. There was a cleat on the gunwale, he noticed. Excess rope was coiled on the bench-seat below it.

"Those, too," said Leftéris, jerking his head at Nick's underpants.

Reluctantly, he slipped them off, too, and made a neat pile of his clothes, espadrilles on top, and placed it on the deck. Then he went forward to hand Leftéris his watch.

"This was a present from my wife. Please take care of it. I'd like my son to have it."

Lefléris was looking at it closely when the next boat lurch came. Nick contrived to topple over backwards and fell against the side with a thump. As he hit the bench, he reached behind him, grabbed the coil of thin rope. Then, as he slid back up, cursing and pretending to have hurt his back, he flipped the bunch of rope backwards, over the side. With any luck, it would still be attached to the cleat but now dangling in the water.

"Oh, Jesus, that hurt," he moaned, still rubbing his back.

The others regained their footing quickly. The machete and the knife were once again pointed at him, but they seemed not to have noticed the rope trick in the semi-darkness. Nick resisted the urge to look back and make sure it worked.

"All right, Fisher, it's time for you to leave. Now move."

He prodded Nick in the stomach with the point of the machete, breaking the skin.

"Turn around, now, and get yourself over the side."

He prodded him again, in the back. A sharp stab. Nick saw black water below. He scanned the horizon and saw only more black water, reflecting moonlight. He took a deep breath and jumped. The water was fresh, but not too cold.

"Now move away twenty metres," called Yiánnis, pointing a torch at him.

After a few strokes, Nick glanced back at the boat. He could just see the slim rope hanging over the side and memorised its position. He appeared to be swimming steadily, but he was hanging back, not using his legs. He was no more than fifteen metres from the boat when Yiánnis yelled: "Okay." He had gone far enough. Then, the man seemed to lose interest. He flicked the torch in Nick's direction once or twice to make sure he was still there, then went below. Nick knew it was now or never. He ducked under and struck out as fast as he could for the bow.

"Okay, Yiánni?" he heard Lefléris call from the wheelhouse.

"Let's go," his brother called back in Greek, and Nick heard the engine revolutions building, then the massive clunk as the gear engaged, but he was still five, maybe six metres away. The boat was moving already. He saw the crest of a bow wave forming as he groped for the side, just back from the bow. He heard the engine surge, felt the boat sliding past his hand and then, thank God, the texture of thin rope in the water. He grabbed it and looped it twice around his right wrist. As the boat accelerated into its course, it swung him round and he hit his head, hard, but he held on as the rope cut into his wrist. As the direction levelled out, the bow wave buffeted him violently and periodically smacked him into the side but, with the engine roaring, there was no way they could hear him. Also, he was below their field of vision unless they took it into their heads to shine the torch over the side. But there was no reason for them to do so. They were rid of him and heading home, scot-free. Or so they thought.

After what felt like an hour, but was probably no more than fifteen minutes, Nick's wrist was burned sore and his arms felt like they were being wrenched from their sockets, but still, he held on, somehow. It occurred to him, if he let go, he could be sucked into the propellers and the thought kept him focused. He was weary from being buffeted by the waves and sick from swallowing seawater. He knew he would not be strong enough to wind himself in and get aboard. Climbing the side of a boat in motion is a Herculean task at the best of times. In his condition, at seven or eight knots and in this swell, it was out of the question. He reckoned the trip out took twenty-five minutes. Another ten minutes to hang on, then. It did not seem possible.

Moments later, he became aware of something. They were changing direction, swinging to port, and he was pivoting wider, away from the side of the boat as they did so. More visible. He could see Leftéris in the wheelhouse but Yiánnis was still below decks. No-one was keeping watch. For the first time, he could glimpse across, beyond the stern. They must have taken more of a dog-leg route back, heading in towards the coast and now cutting across the last few kilometres. He could make out the silhouette of the coastline in the moonlight. There was surf breaking and, as his eyes cleared, he saw they were passing a rocky promontory, perhaps two kilometres away. Was it? Could it be? He looked away and then looked again. No question, there were giant rocks at the end. Even from this angle, those were the unmistakable, slanting towers at Triópetra. The turn had pulled him wide of the boat, away from the propellers, but the angle was narrowing fast as they completed the manoeuvre. It was now or never.

He double-checked the distance, as far as he could, then gritted his teeth and let go of the rope. He kicked hard as he did so, found himself engulfed in a maelstrom of wake and felt panic rising at the thought of those killer blades, but then he was through it. It was okay. He was well clear. He floated on his back for several minutes as the sound of the engine faded and the thudding of his heart slowed. The pain in his arms, shoulders and head welled up, but he was free, safe in the arms of the swell. Thank God.

As his eyes adjusted to the moonlight, he realised he could see surprisingly well. His arms were tortured, but they would have to cope. He would need to pace himself. This was the open sea, not the calm waters of Soúda, and two kilometres would be his longest ever swim – especially on top of the six hundred metres clocked up just five or six hours ago – but he could do it. If he was right about the distance, there was a good chance of making it. He needed, above all, to keep calm, swim steadily and rest frequently. He rolled over onto his front and started a steady, painful breaststroke. He could make out the rocks, now over to his right. They looked farther away now, but he put that out of his mind. *Stay positive! Two kilometres. Eighty lengths*, he thought. *Eighty lengths of the pool.* That's all. Little by little, he could do it. At least the water was not cold, the wind might be easing a fraction, and there was the moonlight. *Thank God for the moonlight.*

CHAPTER 14
THE LONG SWIM

Náni spent most of the afternoon with the Investigating Judge, bringing her up to speed. The judge made it clear she was uncomfortable with a case of such importance being led by a sergeant, especially one new to the area. That she was a woman cut no ice with her. Náni was careful to point out the active support of Lieutenant Stávros Theodórou and the day-to-day involvement of former London DCI, Nick Fisher. She sang Nick's praises in her bid to secure the judge's confidence. The judge remained non-committal but went through the investigation in considerable detail with her. It was not until seven that she was persuaded by Náni's arguments and agreed to issue a warrant to search the Katzatákis premises.

By the time the paperwork was organised and signed, it was ten past eight and Náni was starving. She took herself to a taverna and ordered pastítsio with gigántes, then called her partner to apologise, once again. She would not make it back for dinner. Then she called the station and put together a search team of three constables to join her the following morning.

"I want to go in early, Christó, catch them unawares," she said, "and these are farmers, so I mean early. Let's assemble on the top road above Kardánes at five thirty tomorrow morning. Can you cope?"

Chrístos winced at his apprehensive colleagues.

"I'm sure we can, ma'am," he said.

She finished her dinner and rang Nick's mobile, but it went to voicemail, so she left a message, asking him to call back before eleven. It was not until she put her head on the pillow, at twenty past eleven, that it occurred to her; he had not called.

*

Nick reckoned he was an hour into the swim. His shoulders were aching, and he was thirsty. And he could not be sure he was any nearer. Was it an illusion? He should have covered half the distance by now.

110

Maybe it was his eyes. The saltwater and the buffeting of the waves were making them smart and blur. He struggled to see the rocks, let alone judge their distance with any accuracy.

He tried the crawl, here and there, but it was too exhausting. He tried backstroke but seemed to make little headway. He used side-stroke but found it harder on the shoulders. Every time, he reverted to breaststroke. He swam for fifteen minutes or so, then floated on his back for a couple of minutes before winding himself back into the relentless rhythm of the swim.

There were moments of terror. *Are there sharks in the Mediterranean?* he asked himself in a panic, at one point. He thought the answer was *No,* but he was not certain. Then suddenly every shadow, every wave, concealed a dorsal fin, every splash became an angry, swishing tail until he forced himself back under control, talking to himself and taking deep breaths.

There were moments of despair when he knew it was impossible. What if it was not two kilometres, but five? What made him think he could judge distances across the sea at night? It was notoriously difficult, and now everything was staked on that judgment. He should have clung onto that rope for a few more minutes. And then he cursed himself for his stupidity, his over-confidence.

He thought about dying. About drowning. Was it a subtle, mesmeric thing? Did you reach a point where you accepted death, lulled by the deceitful sea? When your eyes half-closed, your throat opened, and your lungs let the seawater pour in. Would you just forget to choke, then sink with relief into the arms of Poseidon? Or was it a desperate, gasping thrash? Would he feel himself choking, lungs exploding? He did not know. And he had no wish to find out, he decided. Not today. Not ever. And so, he ploughed on, at one with the sea, becoming part of it. Timeless. Lost.

There came a point, when his body was crying out to stop, that he saw something move. It took him several seconds to realise it was a light, over to the right, on the land ahead. No, wait. Two pairs of headlights weaving through the hills, sometimes visible, sometimes not. They were coming down the road to the beach, just this side of the rocks. He could make out two cars, one bigger and darker than the other. They parked and Nick saw a flash of reflected moonlight as a door slammed. He heard it about two seconds later, he reckoned. It was only faint, but it was unmistakable.

Even in his befuddled state, Nick knew sound travelled at about twenty kilometres a minute. That was the same thing as one-third of a kilometre a second, meaning the cars must be something like two-thirds of a kilometre away. Less than seven hundred metres. And that was diagonally across the water. The straight line between him and the shore must be less, perhaps as little as five hundred. Just twenty lengths of the pool. The discovery invigorated him. His aching body grated forward like Yiánnis's gearbox as if all the muscles and cartilage were just so much stripped synchromesh, leaving bone, grinding on bone. But his spirit was stronger now. He just might make it.

As he continued to look, he saw the darker vehicle drive away and he followed its lights as it dodged and weaved up the mountain, leaving the lighter vehicle on the beach, lights off.

Five times in that final stretch, Nick rolled on his back and each time he passed out and woke choking. His throat was raw now, but he sensed he was close. It took him a while, but finally, he heard the sounds of the gentle surf and felt the glorious sensation of shingle scraping his chest and was able to haul himself to his knees in the shallows and crawl, bit by bit, out of the water. A bird was singing not far away, and he was vaguely conscious of the faintest light creeping into the sky as he fell into an immediate, deep sleep.

*

Náni called again at five am. Nick would not welcome a call at this hour, but she was sure he wanted to be part of the search. He wanted to be told when the warrant was through, after all. When the mobile switched to voicemail again, she left a more explicit message, telling him the search was starting in half an hour and asking him to get in touch as soon as he got the message. As she disconnected, she felt uneasy.

*

The sun was well above the horizon when Nick stirred. He figured it was between seven thirty and nine am. His eyes were sore, and his mouth was parched and caked with salt. The wrist on his right arm was red raw, and his shoulders felt like they had been front row, grinding against the All Blacks in some endless scrum. The rest of his body seemed to have spent the night on a medieval torture rack; stretched and strained and aching everywhere. And he was stark naked.

Fortunately, the beach was empty, apart from a small boy and a dog, playing in front of a taverna, perhaps two hundred metres to his left. A taverna he recognised. He staggered to his feet. Now, he knew where he was. This was Lígres beach. He thought about walking to the taverna to get water, perhaps borrow some shorts, but his nakedness deterred him. The owner knew him a little. Nick was not sure he wanted the guy to know him *that* well and then he remembered the young wife and daughter. No. Not on. Even holding a bunch of seaweed. He knew, if he walked in the other direction, east, it was around two kilometres to Triópetra. With luck, the beach would be deserted all the way. He rubbed his aching muscles and started scrunching his way, painfully, along the shingle.

After a few minutes, he came to a small, sand and rock promontory and swam around to the next beach. This was less attractive, part sand, part flat rocks, and deserted. The little swim loosened up his muscles and Nick began to enjoy the walk and the sense of freedom of being alone and alive, as God intended, on this magical island. When he was halfway across, he spotted a green pick-up truck, loaded with tomatoes, and saw that a sandy road was now hugging the rear of the beach. At the end of this next stretch, he realised he would have to scramble over a mass of rocks or take the road briefly to get through to the western end of Triópetra beach. A few minutes later, it was decision time. After listening to silence for a few seconds, he decided to take a chance.

*

Náni decided speed was of the essence, hence the early start. If their search justified it, she would call in the forensics team. It was the grey light of dawn, but the sun was not up. After they rapped on the door, there was a delay before a young man in his late twenties appeared, rubbing his eyes. It was the one without the beard, Náni observed, Andréas.

"What's all this?" he asked, apparently bewildered.

"We are here to search these premises and we would like to ask Grigóri some questions."

"They're all in bed. Can't we do it later?"

"I don't need your permission. I have a warrant. Now step aside, please."

She thrust a copy of the warrant into his hands and pushed past him into the house. She saw the mother, Aléxia, nursing a cup of tea or coffee at the kitchen table.

"Kaliméra, kyría Katzatáki. You will please wake your other sons and bring them here."

"Why are you doing this? What's going on?"

"We are pursuing inquiries into the death of Lukas Hedinger and we have a warrant to search your house and land."

"What for? What are you looking for? What are we supposed to have done?"

"We have information which casts suspicion on your family. The search will help us decide what actions to take."

"What information?" she asked, but Náni was not answering any more questions.

Aléxia rose sullenly to her feet. Náni followed her as she shuffled off to wake the others.

*

The search took two hours. The sons paid scant attention to order or cleanliness and their mother either could not cope or was past caring. The place was a pigsty, inside and out. There were few out-buildings, just a chicken shed with a wired-off run, the ramshackle, fibreglass carport and a larger, concrete building without doors which was one-third store and two-thirds sheep pen, though they saw only a handful of tatty-looking animals. There was nowhere to slaughter animals – or humans.

Grigóris denied both taking the chainsaw and having asked Amalía about it. Then, faced with no choice, he admitted to asking her but claimed he never actually borrowed it. When asked about the pile of fresh-cut logs in the carport, he claimed they used a handsaw.

"Why would you ask to borrow a chainsaw then use a handsaw instead?" asked Náni.

"Theo offered to help. He said we wouldn't need the chainsaw if there were two of us doing it. And anyway, he thought I should *ask* Manóli before I borrowed it."

But this was desperate stuff. And then Stéfanos pointed out that the logs were cleanly cut, with occasional chain marks. No way were they cut by hand.

But the clincher came when Níkos emerged from the bedroom Theo and Grigóris shared. He was holding a small cardboard box and looking pleased with himself.

"What have you got there, Níko?" Náni asked.

"Enough to buy ten or more chainsaws, I reckon, ma'am. It was out of sight, on top of the wardrobe."

Náni did not hesitate. She would take the two younger brothers to Réthymno for further questioning. As they were escorting them to the police car, they encountered Papatónis at the gate.

"Might I have a word, Sergeant?"

She nodded and moved to one side.

"What is it, Papatóni?"

"I see you've switched your attention to my neighbours."

"Our inquiries are ongoing."

"There is something you may not be aware of."

She waited expectantly, hands on hips.

"They have another piece of land, about five or six stremmata, off the top road. You may want to look that over, too."

"What do they have there?"

"A few more animals, a water tank and a sheep barn."

"Would you show my constable, please?"

"Be glad to."

Náni told Stéfanos to take Papatónis, leaving the five of them to squeeze into the other police car. She asked Chrístos to drive slowly through the village, the flashing, blue light bouncing off the white-washed, stone houses. She wanted the village to know. She sensed others were involved and she wanted them scared now.

As they left the village, she checked her watch. Ten minutes to eight. Nick must be awake by now. She called him then, but once again it went to voicemail. This time she called in:

"Déspina? It's Náni. Can you run a trace on this mobile for me?" She read out the number. "It's Nick Fisher's mobile. I've tried to get him three times since last night. Find out where the phone is and, if you still can't get a reply, drive over there for me. I'm getting concerned."

She told her they were on their way back with the Katzatákis boys. She might need Nick's help in questioning them, but she kept that to herself.

CHAPTER 15
OVER-EXPOSURE

There were only two hundred metres of road to negotiate and then he could get down on the gritty sand again. That would be the start of the huge beach, ending with the three massive sandstone rocks that gave Triópetra its name. The first half of the beach, at least, was deserted. Then there was a small café with an empty seating area and, some distance beyond, two stretches of sun loungers with umbrellas. They would be busy later, but they might be empty at this time of day. He could see a small, white car parked behind them, where all the tourists parked. For now, it was the only car.

Whereas he had been comfortable at the water's edge, back here on the sandy tarmac he felt exposed. It was too civilised a setting to be ambling along starkers. When he spotted the feathery leaves of a tamarisk tree, he pulled off a small, broken branch.

He must have been less than fifty metres from safety when he became aware of an engine purring behind him. The sand on the road must have muffled the tyre noise. The driver flipped the siren on and off twice and it sounded almost like a wolf whistle. Nick turned to see a blue and white Skoda and the highly amused face of Constable Déspina Karagiánnis. As she drew up beside him, he deftly positioned the tamarisk branch.

"No fig leaves available, Mr Fisher?" she teased.

"Sorry about this. It's a long story. But you can take me to my clothes if you like."

"I suppose I could. You'd better sit in the back. People might talk."

Nick felt foolish, especially when Déspina said:

"No, I don't want your tree as well, sir! Those things drop tiny needles everywhere. Just get in. I've seen naked men before in my life."

Nick did as he was told, doing his best to arrange his hands strategically in his lap.

"If you could drive to the white car, way over there. I'm hoping it's mine."

"You're not sure?"

"I think it is."

"Don't you remember where you parked it?"

"It wasn't me."

"This *is* going to be an interesting story," she said as they set off around the back of the long beach.

A few minutes later, they pulled up alongside the Suzuki.

"I'd prefer to stay here, for obvious reasons," said Nick. "Perhaps you could check for me if the keys are in the car. If not, I'm hoping you'll find them with a small pile of clothes on one of the sun loungers or somewhere nearby."

Déspina was still smirking as she got out of the car. Nick saw her slip on a forensic glove before testing the door handle of the Suzuki and finding it locked. She peered inside for a moment, then headed down to the sun loungers before veering to her right for thirty metres. Then she looked back and gave him a thumbs up. A minute later, she was back.

"You have shorts, pants, tee-shirt and espadrilles. The watch and keys are in the pockets of the shorts."

"Brilliant."

She passed them through the window, averting her eyes.

"You're lucky to still have your mobile phone. It's sitting on the passenger seat. Now I'll give you a minute, sir."

She walked off in the direction of the first of the tavernas behind the beach.

Nick swung his legs across the back seat and wriggled into his underpants and shorts. He held the watch in his hand for a long moment, then put it on. Then he stepped out of the car to put on the tee shirt and the espadrilles. By the time Déspina returned with an ice-cold bottle of water and a sesame seed dough ring, he had retrieved his phone from the car and was reading messages from Náni.

He took a huge swig, gratefully, and she tore off a chunk of the dough ring for him.

"The guy from the taverna didn't see a thing," she said. "Says the car must have arrived during the night."

"It did. I saw it," said Nick, "from out there." He waved a hand at the sea.

"You were on a boat?"

"Not for the last five hours, no. I *started* on a boat."

She looked shocked and was about to speak again when Nick cut her off:

"I'll explain later. Náni's been trying to reach me."

"I know. She asked me to find you; she was worried."

"I'm touched. What happened with the search this morning? Do you know?"

"Last I heard, they were bringing two of the Katzatákis boys in for questioning."

"What time was that?"

"She called me about eight, I think."

Nick checked his watch. It was nine thirty-five.

"I'll call her now," said Déspina.

There was a rapid exchange in Greek, which was too fast for Nick to follow but involved Déspina raising her voice and then rolling her eyes. Then she put the phone to her chest for a moment.

"She's in the Interview Room with the suspects. I've asked them to drag her out."

She tapped on the car impatiently.

"Yes. Náni?"

More rapid Greek followed, ending in a peal of laughter. She handed the phone to Nick.

"I hear Déspina has you on an indecent exposure charge, Mr Fisher."

"Surely not. I did find a small tamarisk branch."

"A little too small, I'm told."

"Oh, dear." Nick felt himself colouring up like a naughty schoolboy. "Look, Náni, I'll explain everything later. I can come to Réthymno right now if you want me to join the questioning, but first, there are a few things you need to know."

He went on to explain in some detail about Leftéris and Yiánnis and what they did.

"So, they disposed of the body, Nick?"

"No question. Maybe more than that. And then there's what they tried to do to me."

"What's the connection with the Katzatákis brothers?"

"It's all one happy family. Leftéris and Yiánnis are also brothers and they are cousins of the Katzatákis boys in Kardánes."

"All right, Nick, we'll try to bring them in as well … And one other thing?"

"Go on."

There was an ominous pause. Nick knew what was coming.

"Never do this again, Nick Fisher. I'm serious. You spun me some yarn about getting ready for your son. Actually, you lied to me. I had no *idea* what you were up to and you very nearly got yourself killed."

Even through the ether, he could feel her eyes boring into him.

"Did you think, for a single moment, about the shit you'd be dropping *me* in? I'd have to divert very scarce resources to investigate your disappearance, they'd draft in some senior guy from Athína, maybe even put me back to constable for being incompetent. And meanwhile, these nasty bastards would know more about what's going on than the police – and all thanks to you! We'd never catch them."

"But I'd be in even worse shit, in that scenario."

As soon as the words were out, her voice became acid with suppressed fury:

"You just don't get it, do you. That's a risk *you* chose to take, Nick. I'm lost for words, to be honest. It's no way to conduct a police investigation and you know it. We're supposed to be a team. A team works together, helps each other. *Communicates.* This is not some competition where the best cop wins, where the great DCI Fisher has to come out on top to overcome his past failings. It's teamwork, for Christ's sake. Get it into your thick skull. So, next time? You call me first, we discuss and agree your plans *in advance*, then we set up a safety net of some sort, with back up. Agreed?"

"You're absolutely right."

"You'd better mean it, Nick. Be in no doubt, if you pull a stunt like this again, I'll take you off the case and make sure the Greek police never work with you again."

"All right, Náni."

"Good. I hope we understand each other."

She remained silent for a few more seconds to let the message sink in before getting back to the update.

"So, Stéfanos called me. The Katzatákis family owns a separate piece of land, up on the ridge road. There's a sheep barn up there with some dried blood, we think. Forensics are going in."

"It's all coming together, by the sound of it."

"We're even getting the K-9 on Monday."

"Isn't it a bit late for that?"

"They can follow trails up to two weeks old, apparently."

"Astonishing. Did we get confirmation on the various blood samples yet?"

"No. Not yet."

"We need to *prove* it was Lukas's blood on the saw."

"I know. Fingers crossed."

"Meanwhile, we pretend."

"Agreed."

*

It was ten twenty by the time they arrived at Réthymno police station. Nick needed a hot shower and a plate of bacon and eggs, not to mention a deep tissue massage and about twenty-four hours sleep, but he figured this was more important.

"I've made them wait," said Náni, "and I've sent two cars to bring in the cousins."

"They might be armed."

"Our police pistols should be more than a match for a machete or a knife, Nick."

"Ah yes, I was forgetting."

"Are you sure you're okay?" She frowned at his strained, pink eyes.

"I've been better, but I can manage a few hours yet."

"Right then. Just to bring you up to speed, Grigóris has admitted asking Amalía about the chainsaw but claims he did not then borrow it. A lie, we believe. Both he and Theo deny ever meeting Lukas Hedinger. Not sure either way about that."

"And money was found, I gather?"

"Yes. Three thousand, five hundred euros, in cash, hidden in their bedroom."

"Wow. By the look of their place, that must be the largest sum they've ever seen. Did they both know it was there, do you think?"

"Not sure, but my gut tells me Grigóris is the driving force behind this. Maybe Theo knows something about it."

"Why do you say that?"

"Grigóris comes across as fearless and unpleasant, full of animosity. They're all xenophobes, the whole family, which is laughable because they're such a poor example of Greeks. But there's something worse about Grigóris, I feel."

"And the mother and the other brother, Andréas?"

"They may be unaware. It's hard to say."

"They turn the sheep barn into an abattoir, and the others don't know?"

"It's one of the things we need to work out."

"And have you asked them about the disposal of the body parts – about my guys?"

"No. You can do that yourself if you like, but they don't have much English. Can you cope in Greek?"

"I'll have a go. You might have to help me out, here and there."

Nick excused himself and splashed some water on his face, bathed his eyes and combed his hair with his fingers. As he passed back through the main office, Déspina slipped a jar of antiseptic cream into his hands.

"You must rub some of this into that wrist."

"That's very thoughtful. Thanks."

"And this might help, too."

She handed him a coffee cup with a lid and a paper bag. Nick peeped inside and saw a large slice of spanakópita and a small, sugary, apple pastry.

"You," he said, "are an angel."

*

The interview room was air-conditioned but still too warm. The only windows were near the ceiling and were there to let in light rather than air, Nick assumed. It smelled of stale cigarette smoke and body odour. The young men were slouching in insolent postures, particularly the younger one, Grigóris, whose hands were clasped behind his head, legs stretched straight out in front of him. A uniformed constable Nick recognised as Chrístos was standing against the wall.

"I am sorry to have kept you waiting, *gentlemen*," said Náni, with ironic courtesy. "May I introduce Mr Nick Fisher? He is a former British policeman who is assisting us with this investigation."

"Why?" asked Grigóris.

"Why what?"

"Why is a foreigner involved?"

"Mr Fisher has many years of experience. He lives in Crete and has worked with us before."

"Still doesn't make sense."

"Do you have a problem with foreigners, Grigóri? Is that what this case is all about?"

He leered at his brother but said nothing.

"We are going to interview you separately," announced Náni. "The constable will escort you to a waiting room, Theo."

She nodded at Chrístos and Grigóris gave his brother a long look before Theo was led out. Two minutes later, Chrístos returned and Náni started the recording, speaking in Greek:

"Interview with Grigóri Katzatákis re-commenced at ten fifty-two am on Thursday, the twentieth of June. Also in the room are Sergeant Samarákis, Constable Manikákis and Mr Nick Fisher."

"You are the youngest of three brothers living with your mother, Aléxia Katzatákis, in the village of Kardánes. Correct?"

He tilted his head in sullen acknowledgement.

"I need a vocal response for the recording, please."

"I am."

"Good. And you share a bedroom with your brother Theodóris?"

"Yes."

"A police search of your bedroom this morning discovered a cardboard box containing three thousand, five hundred euros. That's a lot of money for a young man from a poor family. Could you explain how you came by it and why it was hidden?"

"If it was there, I know nothing about it."

"*If* it was there?" hissed Nick, in English. "That's an offensive remark, you little prick. It's slanderous, actually, but it's also ridiculous. Do you *really* imagine the police have thousands of euros in a secret stash which they use to incriminate low lifes like you?"

Náni translated for him, toning down the language, no doubt.

"Wouldn't put it past them," said Grigóris.

Nick was shaking his head in despair.

"Anyway, we're testing for fingerprints, so we'll know if you touched it," said Náni.

"If you can dream up an innocent reason for the money being there, I strongly suggest you share it with us now," said Nick.

He remained silent. Nick spoke again:

"Then we will assume the reason is not an innocent one. Did someone pay you to kill Lukas Hedinger, Grigóri?"

"I said already: I never even met this guy Hedinger."

"Tell us about your relationship with Amalía Vernardákis."

"Relationship?"

"You already admitted to seeing her several times," said Náni.

"Yeah. The blob lusts after me so I shagged her a couple of times. So what?"

"What a charmless young man you are. And yet this foolish girl adores you."

"Yeah, I know. It's embarrassing."

"Did you start this *relationship* just so you could get your hands on her father's chainsaw?"

"Of course, not."

"But you knew her father owned a chainsaw?" Nick went on.

"How could I not? We hear it every time he uses it, loud and clear. And Papatónis, too. We're surrounded by the bloody things."

"You admitted to asking Amalía if you could *borrow* the saw."

"Yeah, but I never took it."

"You ring her late at night for this information, wheedle it out of her and then do not act on it? You expect us to believe that?"

"It's the truth."

"How do you explain the traces of human blood we found on the saw?"

"Who knows? Maybe the old boy cut himself. Wouldn't be the first time."

"We expect forensics to confirm it was Lukas Hedinger's blood type and DNA."

He said nothing, just stared ahead with a sceptical look on his face.

"You see, I think you borrowed the saw to cut up Lukas's body after you killed him."

"Not true."

"And then you got your cousins Yiánnis and Leftéris to dispose of the body parts for you."

"No way."

"A job they didn't do very well, given that the torso was found, which was why I saw you berating Yiánni the other day."

"You've got this all wrong."

"Why were you arguing, then?"

"He sold us some bad fish. I told him he should show his family more respect than to unload rotten fish on them. The man is a prick."

Nick and Náni exchanged sceptical looks. Náni was tapping her pen on the table, then she took up the questioning:

"A forensics team is examining your sheep barn, as we speak. The one on the top pasture you failed to mention?"

"What of it?"

"Is that where you cut up the body, Grigóri?"

"I didn't cut up any body."

"I think you did."

"Then you're going to have to prove it, aren't you?"

"Don't worry. We intend to do just that."

The session with Grigóri was terminated, after which they interviewed Theo. He was less confident and more polite. He denied any involvement or knowing anything about the money and no, he did not notice his brother behaving strangely. But when they asked him about the chainsaw, he faltered.

"So, you're telling us you never saw this chainsaw Grigóris took from Manólis's shed?" said Náni.

"That's right."

"So where did the chainsaw come from that was used to cut up the logs in the carport?"

"We did those by hand – Grigóris and me."

"We know they were cut with a chainsaw, Theo. There are distinctive markings."

"Er, … I don't understand."

"I do," cut in Nick. "You're lying to us."

"I'm not."

"You're repeating what Grigóris told you to say. Like a good brother. But in doing so, Theo, you'll share his guilt. Make no mistake. And I'm not talking about the theft of a chainsaw. I'm talking about first-degree murder; a life sentence. Is that what you want? Is that what you signed up for in your secret pact with Grigóris?"

He listened to Náni's translation and said nothing. But it was written all over his face. He was alarmed, no question. Nick went on:

"I don't think you're as guilty as your brother. Maybe you helped. Maybe you knew what was going on but didn't help. I don't know. But I *do* know that you knew about the saw. You knew he filched it and you saw him using it. And you helped. Maybe you also used it. Nothing wrong with that. Saved your mum from struggling with the handsaw, didn't it?"

Theo looked confused. He wanted to agree but did not quite nod. He could see where this would leave his brother.

"I want you to confirm that for us, Theo," said Náni "and then we can help you avoid any serious charges. You saw Grigóris cutting the logs with Manólis's saw, did you not?"

"I think I need a lawyer before I say anything more."

*

Outside, she turned to Nick:

"Nice try, Nick."

"Hmmm. I got him to the water, but he didn't quite drink."

"No, but I think you're right. He's a minor player, at most. We need to nail Grigóri – and it's all down to blood. If we can prove it was Lukas's blood on the saw or forensics find traces of his blood in the sheep barn, then we can move forward and charge him."

"Blood *and* money. Three and a half grand is a huge amount for the average citizen of Kardánes."

"It is."

"Maybe we hold off until we can interview Yiánnis and Leftéris. Question them about where the body parts came from. Try and work backwards."

"Good idea. We'll hold these two for the time being. I'll chase up forensics. And you might need some sleep, Nick."

Nick acquiesced but, before he could escape the office, he was collared by Déspina. She was holding an office phone to her chest.

"I'm sorry, Nick, but it's the garage in Kissós. They want to talk to you about the Jeep."

It was the last thing he wanted, but it had to be sorted out. After a few minutes, it was agreed. They would have to replace all four tyres. They would try to remove the painted message, then respray the bonnet, if necessary. They would try to find a suitable replacement for the driver's seat, but it would not be original, of course. The cost would be between eight hundred and a thousand euros, most likely, but Nick was not to worry. The police's insurers would pay because

127

Náni had designated the Jeep a co-opted police vehicle. The work would be done by early the following week. That was good. Jason was arriving on Tuesday and by then he wanted to be through this case and exploring the island in the Jeep with his son.

*

When Náni caught up with the forensics team, it was very mixed news.

"We've not managed to determine the blood type nor extract any DNA from the earliest blood sample yet, I'm afraid, Sergeant. The traces are so small. I'm sorry."

"That's a big disappointment, sir."

"Yes, I imagine it is. And no fingerprints on the padlock or key, I'm afraid."

"No great surprise. What about the blood samples from the Papatónis farm?"

"Nothing human."

"And the Katzatákis sheep barn?"

"The team are in there now, collecting samples. We should have results for you the day after tomorrow."

She thanked him and disconnected. So, they would not be able to connect Manólis's chainsaw to Lukas, forensically. That was a handicap, no doubt. It raised the stakes on proving that he *borrowed* it. She would keep her fingers crossed for the sheep barn results.

They brought Yiánnis in late afternoon. They found him in Keramés, selling fish, and stayed with him for the last two villages of his round.

"Generous of you," observed Náni.

"Well, ma'am," responded Stéfanos, "it was that or deprive the villagers of their fish and leave it rotting in the van. And it was only thirty-five minutes. He came quietly then."

They found Leftéris asleep at his house. Níkos drew his gun, expecting trouble, but Leftéris chose to play the innocent, co-operative citizen. It was inconvenient, he would lose a night's fishing, and he did not see how he could help but he was happy to answer their questions.

By seven thirty, both were in separate interview rooms at Réthymno police headquarters. Náni had an initial conversation with each of them, but she kept it brief. She would feel more confident when Nick was back on the team. They would turn up the heat tomorrow.

Getting to sleep was a struggle that night. Eventually, her partner made herbal tea and gently massaged her with jojoba oil, mixed with lavender. It relaxed her, but not only that. Sleep was delayed further but in a thoroughly worthwhile manner. Afterwards, she drifted into a cocoon of animal warmth and affection and dreamt of being a child again, her tiny hand slipped into her father's as they walked along the shore in blinding sunlight. He seemed calm and relaxed and his assurance gave her confidence but, when she looked down, she saw that they were walking through a sea of body parts and a hand was reaching up, an old man's pleading face turned up to hers.

CHAPTER 16
CONNIVING COUSINS

Nick woke at five, with the cockerel. He had spent the night on the seabed, under a megaton of water. Or so it felt. He was deaf and muzzy and, though he slept thirteen hours straight, every bone in his body was screaming for more rest. He dismissed their complaints out of hand and staggered to the shower. *A gentle walk and then a huge breakfast will sort me out,* he thought.

*

By eight, he was at the police station, raring to go. But there was no sign of Náni. No matter. Déspina was there and she brought him up to speed over a Ness and a slice of a lemony, custard pie she called galaktoboúreko.

"It's a bit early for this," he said, "but it's gorgeous, Déspina. And you made this yourself? Well done, you."

She grinned happily.

"So, we have four men in custody, to be questioned."

"Correct."

"It's going to be a busy day. And four days till my son arrives."

"You might need to remind Náni."

At that point, Náni burst through the doors, looking flustered.

"Sorry, guys. Give me five," she said, disappearing into the empty office.

Nick and Déspina exchanged glances.

"Maybe she has a private life, after all," he said.

Déspina smirked and her brown eyes widened a fraction.

After a few minutes, Náni called Nick into the office.

"Are you recovered, Nick?"

"I'll live."

"We need to be sharp today. Interrogate these bastards. I'm hoping we can charge them by the end of the day."

"Well, you can charge them anytime you like. Nothing like a murder charge to spring the truth from someone who *didn't* do it."

"An interesting approach."

"Just the sight of me is going to rattle Yiánnis and Leftéris."

"Yes. Maybe that's a good place to start."

They decided to interview Yiánnis and Leftéris together. They were using the same lawyer, an older man from Réthymno called Galánis, and it might save a little time all round. They would conduct it in Greek, with Náni translating for Nick where necessary. But Nick was to stay out of sight, initially. In the interview room, Náni set the recording in motion.

"Gentlemen," said Náni, "I think we can make this simple. I'm ready to charge you both with the murder of Lukas Hedinger, along with your cousins, unless you tell me exactly what your roles were in all this."

"What evidence do you have to support such a charge?" asked the lawyer, but Náni ignored him. She was staring at the two brothers, waiting.

After perhaps ten seconds, there was a knock at the door, as arranged.

"And we can add to that the murder of my colleague, Mr Nick Fisher …"

She opened the door to reveal Nick. They could not have looked more shocked if that other Nick, the devil himself, had been standing there.

"… or, more correctly, *attempted* murder."

"How the hell …?"

"Oh, it was a bloody long swim all right," said Nick, "but I wouldn't have made it without you guys pulling me along for a while." He held up his right hand to show the rope scars on his wrist. "So, thanks for that, at least."

Nick's sarcasm stung them. Leftéris cursed his brother for his incompetence.

"Now, gentlemen, we have all day if necessary, but wouldn't it make sense for you to make a full statement to the Sergeant here? I can help you remember if anything slips your minds."

The lawyer asked for ten minutes with his clients then, and Nick and Náni withdrew. A few minutes later, the lawyer left the room and came over to where they were standing.

"My clients are willing to co-operate if you will drop these trumped-up charges of murder or attempted murder, Sergeant."

"Trumped-up?" spluttered Nick, grabbing the man's lapels and pushing him against the wall of the corridor.

"I think you need to consider the facts, Galáni," he hissed. "Your clients pushed me off their boat at the point of a machete and a hunting knife at least five kilometres from the shore, in the dead of night. It was only my ingenuity, some luck and a feat of extraordinary endurance that enabled me to survive. Now explain to me how the hell that merits the words *trumped-up*?"

Nick's face was fifteen centimetres from Galánis's. The lawyer was stretched to tiptoe, Náni noticed.

"Get this gorilla off me now, Sergeant," he croaked, "or I'll bring an action for assault."

"All right. Calm down, Nick. But I think you have your answer, Galáni. You are dreaming if you think your clients are in a position to bargain."

Nick loosened his grip and the lawyer straightened his lapels and tie, then brushed himself down with his hand.

"Then I will advise my clients against further co-operation."

"And I will arrest them for attempted murder and put them in the cells, pending further investigation. A murder charge in respect of Lukas Hedinger may follow, in due course."

"Let's not be hasty, Sergeant. My clients did not murder Lukas Hedinger, but they may be prepared to tell you everything they know."

"A statement from both of them to that effect with a detailed admission of their involvement, and I can say we will look more favourably on them."

"Meaning?"

"Meaning just that. We will take it into account when framing the charges and we will make the judge aware of their co-operation. You're getting no more, Galáni. Take it or leave it."

"I will consult with my clients."

Galánis went back into the room and the door remained closed for several minutes.

"I need to remind you about my son," said Nick, as they grabbed a coffee from the machine.

"What about him?"

"His name is Jason. He's arriving in four days and I'll need to spend most of my time with him. We have stuff to sort out."

"How long is he here?"

"Three weeks."

"All right, Nick. You'll have to manage that. Just make sure I know what I can expect from you."

"Well, you can expect me to be absent for the first three or four days, at least. After that, there might be space, here and there. We'll have to see. He might want to go off somewhere, do his own thing. He does that."

Before she could respond, the door opened and Galánis waved them inside. When they were all seated, Náni reactivated the recording device and signalled him to speak:

"My clients are prepared to make a joint statement if – and *only* if – you agree to drop the attempted murder charge. They do this believing their willingness to co-operate will also win more lenient treatment in respect of any lesser crimes with which they may be charged. You have said as much, I think."

He looked at Náni, waiting for a response.

Náni sensed Nick squirming in his seat and glanced across. He looked as if he would rather tear them limb from limb than drop the charges, but he said nothing.

"Do they know who killed Lukas Hedinger?"

"They will tell you *everything* they know, Sergeant. Full and frank disclosure."

"We reserve the right to charge them in respect of Lukas Hedinger's death, if not with murder then as accomplices or accessories."

In the silence that followed, Nick saw Leftéris smirking. This bloody woman was bargaining away his suffering. He crushed his plastic coffee cup, kicked away from the table and left the room, slamming the door.

"Well?" Náni asked, sharply.

Galánis raised his eyebrows and looked at each of his clients, then nodded.

"That's understood," he said.

"And we are not judges, Galáni, but we will make the Investigating Judge aware of their co-operation."

"Thank you," said Galánis. "You may now question my clients and they will co-operate to the best of their abilities."

"One moment, please."

*

Náni found Nick staring out of the window at the far end of the corridor.

"They're ready to talk. Are you coming back in?"

"Well of course they are. You've given them back several years of their lives for nothing. Did you see their faces? They can't believe their luck. You've traded an open and shut case of kidnapping and attempted murder worth ten years, for the chance of an accessory charge worth three, probably."

"I understand you're hurting, but it's not for nothing, Nick."

"You don't know that. If it wasn't Grigóris, they may have no idea who killed Lukas."

"That's a risk. But their story should help us convict Grigóri, at least."

"I'm not naïve, Náni. I know how these things work and, as Chief Investigating Officer, it has to be your call. It's just not great to see one's life reduced to a bargaining chip on some lawyer's desk. It would have been nice to be consulted. And I don't think you struck much of a deal with it, either."

"It was a judgment call, Nick. And I felt it was important to get them talking; get this case moving. I'm sorry if you feel hard done by, but you got yourself into that mess. Now, are you ready to stop sulking and listen to what they have to say?"

134

Nick gave her a hard look but acquiesced and followed her back down the corridor and into the interview room, feeling like an ill-treated lapdog.

*

"Were you in Kardánes on the night of Sunday, the eighth of June?" asked Náni.

"I was," said Yiánnis.

"But *you* were not?" Náni asked Leftéris.

"Correct."

"Why were you there, Yiánni?"

"I got a call from my cousin, around two am, asking me to come over. He apologised for calling so late but said I wouldn't regret it. There was a well-paid job in it for me."

"Which cousin are we talking about?"

"I only saw Grigóri that night."

"So, you drove over."

"Yes. I got there about half past two in the morning, I suppose."

"This was in your white van."

"Yes. He asked me to meet him at the sheep barn, up on the ridge road. When I swung in, he was waiting outside for me."

"How was he?"

"He looked very pale in the moonlight, but he seemed calm. He was wearing a leather butcher's apron."

"Go on."

"He said: 'I called you because we're family, Yiánni. Something dreadful has happened, and the family needs your help'.

"I remember he peered at me then until I nodded. 'Inside the barn is a dead body,' he said, 'a foreigner. You don't need to know who it is. We're going to cut it in pieces, you and I.' He could see the horror on my face. 'It's okay, cousin,' he says, 'it's not alive. Just dead meat. We've cut up enough sheep and fish. It's no different. I'll do the cutting, anyway, if you like. You can pack things up.'

"'And then, what?' I asked. 'Then, you will drive the bags to Leftéris,

135

take them out to sea and dump them. Simple as that. You'll be finished by dawn. And fifteen hundred euros richer, between you. Not bad for half a night's work.' And then he took the money out of his pocket to show me. I asked him where he'd got that kind of money, but he wouldn't say."

"Surely you asked him who the victim was and who killed the young man?"

"He said I didn't need to know any of that stuff. And he sure as hell wasn't going to tell me, anyway."

"Did you think Grigóris was the killer?"

"Maybe. He was always a wild kid."

"Tell us what happened next," Nick spoke for the first time. Yiánnis's eyes flicked across to Náni, who nodded once and raised her eyebrows a fraction.

"Well, I felt sick at the whole idea. But he's family and needs help and God knows we need the money. The fish business is getting tougher all the time. There are less and less fish in the sea. More people are going to supermarkets instead of buying fish fresh from me, or not eating fish at all, going vegetarian. We've been struggling for a while now."

"You're breaking my heart," said Nick. Yiánnis scowled but went on:

"I let him take me inside. The light was on and I saw, then. The body was just sitting there; a tall, young guy with glasses, pale and fair-haired. His head was slumped to one side. 'Right,' he says, all business now, 'we'll put his clothes and stuff in this bag'. Then we strip him, there on the floor, and put the clothes into a bag along with his other stuff. 'I propped him up to drain the blood from the head,' he says, 'so we'll start there'. He must have seen the look on my face, because he grins and says, 'Don't worry – after that, it will be easy.'"

"He grinned?" said Nick, appalled.

"Yeah. Well, kind of. Anyway, we lift the body onto the workbench. It's heavy, and I remember wondering if dead bodies weigh more than live ones, and then I see the chainsaw and I say: 'You're not going to use that thing, are you?' and he says, 'Best thing, mate. It'll be quick.'"

"What did the saw look like?" asked Náni.

"Like a chainsaw."

"Make, model, colour?"

"Jesus, I don't know. It might have been orange. Anyway, he dresses me in a plastic coat and has me stand at the end of the bench with a sack. The body is face down with the head next to me. He puts a coat on himself then and some goggles, and then he starts the saw. The noise is tremendous, and I wonder if they'll hear, down in the village or at Papatónis's farm. I try to look away, but he yells at me: 'You have to catch the head, Yiánni,' and then he places the saw on the neck and cuts straight through. Bits of flesh are flying off but there isn't much blood. It takes two, maybe three seconds, and then I feel the weight of the head dropping into the bag. I nearly throw up at the sight of the headless neck. 'It's just dead meat, Yiánni,' he yells and I'm expecting him to go on, do the rest, but he doesn't. He puts down the saw and takes off his goggles.

"'Now, we hang him up,' he says and gets me to help him drag the headless body to the wall. Then we attach ropes to the left wrist and left ankle, pull the ropes through metal rings on the wall and tie them off. The guy's hanging on the wall like a piece of meat, back facing us, mercifully. Now Grigóris hands me a bottle of rakí and I take a large swig and then we smoke cigarettes, though I quit last year. 'We're through the worst of it. Wasn't so bad, was it?' he says. 'It was fucking horrible,' I say. 'Why have we hung him up like that?' I asked. 'The blood will drain from the arm and leg into the torso,' he says, 'then we cut them off. Much less mess.'

Náni and Nick exchanged glances of revulsion.

"So, we wait half an hour and then carry the body back to the bench and he saws off the left arm at the shoulder and then the left leg, close to the hip. There is some blood, of course, but not spurting or anything. Then, he puts extra cloth and paper on the floor by the wall before we hang what's left of the body by the right wrist and ankle. This time it's facing us, and there's blood dripping steadily from the severed limbs and the poor guy's genitals are hanging there, and, for some reason, this makes me cry. And not just the odd tear. Great, heaving sobs. For his gruesome death, his indignity. And for myself, that I have come to this. I never knew if there was a God or a Heaven, but now I know for sure: I'm destined for the other place.

"Grigóris walks me to the sink and tells me to have a splash and another smoke, then he goes back to the bench, wipes the blood off his goggles, and carves the long, severed limbs into smaller pieces to fit in the bags. Then he calls me over and I have to put the pieces in the rubble sacks. We have more rakí while we are waiting for the draining process to complete, and then it's the same again, for the other side. Finally, it's done and just the torso is lying there. It's not bleeding much, which I find amazing, knowing it must be full of blood, but he says the blood has thickened now. It's not going any-where. He's thought it all through, you see.

"I'll never forget that sight. Bloody hideous, it was. I'm feeling dis-gusted and ashamed, but also relieved now. The sawing is over. 'We've used all the sacks,' I say. 'Yeah, but this one's just got his stuff in it, remember?' says Grigóris. 'We can put it in there.' And that was the most disgusting part of the whole job, the two of us trying to fit this limbless torso into the sack. Just a lump of flesh with genitals I was trying hard not to touch. It was a tight fit, but we get it in. And then I throw up. I don't know if it's disgust or relief. Maybe both. I almost made it to the sink.

"When I've sorted myself out, he tells me to fetch pieces of broken concrete from a pile of rubble in the yard to weigh down the sacks, then tie them tight and put each one in a black, plastic refuse sack and tie that tight, too. I'm feeling better now, doing something practical. Meanwhile, he's cleaning the saw and tidying up. Then he checks the sacks and tells me I've done okay, and we load them into the van. Six of them. We strip off our plastic coats and he takes off his apron and then he hugs me close. 'I'll never forget this, cousin,' he says, and he stares at me with this fire in his eyes, like he was loving it – the dan-ger, the gore. He was always like that. Smashing the rule book, riding roughshod over boundaries.

"'And now you must call Leftéri,' he says and presses the money into my hands. 'I'll let you decide how much of this is for him.' I look at my watch then, and I remember thinking: *Is that all it is?* It was just after four. The job took an hour and a half, but it felt like a lifetime. I was exhausted."

"And then you called Leftéri?" asked Náni.

"He called me at ten past four in the morning," said Leftéris.

"And what did he say?"

"He sounded jittery, breathless. And I was half-asleep. I kept on asking him to say things again. He wanted me to meet him at the boat, said there was a family problem he needed help with. Five hundred euros were waiting for me for just an hour's work. Well, I know you don't get that kind of money for nothing, so I asked him what the hell it was all about. He said he'd tell me when I got there."

"And you were happy with that?" asked Náni.

"No, but it was obvious he didn't want to say anything over the phone. Five hundred is a lot to me at the moment, so I agreed.

"We met at the boat, Seirín, just as the first light was coming into the sky. It must have been around a quarter to five. He opened the van doors and showed me the bags. 'We need to dump these,' he said. 'What's in them?' I asked. 'You don't want to know,' he said, but I in-sisted, saying: 'I'm not allowing anything on my boat if I don't know what it is'. Then he told me. Grigóris had killed some German and the body's in the bags. Well, I was shocked and angry, but I wasn't surprised Grigóris was involved.

"'You've no right to dump this on me, Yiánni,' I say, 'no right at all. I resent it. You're presenting me with a *fait accomplit*. And putting me in an impossible position. If I agree, I'll be an accessory to murder and, if I don't, I'm dropping my brother and cousin in the shit.' Then he says: 'You can say you didn't know what was in the bags if it comes to it. Or that I lied about what was in them, even better. Blame it all on me.' And I say: 'Fat chance of anyone believing that.'"

Nick felt himself colouring slightly as he focused on his fingernails.

"Well, then I think for a minute. It's a hell of a risk but the chances of discovery seem quite low and it *is* family. I feel like I have to do it.

In the end, I say: 'I'll do it, but it'll cost you a thousand'. Well, we haggle for a bit, then settle on seven fifty – equal shares, he says. Fair enough, I reckon. Then we get moving because it's getting light; him loading the bags and me preparing the boat. I'm dreading a visit from the harbourmaster, though I doubt he's ever been up so early. Pretty soon we're off, and I'm keeping a look-out for any other vessels, especially coastguard, but there's nothing about, thank God."

"I doubt it's God you have to thank for anything," said Nick.

"Go on, Leftéri," said Náni.

"He asks me for the best place, and I say, 'Off Triópetra would work. The other side of the rocks. It's not far, it's quite deep there and the drift takes things east, away from the busier places.' He agrees and so we motor out there and, when we get there, I hold the boat steady and I say to him, 'It would be safer to spread your little parcels around a bit, wouldn't it, drop them one at a time?' Well, he can see the sense in that and goes to grab the first bag, and I say: 'Hang on, Yiánni. Now, there's nothing in these bags that can identify him, right?' And he gets this worried look. 'You're kidding me,' I say. 'You go through hell to cut the guy up, so he can't be identified, and then what? You slip his passport in there?' 'No passport, no,' he says, 'but there is other stuff: a wallet, a watch, a torch, a water bottle, glasses, clothes'. 'Oh, for the love of God,' I say, 'You fucking idiots. Well, it'll all have to come out. All of it. What were you thinking?' He tells me it's all in the one bag and he knows which one."

"So, you went digging for it?" Náni's question was directed at Yiánnis.

"I did. I know it's all in the torso bag and I can tell which bag that is from the shape, but it's all underneath the body, at the bottom. There's no room to get past it and the idea is just too revolting. So, I cut the bag and the sack to get it out. The stuff's all covered in blood and the sodding wallet is empty anyway. Grigóris must have taken any money and cards."

"So, it was a waste of time."

"I thought it would be, but Leftéris insisted."

"And now the bag is ripped."

140

"Yes. I tied it up as best I could."

"Fuckwit," said Leftéris.

"Well, what was I supposed to do? We should have left it alone like I said."

"Did you see a passport at any time?" asked Náni.

They both shook their heads.

"So, what happened next?" she asked Leftéris.

"We dumped one bag there and then I took the boat round in an arc and we dumped the other five, one by one, maybe two hundred metres apart."

"And the belongings?"

"In the water, on the way back, bit by bit."

"Including the camera?"

"Yes. That was a shame, but we couldn't risk being caught with anything on us at the harbour. I got Yiánnis to swab the decks thoroughly before we got back."

"So, the bags were never in the rear hold?" asked Nick.

"No. A little ruse, Mr Fisher," said Leftéris.

"All right. For now, thank you," said Náni. "I will be questioning you both about the kidnapping of Mr Fisher, but that can wait. You will remain in custody, meanwhile."

And with that, she and Nick stood, left the room, and returned to the Lieutenant's office.

*

"A pretty gruesome tale," Náni said.

"What a pair of bunglers," said Nick. "If they'd left that bag untouched, it would still be at the bottom of the sea. Lukas would be one more unsolved, missing person case."

"I know. I guess I need to organise some divers to find the other bags."

"Hmmm. Probably have to. An expensive and pointless exercise, from our perspective, but you need to try. The Hedingers have a right to expect that. And so do the swimmers and snorkellers at Triópetra, come to that. You don't need more gory bits floating up."

"Not that any of the other bags were ripped."

"Maybe not, but who knows what happens on a rocky seabed?"

She nodded and went out to delegate the thankless task to one of her older constables, Michális. When she returned, several minutes later, it was with coffee and pastries.

"I think we deserve these," she said.

"I don't care if we do or not, they look great," said Nick.

"We should interview Theo, next," she said, handing Nick a plate. "If we can be sure he was *not* involved, even if he thought something was going on, then we can let him go."

"Makes sense."

"And then I want to charge Grigóri with the murder of Lukas."

"Why?"

"Because I think he did it."

"We have no proof yet – no witness, no motive."

"Come on, he was paid to do it and he had the body propped up in his barn."

"Maybe, but by whom, and why? We know none of those things, Náni. We don't even know how Lukas died."

"What do *you* suggest, Nick?"

"Look, I'm not against charging him but that doesn't mean I'm sure he's guilty. If he's facing fifteen or more years in jail, he might decide to enlighten us a little more. Without that, we have a heap more work before any murder charge will stick."

"Are you satisfied Yiánnis and Leftéris told us the truth this morning?"

"I think so."

"So, they weren't involved with the murder itself?"

"Probably not."

"Wasn't it a bit extreme to cart you off and dump you in the sea then?"

"I did point that out at the time, but they weren't impressed by my arguments. Didn't think they'd get caught. And now you've let them off that little misdemeanour anyway."

"Don't be sarcastic, Nick. It doesn't suit you. We've got them for accessories now. No question. And, despite what I said in there, I'll be pushing for the maximum sentence for that, in the circumstances."

"Good. Because those bastards didn't expect me to survive, as you saw."

"I did. Now, it's ten forty-five, shall we do the other two before lunch?"

"Why not."

They were ready to begin the second interview with Theo when they spotted Galánis hovering outside the interview room.

"Can I help you, kýrie Galáni?" asked Náni.

"I have been asked to act for this set of brothers too, Sergeant. I don't feel it's a conflict of interest, so I've agreed, but I thought I'd make sure you're comfortable with that."

"I'm not sure my comfort or otherwise is relevant, Galáni. It's a matter for your clients and your ethics."

"In which case, I'll sit in."

"Quite a scoop, four clients from one case," Nick observed.

*

They asked Theo a string of questions, tried to trip him up a couple of times. He knew Grigóris was up to something. He knew he was out most of the Sunday night and saw him hiding something on top of the wardrobe the following morning. He investigated and found the cash. And yes, he asked him about both things but received monosyllabic answers which gave nothing away. He never met, nor heard mention of, Lukas Hedinger and he was home in bed all that Sunday night. And no, he did not come across any bloodstained clothing. Eventually, Náni took Galánis out of the room. Nick followed.

"Theo was not the killer," said Náni. "We accept this, but he has withheld information on the chainsaw. I'm certain he saw his brother with it, and I want a statement to that effect: where and when, what the saw looked like, whose it was. Given this, I could release him today, get him back to his family."

"What's the point, Sergeant?" asked Galánis. "You already have a statement from Yiánnis that Grigóris was using a chainsaw."

"I want proof that he procured the saw belonging to Vernardákis."

143

"You want me to ask one of my clients to help incriminate the other?"

"That's the deal, Galáni."

"No conflicts of interest, thankfully," said Nick.

"I'll discuss this with my client," said Galánis, ignoring him.

"Just one of the clients?" teased Nick.

*

The second interview with Grigóri took less than ten minutes. Náni charged him with first-degree murder and told him he could expect a life sentence with a recommendation he serve a minimum of fifteen years.

"You'll be middle-aged by the time you get out, Grigóri. The best years of your life gone."

"And good-looking lads like you get a rough time in jail," added Nick. "You'd better watch yourself in the showers."

Náni looked askance at Nick. Grigóris looked sick.

"It might help if you explain the events leading up to the murder of Lukas Hedinger, from the moment you encountered each other to the point where he is a dead body, propped up in your sheep barn at two thirty in the morning," said Náni.

"My client has opted to remain silent at this stage, Sergeant," said Galánis.

"He intends to answer no questions at all?"

"He will answer only: *No comment*. We need time to consider our position."

Náni tapped her upended pen on the table several times.

"Then, Grigóri, you will have to consider your position from one of our cells. O kýrios Galánis will be able to visit you there. Constable? Put him in number three."

Níkos came to attention momentarily, mumbled "Ma'am," then took the boy firmly by the upper arm and marched him out of the room.

"We'll have to leave it with you, then, Galáni. Let us know if and when your client deigns to talk to us."

"So much for that plan," she said when they were back in the corridor.

"Give it time," said Nick, but he was not sure where things went from here.

144

CHAPTER 17
A NOSE FOR IT

"Excuse me, ma'am," said Déspina as they crossed the office, "the K-9 handler just called. There's been a cancellation. He could come this afternoon."

Náni looked at her watch. It was eleven forty.

"Okay with you, Nick?"

"Why not?"

"Let's do it. Have him meet us at the kafenío in Kardánes at two."

She turned to Nick. "Can they cook at this place?"

"It's not bad. Just village fare, but tasty."

"All right. I need half an hour for paperwork, so let's leave at twelve thirty. You can buy me lunch."

"A rare privilege," said Nick.

*

Both Alékos and Varvára were in situ as they drove up in the white Suzuki and the blue and white police Skoda. And they were doing good trade. There were tourists at three tables outside and a larger group of older men, who looked like locals, near the entrance. Náni recognised one or two from her earlier visit, including Vasílios Andréou.

"I see the welcoming committee's here," she said to Nick as they walked up together.

The old men stared at them without smiling, one of them rattling his kombolói. Andréou cleared his throat in an exaggerated manner and spat in their path.

"You're not welcome here," said another of them, in Greek, "I thought we made that clear."

"I have a job to do, gentlemen, and I intend to do it. I think I made *that* clear, too."

"Well, don't expect the villagers to help. And what the hell is *he* doing here? What's the idea, having a foreigner meddle in our affairs? It's not right, Sergeant."

Nick walked over and stood close to the man.

"Were you the cowardly bastard who vandalised my Jeep, by any chance?"

Knowing looks and one or two sniggers passed between the group.

"Not me, my friend, but I applaud the message. Why *don't* you just fuck off back to England, like it said?"

"Because, for one thing, I don't live in England. I live in Crete."

"Oooh-ooh! He's not just a tourist, he's a bloody *invader!*"

This brought a roar of laughter from the others, but not from Andréou, Náni noticed. Then he spoke:

"We are serious, Sergeant Samaráki. You and your Englishman need to stay out of this village. There are some here who wish you harm."

"Threatening the police is a crime, Andréou. Any more of that and I'll arrest you right here and now."

Varvára appeared, looking flushed and wiping her hands on her apron.

"Stop your nonsense now, Vasíli, and let these good people get some lunch." She was trying to make light of a tense situation but, as they followed her around the L-shaped terrace to a table on the far side of the kafenío, she tried to apologise:

"I'm sorry for this. Some of the older villagers have potatoes on their backs."

"Chips? On their shoulders?" suggested Nick.

"Patátes *tigánites*?" Varvára asked, looking puzzled.

"Are they old communists, perhaps?" asked Nick, moving on.

"It's complicated," she said. "Now, what can I get you? I have fresh meatballs, rabbit stifádo, chicken souvláki …"

They ordered and Varvára went away. Soon after, Alékos appeared, hooked a paper tablecloth with a map of Crete onto the table and laid out a small carafe of white wine with two glasses, a plastic bottle of water from the freezer and a basket containing bread, cheap cutlery and condiments.

"Welcome," he said. "Good to see you again." And he gave them a gappy smile as he walked away.

"Well, at least someone thinks so," said Nick.

"What's all this animosity about? Do you get it?" asked Náni.

"Not entirely, no. I know this was a communist village, years ago in the civil war. They lost, of course. There was bitterness, resentment."

"But it's been more than seventy years, Nick."

"I know, but they have long memories in the mountains. They're fiercely independent. But they're also anti-German, anti-fascist, anti-police. Sometimes, I think they dislike all foreigners on principle and, from what I've learned, I can understand why."

"Do you think that's our killer's motivation, then: xenophobia?"

"I don't know, but I'm sure motive is at the heart of this case. If we can't work that out, we'll never find our killer. Why is a perfectly pleasant young man – a stranger – murdered in a Greek village?"

"A village with smouldering resentment and anti-German feeling, it seems, although the people who met Lukas told me they rather liked him."

"Yes. My first thought was a racist, anti-German attack. But I think those old guys are all bluster and bravado. Vandalising a vehicle is a long way from killing a stranger."

"I guess it could have been some random madman. There's a lot of inbreeding up here."

"Or maybe Lukas saw something or found out something or photographed something he shouldn't have."

"Like a drug deal going down, you mean. In Kardánes, Nick?"

"Or somewhere else, before, and they tracked him to Kardánes."

"You make it sound like a gangland killing, but the Katzatákis cousins seem like rank amateurs. I doubt professionals would use them to clean up their dirty work."

"Out-of-town professionals might have to rely on available local talent."

"So, you think Lukas found himself in the wrong place at the wrong time."

"Perhaps. Or they hit the wrong man."

"Mistaken identity? But he looked so different from the young men around here. It would be hard to mistake him for anyone else."

"But there's another side to that coin, Náni. If they were looking for some tall, blond kid, they could have *assumed* he was their boy."

Nick took a gulp of wine.

"Whatever it is, we need to get to the bottom of it, somehow."

"I know. You were sounding quite empathetic there about the villagers and their past."

"I see where they're coming from, at least. My understanding doesn't extend to them trashing my bloody Jeep, though. I'll crack some heads if I find out who did that."

"Is it being fixed up?"

"Should get it back early next week."

"In time for Jason."

"More or less."

"Tell me about your son."

They chatted happily for several minutes as the sun glinted through the plane trees and the wine relaxed them. The gentle murmur of other conversations and the hissing of the cicadas was reassuring, but Nick could still hear the clacking of the komboloi as the beads smacked the hands of bitter, old men.

As they came to the end of their lunch, they heard more raised voices and jeering from the old men and saw a uniformed police officer hesitating at the kafenío entrance. They waved him over.

"Sergeant Samaráki?" he said to Nick.

"*I* am Náni Samarákis," said Náni.

"Ah. Signómi." The constable rubbed his beard in embarrassment. "Constable Vangélis Theodorákis, ma'am."

"Sit down, Constable, we're nearly done here and we're speaking English today if that's all right with you. You have a dog for us?"

"I do, ma'am, and English is no problem."

"Is it a bloodhound?"

"She's a Malinois called Tzíka."

"What's a Malinois?" asked Nick.

"I'm sorry," said Náni, "this is Mr Nick Fisher, a senior British policeman who is working with us."

They shook hands.

"They are a little like German Shepherds, Mr Fisher, but smaller, with shorter fur. They are originally from Belgium."

"I've never heard of them. Are they any good?"

"They are excellent track and search dogs, sir. Amazing olfactory sense. And Tzíka is PDTI trained – two hundred and fifty hours of training over ten weeks."

"Olfactory sense?" asked Náni.

"Sense of smell. We, humans, have about six million olfactory receptors in our noses."

"I must be more careful when I blow my nose," said Nick.

"Ha-ha. Don't worry about that, sir. My point is, Tzíka has getting on for three *hundred* million. Fifty times as many. Her ability to analyse and recognise smells is on a different scale to ours."

"All right," said Náni, tucking a twenty euro note under the half-full carafe, "Let's go meet the wonder dog."

"I thought I was buying," protested Nick as he downed the rest of his rakí and followed them out of the kafenío, waving farewell to Alékos. There were fewer old men now, but they maintained a stony silence as they passed.

The white police van was parked behind Náni's Skoda.

"Our task for Tzíka is a simple one," said Náni. "I have some used clothing belonging to a murder victim – a young Swiss man named Lukas. We know he left this kafenío on the night of the murder and we'd like to know where he went. The challenge for her is that this was almost two weeks ago."

"But it hasn't rained, ma'am, so we might be okay."

Náni opened the Skoda and pulled out the bag of clothing from Hedinger, then Vangélis opened the van door to reveal a cage containing a smart, powerful-looking beast. She might be smaller than an Alsatian, but she was still a big dog, Nick saw. Her face was black with orange eyes, the fur colouring ranging from fawn to dark tan. She looked alert and intelligent. She also looked like she could tear your arm off if the mood took her.

She did not bark as Vangélis attached her harness, then she jumped down from the bumper, sniffing at Nick and Náni.

"Don't worry," he said, "she's just getting to know you."

By now, a few locals were admiring the dog or using her as a pretext to find out what was going on.

"Move on, please," called Náni, "this is police business. There's nothing to see here."

They shuffled off, glancing back over their shoulders. Nick recognised María and gave her a grin and a wave, but she did not respond. He felt slighted, for a moment, then it dawned on him; she would be afraid to acknowledge their acquaintance. He scanned the rest of the group as they moved away and thought he recognised Andréou from the back. And then he cursed himself for his stupidity and hoped he had not put her in danger.

Now, the constable was mumbling to the dog as she immersed her nose in the fabrics.

"Go on, girl. That's it. Take it all in."

Then he locked the van and handed the bag of clothing back to Náni.

"Ready?" he asked them. They nodded, and he turned back to the dog. Her ears were pricked, eyes watching her handler's every move.

"Seek, Tzíka, seek," he hissed, and she gave a small yelp. It was the first sound from her. As they watched, she lowered her body, put her nose to the ground and crept her way back to the threshold of the kafenío, concentrating and analysing. Then she lifted her head, tongue lolling, and looked up at the constable.

"I think she's picked up the scent," he said, patting her and slipping off the harness.

"Now go, girl," he said, and the dog put her nose to the ground once again and trotted up the lane towards the church. They followed. She went on past the Spíli turning, and up to Nikki's house. Little Mísha hurtled out to the gate, barking furiously, but Tzíka remained serene and focused, moving on past Andréou's cottage. They followed her past the James's house, which looked empty now, the green Jeep gone, garden furniture cleared from the roof terrace. At the ruined house, the dog hesitated. She trotted into the ruin and then out again. She ran in circles, almost chasing her tail and then she gave a small yelp again and accelerated down the alley opposite the ruin.

After thirty or forty metres she stopped at a set of ancient, stone steps leading up to the left. This time she barked once, before climbing them. They mounted the steps to a gate, beyond which a short, concrete path led to the front door of an old, stone cottage.

"Whose house is this?" asked Nick.

Náni was checking her map of the village.

"I think it belongs to the old lady, Eléni Fotákis."

Náni went to the front door and used the heavy, iron knocker. The dog did not follow, however, and whimpered slightly. When there was no answer, Náni rejoined the group and then Tzíka led them to a garden wall, part of which had collapsed. Here she seemed to lose interest and took to sniffing the nearby garden beds and marking her territory. They saw that the stone wall stretched along two sides of a once beautiful garden. It ran parallel to the alley but some five metres above it, then angled left to form a boundary at the back of the garden where several oleander bushes grew.

While Vangélis reattached Tzíka's harness, Nick went to the fallen part of the wall and found he could climb to the top without difficulty. Then he stood, staring at the sky, looking back and forth.

"I'm trying to work out which way I'm facing," he called to Náni.

She saw him looking away from the house, toward a giant pair of walnut trees on the other side of the alley.

"I think north, maybe north-west," she said.

Nick walked along the top of the wall and followed it around to the left. "And now?"

"That would have to be south-west."

"Get up here, Náni."

She scrambled up tentatively and followed the wall to join him as he gazed across the valley.

"It's quite something, isn't it?" she said.

"Yes, it is. But I think, for Lukas, it was also the last thing he ever saw."

"Go on."

"We know he was a keen photographer. The Polish guys told us there was a spectacular sunset that night. We know Lukas walked past little Mati's bedroom with a camera around his neck. Tzíka is telling us he came to this wall. He was looking for the perfect spot from which to photograph the sunset. Well, this is it."

"Somewhere along this wall?"

"No. *Right here.* The walnut trees obscure the view from the wall above the alley. Here, it's clear and the further towards this corner he went, the closer to the sun – and the easier to avoid the telegraph pole over there."

Nick was framing a rectangle with the fingers of both hands.

"Perfect," he said. "In about six hours, this will be the ideal shot. The mountains in the distance, the most attractive part of the village below. Beautiful."

Náni could see his point, but she was keen to get down. She was no good with heights and there was a drop of five or six metres on the other side of the wall. When they were safely back in the garden, she said:

"If you're correct, Nick, where did he go next?"

"That's the big question, isn't it? Can Tzíka tell us?"

"I can run her along the top of the wall if you like, sir," said the constable.

"Yes, give it a try."

They watched as Vangélis and the dog shuffled and sniffed their way in silence around the wall and then returned. Nick heard the throb of cicadas intensifying. Chickens were clucking not far away.

"She has nothing more to give us, sir. I thought so when she barked. Usually means *job done.*"

"So, we *know* Lukas came to the wall. We *think* he climbed up on it to take a photograph, and then what? Just vanished?" said Náni.

"Maybe he jumped off?" suggested the constable.

"It's too high," said Náni. "Perhaps he fell."

"Or was pushed," said Nick, and they both turned towards him.

The constable took the dog around to the base of the wall on the other side, but this time Tzíka circled several times, her nose amongst the stones and leaves and did not bark.

"She's not sure," called Vangélis.

"Pity. I thought we were on to something," said Náni.

"Does that mean Lukas was *not* there?" Nick asked the constable.

"No, sir. I wouldn't like to say. Not after two weeks. There could be other smells confusing her, other animal scents: cats, vine rats, pine martens."

"What the hell is a vine rat?"

"That's what we call them, sir. It's really a large mouse – a broad-toothed field mouse, to be precise. They're rather cute, but they upset the locals by eating the grapes and walnuts."

"You should get the forensics boys to check out the base of this wall, Náni," said Nick. "If he fell, or was pushed, he would certainly have hurt himself, maybe fatally. There could well be blood traces that the dog can't isolate."

Náni nodded and walked off a few paces to make the call. When she returned, she said:

"Well done, Constable, and well done you," patting the dog. "Now, while we have you both here, I'd like us to try the same trick at the Katzatákis home. I want to know if Lukas was ever there – in the house or the outbuildings – and then we can do the same thing at the sheep barn on the top road."

"We already know his body was at the sheep barn," said Nick.

"According to Yiánnis Katzatákis. I'd rather trust Tzíka's nose, wouldn't you? And we don't know if Lukas was at Grigóris's home beforehand. It's just a precaution, Nick, while we have the dog. Let's fill in some blanks in the story."

"Okay. Makes sense."

*

They walked back up the alley to the lane and turned right, past the Vernardákis house to the ramshackle mess of the Katzatákis smallholding. The eldest son, Andréas, was at the gate.

"Kalispéra, kýrie Katzatáki. Under the terms of the existing search warrant, we have come to search your premises with this dog," said Náni, in Greek.

"Where are my brothers?"

"They remain in custody. We hope to be in a position to release Theo later today or tomorrow."

"And Grigóris?"

"We have more questions for him."

"Is big problem for me. So much work and now my mother is ill."

"I'm sorry to hear that, but we won't take up much of your time."

Náni pushed past Andréas, followed by Vangélis and Tzíka. Nick hung back and found himself standing with the young man, watching the others exploring the yard and the outbuildings. The dog was off the leash again, nose to the ground, tail wagging.

"It's just a precaution," said Nick.

"What the hell are they looking for?"

"Traces of the Swiss man."

"They think he was here? Why would he be here?"

"I don't know. I guess they want to be sure he wasn't."

Andréas blinked at him incredulously, then shook his head.

Nick let his gaze wander in the direction of the carport.

"That's quite a pile. It must get cold here, in the winter."

"The logs? Oh, we'll need all of those. The wood burner chews through them. We're more than six hundred metres up, here. Sometimes there is snow, January or February."

"Looks like a lot of work. Did you cut them all yourself?"

"Actually no, my brothers did this."

"I didn't realise you owned a chainsaw."

"We don't. Grigóris borrowed one."

"Sensible lad. Was this from Papatónis?"

He looked back at Nick with a scornful grin.

"You could be on fire, but that smart-ass wouldn't cross the street to piss on you. No, Grigóris would have used Manólis's old machine."

"Did you see it?"

"Why do you ask?"

"Just curious. I've been looking to buy one myself. Is it a good one, not too expensive?"

"It's a Stihl, a few years old now. I don't know which model."

"It must be a good one to cope with that lot."

"It's okay."

Nick was looking around now, at the sorry piece of land and the few mangy sheep.

"What do you have here, ten or twelve stremmata?"

"No, it's only seven and a half."

"And this is all you have?"

"There's another five stremmata of sheep pasture on the top road."

"Ah, yes. I know. I think I saw the sheep barn."

Andréas was nodding, innocently enough.

"Do you get up there much?"

"Sheep are Grigóris's job, so no. I've enough to do here."

There was another pause. The others were picking their way across the yard towards them. Tzíka was back in harness. Then Vangélis walked her over to the front porch but she just whimpered faintly and looked up at him with those big, orange eyes.

"I'd rather you didn't go inside," said Andréas. "My mother …"

Náni raised her eyes to Vangélis who made a face and shook his head.

"That won't be necessary thank you, kýrie Katzatáki. I think we can leave you in peace, for now."

"Are you going to charge my brother with something?"

"Grigóri has already been charged. With murder."

"Are you serious?"

"We have many questions for him, but he has chosen to remain silent. We have a witness who saw him with the Swiss man's body and claims he cut it up with a chainsaw."

"Oh, my God."

"I'm sorry, Andréa, but I don't think you'll be seeing your little brother for some time. As I said, Theo should be back with you very soon."

They left him staring at the ground. Nick wondered if it was dawning on him just how helpful he had been. On the walk up to the sheep barn, Nick shared what he had learned.

"Good work, Nick," said Náni. "Theo should confirm what Andréas said about the saw – but as an eyewitness. And, with Grigóris being the sheep guy, the barn is his territory. Explains how he could do this without the family knowing, maybe."

"That's what I was thinking."

They were walking past the Papatónis farm now, but there was no sign of him.

"I'd love to give Tzíka a run in there and see what she turns up," said Náni.

"You'd need a warrant."

"I know. And we'd have to reprogram the dog for the missing wife."

Nick saw Vangélis wince with irritation. Clearly, he did not see his beloved Tzíka resembling any kind of computer.

"You think he killed her and buried her on the farm?"

"I don't know, Nick. Maybe. Something's not right with the guy. I can smell it."

*

By the time they reached the sheep barn, it was after seven, but the sun was still high in the sky, the temperature in the high twenties. Insects were everywhere and Nick could feel the shirt clinging to his back. At the gate, Vangélis slipped Tzíka off the lead. Her ears pricked up and she yelped. They saw her drop her nose to the ground, then follow a circuitous but purposeful route to the rusty, corrugated door where she barked once and stood on her hind legs, scraping her paws against the metal and looking back at them, pink tongue lolling.

"Is it open?" asked Nick.

"Stéfanos took bolt cutters to the padlock. This is covered by the warrant. Don't worry."

I'm not in the least bit worried, thought Nick. *I'm all for a bit of direct action.*

The door clanked and scraped as Vangélis pulled it back and let the dog in. Fierce sunlight pierced the gloom and they saw the workbench and the metal rings on the wall. They saw brown stains at the base of the wall where Tzíka now stood, barking happily. Job done. They saw the sink Yiánnis almost reached as he threw up. Nick walked over to the workbench. It looked clean. They must have put sheeting of some kind beneath the body but there were many brown spots on the floor. *Plenty for the forensics boys to get their teeth into here*, he thought.

"Happy, Constable?" asked Náni.

"Yes, ma'am. Tzíka's reaction is conclusive. The young man was here, as you expected."

"Well, his body was. Was he killed here though; I wonder?"

"Even Tzíka can't tell you that, ma'am."

"What we *do* know," said Náni, "is someone paid Grigóris five thousand euros. That's big money round here. Did they pay him to kill Lukas or just to dispose of the body?"

"Why would anyone pay a substantial sum of money to kill a stranger. It doesn't make sense," said Nick.

"Assuming he *was* a stranger, I agree. So, our hypothesis must be that the money was paid to dispose of the body by someone relatively prosperous who had *already* killed Lukas."

"Sounds more like it."

"We need to get the lad talking."

It was coming up to eight pm now and the sun was beginning its long descent to the horizon. The face of Mount Kédros was a dusty pink and birds were hurrying to roosting spots in the village trees. They decided to call it a day. Tzíka was patted and Vangélis thanked. Nick and Náni agreed to meet at Réthymno early the next morning.

Back in the car, Nick checked his phone. There was a voicemail message. The husky voice with the faint Swedish intonation and the ever-present hint of suggestiveness was instantly recognisable:

I hear you're pretending to be a detective again, Nick Fisher. This means you'll be working too hard, missing your Greek lessons and eating garbage. I know. So, for tonight, I thought you might enjoy fried peppers, an octopus salad and some home-made walnut cake with honey rakí? If you can get here by nine, I'll feed you. Bring some of that wonderful Vidianó if you have any left – what was it called? And we can talk about what you're going to do with Jason while he's here. I have some ideas for you. Anyway, let me know.

Good old Lena. Nick glanced at his watch. He might just have time to shower, change, and grab a bottle of the wonderful White Rabbit. *I'm late, I'm late, for a very important date*, he chuckled to himself.

CHAPTER 18
THE HOODED MAN

Nick could see this was one of her difficult days. It was five past eight and she was already on the phone, looking exasperated and clicking her pen in and out, then tapping it on the desk. It did not help when he slopped the coffee as he handed it to her and then used a fistful of her tissues to mop some official-looking papers.

"Helpful, but no more than that," Náni was saying in Greek as she glared at him. "The saw and the base of the wall are much more important."

Nick sat down heavily as she continued to stab the desk in frustration.

"You're quite sure? Should I take it somewhere else? … What about the wall? … Okay. You're promising me, right? … Yes, as soon as you can, please."

She lifted her head, eyes closed for a moment, before slamming the phone into its cradle and looking straight at Nick.

"Good morning," he said.

"The blood in the sheep barn is Lukas's. No question. That's the good news."

"And the bad news?"

"They've concluded that the blood traces on the chainsaw can't be identified with any certainty. There's just not enough of it."

"They already told us this, didn't they?"

"They were still trying. Now they've given up."

"Right."

"And the other thing?"

Nick raised his eyebrows.

"They haven't been out to the base of the wall yet."

"Why didn't they do that while they were there?"

"I don't know. They gave me some crap about the light and the dewpoint. They're going back later this morning."

"Not the end of the world."

"I suppose not."

She glanced at her watch.

"Galánis wants to see me at eight thirty. Do you want to sit in?"

*

They must be about the same age, but this guy looks like he never sees the light of day, Nick thought. *Probably never exercises beyond lugging files about.* He was dishevelled and disorganised. And he was late. And flustered.

"Perhaps we could start with Theodóris Katzatákis?" he said. "I have a form of words for a statement he's willing to sign." He handed each of them a piece of paper in Greek.

Náni cast her eyes over it, frowning.

"This doesn't go far enough," she said. "And we already have this from Andréas. I want to *prove* beyond doubt the saw came from Manólis."

"If he doesn't know, what can I do?"

"Oh, come on, Galáni. There's a pile of logs as big as a house. He must be able to give us a good description – colour, make, model, fuel type – even if he claims not to know whose it was."

"All right, Sergeant. I'll ask him again. Now, turning to Leftéris and Yiánnis Katzatákis, you said you wanted to question them further. Will that be today?"

"They will be charged as accessories today, but any further charges will be held in abeyance for now. You may apply for bail, pending trial, and the police will not oppose that."

"If it were up to me, they'd be charged with attempted murder right now and put away for ten years," said Nick.

Náni threw him a glare, before continuing:

"I will bring their co-operation to the attention of the prosecutors and encourage them to take a more lenient view, but I can't promise that they will, given Mr Fisher's ordeal. This is all I can give you, Galáni."

Galánis shrugged slightly and shuffled some papers.

"Then we come to Grigóris Katzatákis … He is not a murderer, Sergeant. He says he didn't kill him. He was a stranger. There was no reason for him to do the man any harm."

"Grigóris is a racist thug. He believed Lukas to be German. And he may have been egged on by other racist elements in the village."

"Racists who would pay him a large sum of money to kill a stranger. Does that sound likely to you, Sergeant?"

"If Grigóris is ready to talk, we'll listen, Galáni, but I refuse to waste time with him. If he wants us to believe he's not the killer, he must tell us what happened, and he must give up those who contacted him and gave him the money. Until then, he can remain in our cells. He will not be granted bail and, as you know, a trial could be twelve or eighteen months away, these days. I hope he enjoys his own company."

Galánis gave a curt nod, gathered up his papers and withdrew to lick his wounds.

"That was well done," said Nick, when the lawyer was gone.

"No thanks to you, Nick Fisher."

"Just saying it how it is."

"Let's get some coffee."

As they were wandering back, Níkos caught Nick's eye.

"I have good news, Mr Fisher. Your Jeep will be ready to collect on Tuesday."

"Excellent, but I can't collect Tuesday. I have to pick my son up from the airport."

"Then I will have them bring it here. And shall I arrange for the car hire people to collect from here, Wednesday morning?"

"That should work. Thank you, Níko."

When they were back in the Lieutenant's office, Náni said:

"So, this Eléni woman who owns the house with the wall. What do we know?"

"She's in her early nineties and losing her marbles. Has a son in Réthymno."

"Losing her marbles?"

"Going a bit doolally."

Nick was drawing circles in the air with his index finger, pointing at his head.

"She suffers from dementia, you mean?"

"So, I've been told."

Náni was shaking her head, shuffling back through her notes.

"Ah, yes. Eléni Fotákis. The son is Pandelís."

"We might need to talk to them quite soon."

"And there's a daughter, Roúla. Working in England."

Nick jolted at the name. How did he miss that connection? Then his conversation with Alékos floated back to him. *There's only one Eléni in Kardánes, Nick.* Perhaps his subconscious had been blocking what was staring him in the face.

"Yes, I met her briefly. Do you have an address for the son?" he said.

"I'll get one. Maybe the old lady is with him."

"She often is, I believe."

"So, let's pay a visit to this Pandelís Fotákis tomorrow morning. I'll chase the forensics team to get something to us before then."

Déspina knocked and put her head around the door:

"The lawyer Galánis wants to see you again, ma'am. Shall I tell him he has to wait?"

"No. It's okay, Déspina. Send him in."

*

They were able to deal quickly with Theo. The statement now referred to a cordless electric chainsaw, orange and white, matching the one Náni remembered. That would do, she said and agreed to his release, once the document was signed.

"And Grigóris would like another interview, Sergeant."

"Hooray. One at which he plans to speak, perhaps?"

"He'll tell you everything he knows. He wants the murder charge lifted."

"All right. Well, as you're here, let's do it right away. Shall we say fifteen minutes?"

*

The cocky gestures were gone now, replaced by sullenness. Náni got straight to the point:

"So, Grigóri. Did you kill Lukas Hedinger?"

"No."

"Who did?"

"I don't know."

"I find that hard to believe."

He shrugged insolently as if what she chose to believe was her problem.

"I think you'd better start from the beginning, Grigóri," she said.

His lawyer looked at him for a few seconds, eyebrows raised. Finally, he began to speak:

"I got a text, about ten o'clock on the Sunday night. No name showed and it wasn't a number I recognised. All it said was: *If you want to make three thousand euros tonight, meet me at the cemetery in fifteen minutes.*"

"This was from a Greek phone?"

"A Greek mobile, yes. A number starting 697."

"Like half a million others. Is your phone here?"

"He destroyed it."

"Who did?"

"The bloke I met, later."

"So, you went to meet this person without knowing who it was?"

"Sure, that sort of money is huge for me."

"And who was it?"

"It was a man. I know that much, but he was wearing a makeshift hood, cut from a sack or something with holes for the eyes."

"Oh, come on, Grigóri. You expect us to believe that?"

"It's true. I swear."

"How could you be sure it was a man, then?"

"He was wearing men's shoes, and it became clearer later when he threatened me."

"What did he say?"

"Nothing."

"Oh, come on, Grigóri!"

"No, I swear. He never spoke. He'd written out these cards. The first one said: *I need your help*. So, I said, 'Okay'. And then he showed me the second one. It said: *I have a dead body*. I could feel him staring at me, seeing whether I was fazed by that. I just said, 'Right.'"

"Did you see his eyes?"

"Too dark. Felt them more than saw them – just staring at me, you know?"

"Then what happened? Card number three?"

"Yes. It said: *It must never be identified* and the *never* was in red, underlined. I said, 'Who is it?' but he just shook his head, so I said, 'Aren't you going to tell me?' and he shook his head again. 'Do I know this person?' I asked, and he shook his head a third time."

"What are you sensing about this guy?" asked Nick, in English. "Is he young or old, fat or thin, tall or short? Anything you noticed at all?" Náni dutifully translated.

"He didn't seem young or old – somewhere in between. Average height and weight. I remember he was wearing a check shirt and jeans."

"Did you smell anything, hear anything?"

"Nothing I remember. Then the next card said *Three grand – will you do it?* Well, I can feel his desperation, so I say: 'No, five' and raise my hand like this. Well this gets him riled and he's stomping about making exasperated noises, so I say, 'I'll do it tonight for five grand, no questions asked'. And after a little while, he calms down and raises his hand with the five fingers splayed and I say, 'Okay, deal. When?' And he just stares at me, so I say, 'Now?' and he nods. Then he reveals the next card, *Where?* Well, I've already been thinking about this, so I say, 'My sheep barn, on the top road. You know it?' and he nods."

"So, he's a local, someone from the village."

"Someone who *knows* the village, for sure. And someone who knew how long it would take me to walk from the cemetery to the barn."

"Why do you say that?"

"Because the next thing, he pockets the keys from my truck, then he points up the hill and raises both hands with the fingers splayed.

164

I figure it out: 'You want to meet at the barn in ten minutes?' and he nods, 'and I've got to walk there?' and he nods again. Then he disappears down the hill, back into the village."

"He didn't have a vehicle there, then."

"No. And that was the point of his little charade. He gives himself enough time to get the body and drive it up to the sheep barn before I can get there. By the time I arrive, he's standing at the gate, no vehicle in sight, and I see something bundled in black refuse bags, propped up against the side of the barn."

"Could he have done that alone?"

"I doubt it, but I never saw anyone else."

"So, what happens next?"

"I walk over to the body and take a look. It's a young guy I've never seen before and he doesn't look Greek. Meanwhile, our friend has brought out his cards again. The next one says, *Can I trust you?* and then he shuffles back to the earlier one, *It must never be identified* and then a new one, *And it must never be found!* and the *never* is in red and underlined again. Then he puts down the cards and grabs my wrist hard, and it hurts. He comes up close and stares at me and draws a line across his throat with his forefinger, slowly. Chills me to the bone, that. I get the message. Then he searches me, takes my phone and smashes it to pieces with a rock, sifts through the bits with a torch and I see him slip something into his pocket. Then there's a pause. I'm guessing it's a tough decision for him, but it's one he's already made by bringing the body, so he reaches into his shirt and pulls out five small packages and hands them to me. I signal for him to wait while I walk to the streetlight and check. Each one is wrapped in brown paper with *20 x 50* handwritten on the outside. I check a couple of them."

"And then what?"

"He just picks up the cards, throws me my keys and leaves. A couple of minutes later, I hear an engine start so he must have parked just past the turning."

"A car or a truck?"

"I'd guess a car. It wasn't loud."

"Then what did you do?"

"I open the barn and drag the body inside, take off the bags and lean it against the wall. It feels like a dead weight and a huge risk. Suddenly, the five grand doesn't seem so much and I start wondering what the hell I've taken on. In one way, I'm relieved it's a foreigner and not a Greek, but I know there'll be big trouble when he's missed. I know I have to get moving. I think about piling the body into the truck and driving it to some remote part of the island and dumping it, just dropping it into a gorge or something, but then I see that finger again, drawing the line across his throat and I know he'll come for me if the body is found. No, I need to make it unrecognisable and I need to get it somewhere it will never be found as he wanted. Otherwise, I might not get a good night's sleep, ever again.

"On the walk back to the truck, I came up with the idea of the chainsaw. I was sure I could get it from Amalía with a plausible cover story, but I knew I needed help, too. I couldn't do everything myself and a boat would be useful. My cousins were the obvious choice. I guess you know the rest by now."

"How do you think this person picked you out, Grigóri?" asked Nick. "How did he know you were the right guy to approach."

"I've no idea."

"Sounds like he knew you pretty well. And yet you don't have a clue who you were talking to."

"Well, I couldn't see his face, could I, and *he* wasn't doing any talking, was he?"

"It's not a big village though, is it? I bet we could make a list of all the men in the village and you could narrow it down to a handful."

"Why would I do that?"

"Because we ask you to," said Náni, "and because you've done something appalling and horrendous that is an offence to humanity and you're going to need all the help you can get if you're to avoid a very long time in prison. Isn't that so, kýrie Galáni?"

"I think it's in your best interests to co-operate, Grigóri," said the lawyer.

"When will I get my money back? Then I might co-operate."

"*Your* money? Money from criminal activities is forfeit, Grigóri. You won't be getting it back," said Náni.

"What the fuck?"

"It goes to the state. To help catch more villains like you."

"You mean, I went through all this for nothing?"

"For nothing, plus five years inside, with luck," said Nick.

*

Grigóris was sent to Chrístos and his list of one hundred and forty-eight Kardánes residents. Of those, seventy-nine were female and fifteen of the sixty-nine males were under eighteen. They would go through the remaining fifty-four one by one, trying to eliminate them and outlining their reasons for doing so.

Nick made an excuse and left mid-afternoon. Within half an hour, he was ringing the bell at María's little yellow house in Kardánes. She glanced around nervously as she let him in.

"You should have called, Mr Fisher. I would have met you somewhere else."

"Have you been threatened?"

"Not threatened, no. Not quite. It's more the way the villagers look at me. Some have ostracised me; I think."

"Shall I tell the police?"

"Tell them what? It's not a crime, and squealing could make things worse for me. Anyway, you're here now. You'd better come through."

Nick followed her through the living room to the terrace.

"Can I get you anything?"

"No, thank you."

"You remember my mother?"

Nick had not noticed the old lady sitting in an armchair with a book. Now she looked up and smiled faintly.

"Of course. It's Evangelíne, isn't it?"

This brought a watery smile and she extended a bony hand which Nick shook gently.

María pulled forward an awning and they sat at the metal table.

"I'll come straight to the point, María. What do you know of the Fotákis family?"

"Well, let me see. Nice family. There's Eléni and her son Pandelís. He is an estate agent in Réthymno, married to Giorgía. They have two boys – young men now."

"And there's a daughter too, I believe."

"Yes. Lovely woman, very bright. Roúla works in London these days. Some kind of lawyer, I think."

"Does *she* have a family?"

Nick was going off-piste and he knew it.

"No. It's a shame. She'd make a lovely mother. I suppose she was always driven to work hard and now her chance has slipped away."

María looked off into the distance, at the arid slopes of the mountain and the fields below, dotted with spring flowers.

"I'm sorry. I mustn't judge others by myself," she said, "but I just couldn't imagine life without my children."

"Some people find fulfilment in careers," Nick said, "especially if they're doing something worthwhile, helping others."

"I'm sure you're right," she said, but she didn't look convinced.

"I didn't get my coffee, dear," Evangelíne piped up, in Greek.

"Oh, sorry, Mum. I'll go and get it. And would you like a Ness while I'm there, Mr Fisher?"

"Why not? Thank you."

As soon as her daughter disappeared into the kitchen, the old lady leaned across.

"I will try to speak English with you, Mr Fisher, but I'm out of practice."

"Sounds pretty good to me, Evangelíne."

"Well, thank you," she smiled. "She's quite wrong, you know."

"What do you mean?"

"Eléni is not their mother. I was born in this village, you see."

"And María moved here – what? Five years ago?"

The old lady nodded and swung her chair around a little, so she could look him straight in the eyes.

"She's not their mother. She's their aunt: Aunt Eléni."

There was a triumphant gleam in her eyes.

"What can you tell me about her?" Nick asked.

"Eléni had a difficult war, shall we say, and then she went off to fight with the Communists."

"What do you mean by *a difficult war*?"

But the old lady continued without seeming to hear.

"When the civil war was over, she came back to her parents, here, in the village. Years later, when they died, she went to live with her sister and her young family."

"Where was this?"

"Still here, in Kardánes. The kids were only little then, and they loved having her there. And then, I heard the sister died. She was only in her forties, poor thing, but she'd been ailing since she was a girl, pretty much. Much later, when the children left home, Eléni got herself the little place down the alley. Got it fixed up quite nicely."

"Why did she leave?"

"Living with just her dead sister's husband? Not done in those days, Mr Fisher."

"What happened to him?"

"A sad story, I'm afraid. He struggled, without his wife. And when Eléni left too, he couldn't cope. Eléni tried to help him, but he wouldn't be helped. Drank himself to death inside two years."

"That would have been rough on the kids," said Nick.

She just went on looking at him, an eyebrow slightly raised.

"You don't have sugar, do you, Mr Fisher?" said María, emerging from the living room with a tray.

"Er … no. I don't, thanks. And please call me Nick."

She smiled as she passed around the cups.

"No more simnel cakes, I'm afraid, but I do have home-made cookies."

"How wonderful," said Nick.

With her coffee and cookie delivered, the old lady turned back to her book. Nick guessed he was not expected to share her revelations with María. Instead, he asked about Eléni's nephew.

"Pandelís is a nice man, what I've seen of him. A quiet, introspective type."

"Rare, for an estate agent," said Nick with a grin.

"You know, that never crossed my mind! And yet he must be quite good at it. He's hardly a go-getter but he's done all right for himself. I often see him fixing up the garden for her, when they're here. We have a little chat. Looks after his mum, he does, and Giorgía's lovely with her, too."

The old lady shot him a glare over her spectacles at the word *mum*, but Nick wasn't about to correct María's happy ramblings.

*

It was after six by the time Nick found himself in a bar in Spíli with a large beer and a dish of spicy peanut mix in front of him. He avoided the kafenío in Kardánes so as not to stir up more trouble for María, but he needed time to sit and think things through. It was pleasant enough here, a modern, paved area under the local mountain, shaded by giant plane trees with a hubbub of chatter, some piped music and the sound of running water. A little torrent rushed down the mountain to spout from the mouths of a row of Venetian lions' heads. Here, tourists filled their water bottles with spring water and, occasionally, a donkey would dip its head to drink from the trough below. Several cafes and bars converged on the square. There were tables of locals and tables of tourists. Separate, but mutually accepting. The quiet tourists were fascinated by the noisy, convivial locals; the Greeks ignored the tourists. Not belonging to either camp, Nick kept himself to himself.

He was thinking about Roúla and wishing she was sitting there with him, right now. He wondered if she was like her Aunt Eléni – a tough character moulded from battle, hardship and loss. It seemed likely. Roúla lost her parents early, worked hard and forged a profession for herself and a life in another country. A demanding country. She must be resilient, independent and strong. He liked strong women, the more so if they were feminine, too. They could be hard work, but he believed in full, sharing relationships, not stereotypical male and female roles. Jen felt that way too. Perhaps Roúla was the same. So much the better.

He ordered a second beer and turned his thoughts to the case. He was not sure whether to believe in Grigóris's mystery man with the sacking mask and the carefully thought-out prompt cards. It was all a bit too clever for a man who had just killed someone, a man who was likely to be in a state of panic. And, if Grigóris was trying to avoid revealing the identity of the person who hired him, it would be a handy story to tell. How could he be expected to recognise a guy who hid his face and never spoke? And he would have had plenty of time to put these ideas together while waiting to be interrogated.

And what about this guy they were going to see in the morning, Pandelís? He didn't sound much of a killer. An estate agent all his life, a family man who was kind to his ageing aunt? What would he be doing murdering a young Swiss guy at random or in some fit of racist rage?

No, the more he thought about it, the more Nick was convinced. They were missing something. Something vital. And, when they found it, whatever it was, they might just have themselves a motive.

CHAPTER 19
THE RUSSIAN DOLL

"Does he know we're coming?" Nick asked as he settled into the blue and white Skoda outside Réthymno police headquarters on Saturday morning.

"And give him a chance to run? Of course, not, Nick."

"Let's hope he's in, then. Anything from forensics?"

"Yes. Good news for once. They found blood traces near the base of the wall."

"Human blood?"

"We'll know, later today."

"Enough to identify it, this time?"

"They're hopeful, but it will take a while. And they want swabs from those present at Eléni's house to identify and eliminate any other DNA profiles. They're going to meet us there."

"Roúla could be a challenge."

"Yes. Maybe we can get to her later if we need to."

They chatted about the case as Náni drove the five kilometres out of the city and up the steep road to the village of Roussospíti. Nick saw a rash of new building, scarring the landscape, but then concrete and glass gave way to old stone, draped with purple flowering succulents and great swathes of bougainvillea in white, lilac or red.

The Fotákis house was modern, but in keeping with the older structures nearby, being largely stone and glass. It looked architect-designed, the conservative style radicalised by a useless, but impressive, concrete arch, angled out to one side and painted a contrasting dove grey. The house was not large, but it looked neat, stylish and comfortable.

Náni was not in uniform, but the police car was visible, and Nick saw the woman's eyes glance at it in consternation as she opened the door.

"Kaliméra, kyría Fotáki," said Náni, holding out her identity card. "I am Sergeant Samarákis and this is Mr Nick Fisher. May we come in, please?"

The woman scrutinised the card, then glanced at Nick.

"What's this about?" she said.

"May we come in?" persisted Náni and the woman acquiesced. They followed her through to a front-facing living-room with net curtains covering the lower half of the windows.

"Please sit," she said.

"We are pursuing enquiries into the murder of a young Swiss man who was last seen in Kardánes almost two weeks ago: Sunday evening, the eighth of June. We have reason to believe he was in the vicinity of Eléni Fotákis's house at around nine pm."

"I don't think I was there that weekend, Sergeant."

"And your husband?"

"Shall I get him?"

Giorgía glanced nervously at each of them.

"Yes. Thank you," said Náni.

"Did you see her hands?" whispered Nick after she left the room. Náni widened her eyes and nodded.

Pandelís breezed in smiling, followed by his wife, shook hands and sat down facing them with an open expression. *An estate agent should have a professional front*, thought Nick, *but this one looks impenetrable.*

"You know, I think I *was* there with Mum, that night," he said, in answer to Náni's question, "but I'm sure we didn't see any strangers around. It's a very quiet village. I'm sure I'd remember."

"By *Mum*, you mean your Aunt Eléni."

"Sorry, yes. We've always called her Mum."

"Were you there *all* evening?" asked Nick.

"Actually, no. I don't think I got there until nine thirty or so. I came to collect Eléni and bring her back here, but then I stayed an hour or two for a natter with Roúla."

"Your sister."

"Yes. And she really is my sister. She tries to get over every few weeks. This was one of those weeks."

"The two of them were there all evening?"

"I imagine so."

"But you saw nothing and heard nothing? No noises from the garden, for example?"

"No, nothing. I'm sorry I can't be more help, Sergeant. What they did to the young man was terrible. Unforgivable."

"Could you let me have a number for Roúla, please? We'd like to give her a call."

"I'm sure she'd have told me if someone was snooping around."

"Perhaps, but we need to hear it from her."

"Very well," he said.

"Give me your mobile numbers and I'll share her contact details," said Giorgía, to Nick's delight.

"Just write it on a piece of paper, please," said Náni. "My number's not in the public domain."

"Sorry, no, it wouldn't be, would it?" said Giorgía. "I'll dig out a notepad before you leave."

At that point, the doorbell rang.

"I think that will be the gentleman from our forensics team," said Náni. "We're doing some analysis of samples taken at your mother's house. He needs to take swabs from you and your aunt, Pandelí. It will only take a minute or two and will help us isolate any foreign DNA in the samples."

"Foreign?" said Pandelís.

"DNA from anyone outside the family."

"I see."

"Would that be okay?"

He shrugged and nodded acquiescence and Giorgía went to let the man in. A bespectacled, young man took less than two minutes to confirm Pandelís's identity and have him sign a consent form, then rinse his mouth with clean water. Then he donned polythene gloves and tore back a strip to extract what looked like a tiny toilet brush with a long handle from a wrapper. He then checked his watch and asked Pandelís to open his mouth before inserting the thing and rubbing it around the inside of his left cheek for a good twenty seconds before placing it in a special envelope. He then repeated the process with the right cheek before thanking his patient.

"Are you my second patient?" he asked Giorgía.

"No. Through here," she said, and he followed her out.

"When he's finished, we'd like to talk to Eléni," Náni said.

"I'm not sure that's a good idea," said Pandelís. "You see, my aunt is ninety-two now. She's frail and suffers from dementia. I'm not sure you could rely on her to understand your questions or give you truthful – or even sensible – answers, I'm afraid."

"I do understand," said Náni, leaning forward, "nevertheless, we'd like to try. We'll treat her with respect and weigh her answers carefully."

"I'm afraid she would find it upsetting. She is very weak, Sergeant."

"We won't take much of her time and we'll go to her if that's easier."

Despite the squirming, Náni's insistence brooked no refusal. Nick admired her quiet determination.

"All right, then. If you must, but let's keep it to a couple of minutes, please."

After the young man left with his DNA swabs, they followed Giorgía and Pandelís to a large kitchen at the rear of the house which gave onto a small, neat garden. A very old lady, all in black, was sitting at the kitchen table. A photograph album was open in front of her and a few sepia-tinted, black and white photos were scattered across the table. Nick was astonished to see her smoking, and alongside her glass of water was another, much smaller, glass containing a pale brown liquid.

"What's this Pandelí. More excitement?" she said.

Pandelís bent down in front of her, bringing his eyes to her level.

"These people are from the police, Mum. They'd like to ask you a couple of quick questions."

Náni and Nick slid into chairs in front of her. Pandelís sat next to his aunt, to one side.

The old lady looked at Nick with a wicked smile.

"Will you take a rakí with me, young man?" she said, in Greek.

"It's honey rakí," said Pandelís. "She often has one or two mid-morning."

It sounded like she might have a problem with the booze, *but, if you're ninety-two, who gives a damn?* thought Nick.

"A little … lígo, efcharistó," he said. And then, seeing her wavering hands reaching for the almost full bottle, "Shall I help myself?"

He took a sip to appease her. It was far too sweet and bore no resemblance to the rakí he was accustomed to having at the end of a meal.

"Eínai glikós!" he winced, grinning.

She beamed, showing her three or four remaining teeth, and patted his arm with a liver-spotted hand.

"Have you found some memories?" said Nick, raising his voice and gesturing at the photos. Náni translated for him and then Eléni started chattering in Greek and arranging pictures in front of them.

"She says these are from the civil war. This is her."

Nick saw a stunning, dark-haired woman of about twenty with her foot on the bumper of a light armoured vehicle, a cigarette in her mouth. She was wearing battle fatigues with a paler scarf, knotted loosely around her neck. She looked exhausted but triumphant.

"They just captured the truck," said Náni as the old lady rambled on.

Only then did Nick register the bloodstained knife in Eléni's young hand and see a body, face down towards the rear of the truck, in a fresh, dark pool of blood. He was momentarily shocked, the more so when he looked up to see Eléni drawing her wrinkled hand across her throat, eyes wide, then cackling at his discomfort.

He scanned the other photos briefly but Eléni was now looking at the album, he saw. Pandelís reached across and took it from her.

"They're not here to look at your old war pictures, Mum. These are busy people."

The old lady gave Nick a knowing look, as if to say: *See what I have to cope with – my idiot nephew – what does he know of the things that matter in life?*

"Now, ask your questions, Sergeant," said Pandelís.

"Thank you for seeing us, Eléni. You must have been a very brave, young woman. Now, I'd like you to cast your mind back to Sunday the eighth, almost two weeks ago, in Kardánes. Do you remember?"

Her cigarette was still burning, forgotten in the ashtray and it was stinking. Mercifully, Pandelís stretched behind her to put it out.

But Eléni was looking bewildered now and suddenly very old.

"You remember, Mum. Roúla was here. The last time you saw Roúla?" said Pandelís.

She was nodding but her mind seemed to be elsewhere. Náni persevered:

"Did you see a young man at your house, that evening?"

Fear seemed to have crept into Eléni's eyes or was it just confusion? Nick could not be sure. Náni put her phone on the table and brought up a picture of Lukas.

"This young man."

Eléni jerked back, pushing against the table so it scraped on the floor tiles. Her water glass toppled over and broke, and Nick and Náni had to jump back in their chairs to avoid the stream of water. Then she raised her head and chattered wildly in Greek, or was it German? There was a touch of madness in those eyes now, as she struggled against Pandelís's restraining arms. Náni hurriedly recovered the dripping phone and accepted some tissues from Nick. He was surprised by the old lady's reaction, as they all were. *Was it fear or hatred,* he wondered? *Perhaps both.* Whatever it was, gave her extraordinary strength for someone her age, albeit briefly.

Gradually, she seemed to regain some kind of equilibrium.

"What on earth's going on?" said Giorgía from the door.

"Mum had one of her turns," said Pandelís, gathering up the shards of broken glass.

But Eléni was staring fiercely at Nick as if to say: *We know different, don't we?*

The rakí glass did not fall over, miraculously, and now she downed the rest of the brown liquor and smacked the glass down.

"Right. That's it," said Giorgía. "I don't think she can take much more of this. We'll have to ask you to leave now."

"Perhaps we could come back another time," said Náni, but received no reply.

Eléni was looking strangely pleased with herself, Nick thought, as they were hurried from her presence.

Náni asked a second time for Roúla's phone number and Giorgía slipped her a piece of paper before closing the door on them. Neither spoke until they were back in the car.

"Frail, my arse," said Nick. "The old girl's as tough as they come, for ninety-two."

"I agree, but she seems a little crazy."

"Maybe she is. What was it she yelled, Náni?"

"I can't be sure. It seemed garbled. When she was speaking Greek, I heard Ángelos, which means *Angel*. Then there was a burst of German, I think it was."

"And did you see the photos in the album, before he snatched it away? Someone took a pair of scissors to them. Six of the eight we could see. Someone was cut out of those photos."

"And out of her life?"

"There's so much more we need to ask her, Náni."

*

When Nick got back to Saktoúria, it was lunchtime. But, before heading down to the kafenío, he called Sofía.

"Just wanted to check. Are you okay for Tuesday, Sofía?"

"Big clean for Mister Jason, I know. Don't worry."

"Only, I might not be here."

"No problem. I have key. You pay me next time."

"Great. And one more thing. Your auntie, Aunt Evangelíne …"

Ten minutes later, Nick knew the whole story. The old lady's birthday was the very next day, as it happened. She would be eighty-eight. She was born in the village and lived there until the late 1950s when she married and moved away. She returned thirty or forty years later after her husband died, and then María moved there, with *her* husband, just a few years ago and they all decided to live together.

"She want take care of her mum. Evangelíne not so young now."

"And a little bit crazy?"

"She *no* crazy, Níko. She nice lady. Wise."

"So, she would know about the village and its people during the war and the civil war?"

"She was young then, but yes, she must."

"And she would have known Eléni?"

"Which Eléni?"

"The Eléni in Kardánes."

"I don't know her, Níko."

"Of course, it's not your village, is it?"

"I know people there because of my cousin, but no Eléni. There are two Elénis here—"

"Entáxi, Sofía," interrupted Nick.

He thanked her and ended the call.

*

Rather than go to the kafenío, he decided to drive to the coast. The thermometer on the back wall crept past thirty-six, the hottest day of the year so far, and Nick needed a swim. He reckoned he was overdue some exercise and a little Vitamin D. Skinária was *west* of Triópetra, so no risk of body parts, and there was a pleasant, shady taverna on a lawn of sorts where they served an excellent shrimp and avocado salad, he remembered.

The call from Náni came as he was dripping from his first swim and fumbling for five euros to give the sun lounger guy.

"Just checking, Nick. Are you okay to join me Monday afternoon? I want us to go back to Pandelís and have a more serious talk."

"On what basis? Do you have an answer on the blood already?"

"No, but we'll get that Monday lunchtime and I want to be ready to move right away if it's Lukas's. I'm going to try for a search warrant, too."

"Sure, I'm up for that. His reactions today seemed a bit glib; there might well be something there. And it would be good to get more time with Eléni if we can. Did you get hold of Roúla?"

"Rang twice, left a message."

179

"Want me to have a go, let you enjoy your weekend?"

"Oh yes, you met her, didn't you? I guess it can't do any harm. The number is—"

"Hang on, can you just share the contact? I'm on the beach."

"Lucky you."

Nick went on to tell her about Evangelíne.

"Okay, might be useful background for us. Bring her in Monday morning, if she's willing. I think I'll need to be in the office, the way this is going."

Nick agreed to try.

*

He added Roúla's number to his contacts and called her that evening but disconnected after being directed to voicemail. On Sunday morning, he called María. The damned village dogs were enjoying a barkathon and he swore quietly to himself. Thirty degrees already and he was having to shut the window.

"María. Kaliméra. How are you?"

"Hello again, Mr Fisher. We are quite well, thank you."

"A little bird told me it was Evangelíne's birthday today. Is that right?"

"That Sofía could never keep a thing to herself."

He chuckled.

"Will you give your mum my best wishes, María?"

"I will."

"And there's a favour I'd like to ask."

"Go on."

"Would she be able to come to Réthymno with me tomorrow, to police headquarters? It would be very helpful to our investigation to get all the background we can on the village history and characters from someone who remembers the war."

"She's eighty-eight today, Mr Fisher. She doesn't go anywhere, anymore. I think it would be frightening for her."

"Could you ask her for me? She might enjoy a little adventure. You never know. And the Investigations Sergeant would like to meet her."

"No, I'm sorry. I'm not going to ask her. I don't want her exhausted or upset. And she might be seen with you. People would put two and two together. I'm not having my mother put at risk like that."

"Okay. I didn't think about that."

"You can come here again if you're careful. Just you. No uniforms, no police cars."

"All right, thank you. I'd prefer to interview her alone, María, if that's okay."

"If she's comfortable with that, I won't object."

Nick thanked her again and arranged to be there for nine thirty the following morning. Then he called Náni.

"Okay, Nick. I think it's more important for me to focus on getting the search warrant, and there's no way I can afford three or four hours out of the office on Monday morning. Could you record it? Just use your phone and we can get a transcript made for the file."

"Is it easy to do?"

"Just Google it, for Heaven's sake. It'll be straightforward, even for you, but practise first. You don't want to put the old dear through a long interview and come away with nothing."

"I'm sure I can work it out."

There was nothing more to be done on the case, and it was Sunday, after all, so Nick decided to have a day pottering around the little stone house, making sure everything was ready for Jason's visit. He would start by watering the parched garden, before it got even hotter, maybe set up the speakers outside and float some Brubeck over the village. He could stroll down to the kafenío later, have a couple of beers with Kóstas and Yiórgos or pop in to see Lena. He should also give Lauren a call. Before doing any of that, though, he tried Roúla's number again. This time he left a message at the prompt:

Hi Roúla. Nick Fisher here. We met briefly in Kardánes. I hope you remember because I certainly do, and I was hoping we could meet up again. Are you planning to come back soon? Please let me know when you have a moment. It would be great to see you.

CHAPTER 20
WAR STORIES

María was being overly solicitous. She plumped up her mother's cushions, lined up tea and biscuits, asked again if she was entirely happy to be interviewed.

"How was your birthday party?" asked Nick, when she finally left them alone.

"I'm too old for parties now," said Evangelíne.

"That sounds like María talking."

"Don't misunderstand me. I'd *like* one, but I'd just fall asleep as soon as the fun started. And who would come? Most of my friends are gone, now."

Nick made a rueful face and patted her hand.

"I'm just going to set this up if that's okay?" he said, placing his phone on the table in front of them. "It's for the Sergeant, so she can hear what you have to say, later."

"The Sergeant is a woman?"

"Yes, she is. And quite a young woman, too."

"Good. About time."

He grinned and pressed the red circle. A reassuring counter started.

"Interview with Ms Evangelíne Vókos commenced at nine forty-two am on the twenty-third of June. Interviewer Nick Fisher, seconded to Réthymno police."

"Sounds rather formal, Mr Fisher."

"Don't worry about that. It's just standard procedure. Now relax – and please call me Nick."

"All right."

"So, Evangelíne, you were born in the village of Kardánes and lived here from 1932 until the late 1950s. Is that correct?"

"Yes, and then I came back, later."

"Did you know Eléni Fotákis then?"

"I knew everyone in the village. Eléni was four years older, so we weren't friends when we were kids. I was more friends with her sister, but I was aware of her. More so later, of course."

Nick's antennae picked up on that, but he decided to stick with the order of questions, for the recording.

"Tell me what you remember of her, during the German war."

The old lady pushed at the loose skin on the back of her hand with her right thumb, then took off her glasses and let them dangle on their silver chain as if she could see the past more clearly without them. Then she started to speak:

"Nothing happened at first. There was a war going on somewhere, but not here. But then the Germans invaded, spring 1941. The powers that be were expecting an invasion from the sea and they'd prepared for it, supposedly. But the Germans sent in paratroopers. Thousands of them. Never been done before. At least, not with any success. They landed at Máleme, near Chaniá and over in Iráklio. The people were out at the airfields with anything they could find, trying to fight them off. Ordinary people with machetes or axes or just throwing rocks. Terrible. The Germans were hacked to pieces, to begin with, but wave after wave kept coming and eventually, they overwhelmed us. Within a few weeks, they were all over the island. I remember when they first came *here*. I was nine years old."

"And Eléni would have been thirteen," Nick prompted.

"Yes, I suppose she would. They set up camps, the Nazis, started acting like they owned the place. Some of the village men joined the partisans, living up in the mountains, attacking the Germans whenever they could, but every attack brought harsh reprisals. Men were shot, villages burned, right the way down the Amári Valley."

"I've read something about this. Was it like that here, in Kardánes?"

"They were brutal at first. Two of the villagers were shot for so-called acts of resistance, but, after a while, things settled down, people were toeing the line, or at least making the Germans think they were. Some of the men were still hiding and we sent supplies whenever we could. That was the most dangerous thing."

She took a sip of tea and pressed a napkin against her mouth before continuing:

"Some of the Germans were quite friendly to us kids, after a while. I don't think we got the hardened Nazis so much, being a distant outpost. Most were just ordinary lads, trying to make the occupation a little less adversarial. Trying to be human beings rather than uniforms. It was sweet of them to try, but it was impossible."

"How do you mean?"

"You can't have some village women with husbands fighting and dying with the partisans while others let their kids make friends with the occupying forces. It was made abundantly clear to us – fraternising with the enemy was unacceptable. Eléni knew this."

"Tell me more about Eléni, please."

"I'll tell you what I know, Mr Fisher. She's quite beautiful by now but seems unaware of it. She's slim, with long, dark, wavy hair and eyes soft, like dark blue pools. And she's pure, quietly devout, like the Virgin Mary." She chuckled. "Not like me at all. The German boys notice her. Some try to speak to her, but she'll have none of it. But then there's this one boy. Very good-looking in the classical German way: tall, blond, blue-eyed, but there seems to be a softness about him, an uncommon warmth and intelligence. And he starts doing things for her, helping her carry water, mending the pail, fixing the gate. That sort of thing. He tells the other lads off for harassing her. He makes little gifts for her which he's fashioned out of odds and ends, and he makes her laugh, even though they don't speak the same language. And laughter, in those times? It's like being thrown a rope when you're drowning, Mr Fisher."

And I know something about that, thought Nick.

"She starts looking out for him and, before too long, I notice they are both absent at the same time, every once in a while. They must be meeting somewhere. One or two of my friends notice, too, but we keep it between ourselves. It's *so* dangerous, you understand."

Nick pursed his lips and nodded.

"It's now the summer of forty-three and I think she's fallen for him. It's getting so obvious – to me, at any rate – and still, it goes on. I wonder if the other soldiers know. Perhaps it's getting back to the officers. And then, one day, her young man vanishes, and we ask the soldiers, but they just shrug until Werner tells us, weeks later. He was transferred to the Italian front."

"Who was Werner?"

"He was a nice guy. A different kind of German. Quieter, more educated. He was friendly to us. He liked Eléni, too, I think."

"How did his news affect Eléni?"

"Well, she's devastated of course, but we all think the stupid girl has the Nazis to thank for her life. They must have been a whisker away from being discovered. Some in the village suspected, I think. When German command got a whiff of it, they shipped him out, just like that. His feet didn't touch the ground."

"Did you ever see him again?"

"No."

"Do you know what happened to him?"

"Went back to his wife and kids, I imagine. After the war."

"He was married?" Nick was genuinely shocked.

"Oh yes. None of us knew at the time, but we found out later."

"How?"

"It must have been from chatting to the German boys. There was a young family in Lübeck, I think it was. A wife and two little girls."

"And Eléni knew this?"

"I think we found out while she was away, but someone would have told her, later."

"When was she away? Where did she go?"

"We started noticing she wasn't around at Christmas. Her lovely voice wasn't there to sing with us that year and we missed her."

"Where had she gone?"

"There were rumours, but I can't say for sure. She was away for about six months."

"What did the rumours say?"

"A breakdown of some sort, then sent to the mainland for treatment. The whole family's a bit fragile upstairs, mind you, what with her sister and then Pandelís later."

"Pandelís?"

"Her sister's boy. He had problems as a teenager after his mum died. I believe he was sent away for a while, too."

"I didn't know that. Go on, Evangelíne."

"I think the rumours about Eléni must have been true because she wasn't the same person when she came back. She was angry, tearful, withdrawn. She wanted to be left alone. Lashed out sometimes. And she seemed older. A lot older. We all seemed to irritate her with our childishness. And she no longer spoke to the Germans, I noticed. Not a word."

"What did you put that down to?"

"That he'd broken her heart and she'd gone crazy with it."

"Did she recover?"

"She never went back to how she was before. And something else happened which didn't help. When the German war ended, some women in the village grabbed her, stripped her almost naked and cut off her beautiful hair. They must have known, or strongly suspected, and now the whole village could see: Eléni the collaborator; Eléni the Nazi whore. It was disgrace for her, but some said she was lucky. Many collaborators were killed, right across Europe. There were lynchings. Vigilantes hung them from lampposts in Paris. But all the poor girl did was fall in love with the wrong man. When her hair grew back, it was coarse and thick, all the soft beauty gone from it, as it had from her.

"The country was in turmoil again as soon as the Germans left. Maybe she needed to do something with her anger, or she had a point to prove. I don't know, but, at the age of seventeen, she joined the Communist forces and left to fight with them. She was stationed in Bulgaria at one point, I believe. She was away three and a half years."

At this point, María popped her head around the door.

"You're not getting too tired are you, Mum? Shall I bring more tea – and perhaps a Ness for you, Mr Fisher?"

The old lady reassured her with a bright smile and neither took up her offer. *She's relishing this*, thought Nick. *A rare chance to talk about her youth to someone who seems genuinely interested, for once.*

"Were you here when she came back?" asked Nick, as soon as María retreated.

"We all were. By then, she was a heroine. They'd lost the war, but she fought bravely and made a name for herself. And some said they only lost because Stalin sold them down the river."

"Yes, your daughter told me."

"We were pawns, sacrificed for the greater cause …"

And for the first time, Nick saw cynicism in her eyes.

"But Eléni was reprieved, then? The collaborator label expunged?" he asked.

"More than that. She was much admired, Mr Fisher. This woman was still only twenty-one, but she'd done what many in the village failed to do: fight for her beliefs, endure hardship, risk her life, and kill many fascists, no doubt. No, they welcomed her back without reservation."

"And how was she, in herself, do you think?"

"Well, I didn't expect her to stay in the village. All that travel and excitement would have made the place too small for her, I thought. But I was quite wrong. It was as if, at that tender age, she'd seen all she ever wanted to see of the world. She went back to living with her parents. The quiet and dutiful daughter. She became withdrawn again. More so. Reclusive. We were never friends, as I told you, but I rarely saw her then. We hardly exchanged a word."

"There must have been other young men. I've seen photographs; she was still a stunningly attractive woman."

"She was, but I don't think there was anyone. Some were frightened off by her fearsome reputation, I suppose – she would have killed many men – others by the shadows in her past. I know there was no-one before I left to marry María's father, in 1958. By all accounts, nothing changed after that. And she hardly ever left Kardánes. All those years, getting a little crazier every year."

"And no children."

"No. And it's unnatural for a Greek woman not to have children, Mr Fisher. That would have been a factor."

Nick's thoughts went to Roúla. She did not have children either, but she seemed sane enough, so far.

"I'm told Eléni has a touch of Alzheimer's, these days."

"Does she? Maybe, maybe not. She's always been certifiable, in my opinion, but her family is very protective."

"How do you mean, Evangelíne?"

"You have a term in Britain, I read somewhere: *Care in the Community*? Our version was more like: *Keep them out of the Asylum*. Our mental health services were appalling then, Mr Fisher. The mentally ill were simply removed from their communities and hidden away. Out of sight, out of mind. Like the poor lepers at Spinalónga. The few facilities were hopelessly overcrowded and the treatments, if any, were horrendous. Any family with a mentally ill member would do their best to play it down, keep the person safe and out of harm's way, so they didn't have to go there."

"Sounds like Bedlam."

"I don't know this word."

"Saint Mary of Bethlehem was a mental hospital in London. The name was corrupted over the years, I guess."

"And it was a terrible place?"

"Feared and derided in equal measure, I think. To be avoided, at all costs. Things are better now, thank God. Here too, I'm sure."

"Yes," she said uncertainly, "but in Greece, things didn't *start* to improve until the late seventies and eighties. We're still in catch-up now, I think."

Nick glanced at his watch. It was almost half past ten.

"Well, Evangelíne. You've been tremendously helpful. Thank you. One last question, if I may. Did you know the name of Eléni's young German?"

"You know, I must have done, Mr Fisher, but I can't remember now. Was it Jürgen or Hans or Fritz? Could be any of those – or something else altogether. Sorry."

"Perhaps you could let me know, if you remember."

"Oh, I'm not going to remember now, not after nearly eighty years. Some days I struggle to remember my own name, Mr Fisher."

"I don't believe that."

There was a brief knock at the door and María appeared again.

"Are you nearly finished, Mr Fisher? Only, I think you're wearing Mum out."

"I'm fine," protested Evangelíne.

"We're done, anyway," said Nick. "It's been a great pleasure, Evangelíne," and he patted her hand again and received a beaming smile, before gingerly tapping the little screen. The icon changed shape, which he took to be good news, and he slipped the phone into his pocket.

"Won't you stay for some coffee?" asked María.

"Thanks, but I need to get going," said Nick.

He grinned and waved as he made his way back to the car, relieved to find it unmarked. He tried to reach Náni but was directed to Déspina instead.

"She's with the Investigating Judge, Nick. Sorry."

"Never mind. Just let her know, will you? I've finished interviewing Evangelíne, but there's something I need to do on the way in. I should be with you by lunchtime."

CHAPTER 21
A SUDDEN HOLIDAY

Nick parked the Suzuki along the main street and walked up to the small hotel.

"Yes, Mr Fisher," said the receptionist, glancing at his card, "they *are* still here." Nick heard sadness but also resignation in her voice. And then she leaned over the counter to speak softly, "Perhaps you could persuade them to go home now? I feel for them – we *all* do – but it's not healthy to stay on like this."

Nick wondered if her concerns were wholly empathetic. More likely, their continuing presence was impacting her other guests. She led him through to where Hedinger sat, gazing vacantly over the pool where two young boys were playing with a multi-coloured ball twice the size of their heads.

"Hello, Herr Hedinger."

The blue eyes came alert, and he made some effort to stand.

"No, please don't get up," said Nick, sitting down and smiling faintly.

"Do you have news, Mr Fisher?"

"We are making progress, sir. The men who disposed of the body are in custody. We don't think they killed Lukas, but we are closing in on the murderer, I believe."

"Have you found the rest of my grandson's body?"

"Not yet, no. The police have divers working on it."

"Can't you make these bastards tell you where they dumped him?"

"We know the general area of the sea-bed, but it's a large area and things move. I'm sure they'll succeed, in time."

"We are still here because we want to take my grandson home."

"I know. It's a difficult time for you."

"Thank you, but it's results we need, Mr Fisher, not platitudes."

"We're doing all we can, I'm sure, but I'll check when I'm back in the office, later today. Now, may I ask you one or two questions?"

The boys were getting rowdy now and some pool water splashed near the old man.

"I think you'd better come inside," he said, and Nick followed him through a glass door and down a carpeted corridor to room number three. It was, in fact, a small suite with a private patio. An elegant, elderly lady looked up from a writing desk as they entered.

"Mr Fisher has come to see us," announced Hedinger, and she extended her hand.

"I thought the police had forgotten all about us," she said.

"You should be getting regular updates," said Nick. "I'll chase things up. Sorry."

"Please, have a seat," she said, indicating a round wooden table by a curtained window. "It's too hot for me outside, I'm afraid. Would you like some coffee or water?"

Nick accepted a glass of sparkling, mineral water and they all sat. Hedinger told Ilse about the fruitless underwater search.

"Who'd have thought, two weeks ago, we'd be having such a ghastly conversation?" She was dabbing at her eyes with a handkerchief and then she looked straight into Nick's. "We are mild people, Heinrich and I, but we are angry, Mr Fisher. We have a cold fury in us now and it may never go away. This is not what we wanted in our hearts, at our age."

She clutched his arm.

"Help us, please. We need to know *who* did this, but even more, we need to know *why*. Without this, we may never rest. Do you understand?"

Nick nodded and placed his hand on hers. She went on:

"Bring us this and we can go home, with what we have of Lukas, and try to live the rest of our lives."

"I understand, Frau Hedinger. This is what I want, too, and I will work very hard to get us there, I promise you."

They both looked at him steadily for a few more moments. Nick saw the desperation in their eyes, felt the weight of their trust settling on his shoulders.

"All right, Nick," said Heinrich. "Thank you. And you will please call us Ilse and Heinrich."

"I will. Now, might I look through your grandson's things?"

"What is it you're looking for? There's not much. The documents, phone and camera are all lost. The police have some bits and pieces of clothing."

"I'm interested in his research. The history. The stuff he worked on before he came here, after he lost his parents."

"What does history have to do with any of this?"

"Maybe nothing. I don't know yet, Heinrich, but my instincts are telling me to find out more."

"It'll all be on his laptop."

"With the police?"

"No, it's here. Someone technical came to look at it, but they didn't take it away. They were looking for communications, I think, but he did all that on his phone. The laptop he used as an archive. How's your German?"

"Not good."

"Then I will help you," said Hedinger. "Bring us the laptop, Ilse."

A few moments later, she placed the laptop on the table. Heinrich signed in and then opened a file. A photograph of a young soldier filled the screen.

"Wow. That's a strong family likeness," said Nick.

"You think so? It's my father, of course."

"And that's his name, Franz Engel? Why did your father have a different surname, Heinrich?"

Nick saw the old man's chest rise and fall, his lips compress into a thin line.

"I was adopted, obviously."

"So, that's how you came to be Swiss, not German."

"I was eighteen when they told me. They said they'd always loved me as a son, but I was not, in fact, their son. My birth father was a German soldier who died in the war."

"And your mother?"

"They didn't know. My birth certificate shows only my adoptive parents. We never found the original, if there was one."

"Must have been a massive shock for you."

"To discover you have no genetic connection to the people you've lived with, loved, admired – all your life? It's a terrible thing, Nick. Suddenly, there are no benchmarks, no measuring sticks, no ways to understand yourself or judge yourself. On good days, I felt like a boat without a rudder; on bad days, like the victim of a fraud. I still loved them, and they me, but something fundamental changed that day. To find out your father was a Nazi who died years ago and that you are his bastard, that you will never know your mother? It's a lot for an eighteen-year-old to face. I was a little crazy for a while."

"I'm not surprised."

"And then, with a little help, you find a compartment in your mind, somewhere to hide it all away, and you try to get on with your life."

"You must have had mixed feelings about this trip, then."

"For myself? A little. But all this research – it was so good for Lukas. Absorbed him. Helped him deal with the death of his parents. When he came up with the idea of the trip, it seemed like the natural, next step. We didn't want to discourage him and for us, it was good, too. We've been in love with Crete for many years and this was our chance to show him this beautiful island, help him discover it, too."

"I can understand that. My son is coming to Crete very soon."

"His first visit?"

"He came here once before but that didn't end well. This time will be different."

*

Déspina had not seen Náni this angry before. She stormed across the office, tore a strip off Chrístos, who seemed to be chatting to Stéfanos instead of working, then disappeared into the Lieutenant's office, slamming the door. Moments later, she was shouting at someone on the phone, then she threw a file against the wall. Déspina knocked softly and entered:

193

"Is everything all right, ma'am?"

"No, of course, it isn't. Next stupid, bloody question?"

"What's happened?"

"*Nothing.* That's the problem. We're starting the third week of this murder investigation and we still don't have a prime suspect."

"Have you been through Chrístos's list, ma'am? Only they'd got it down to about a dozen names, last I heard."

"Was Pandelís Fotákis one of them?"

"I don't know. Shall I get Chrístos?"

"No, I'll check with him in a minute. I might owe him an apology."

"You think the hooded man was this Pandelís, then?"

"If there was a hooded man at all, he was my best bet, yes."

"Why do you say *was*, ma'am?"

"Because I've failed to convince the Investigating Judge of that, and she won't give me the search warrant I need."

"No wonder you're upset. How about some coffee?"

"Thank you, Déspina. And ask Chrístos to step in, would you?"

"I will. Also, Mr Fisher called about half an hour ago. He won't be here till lunchtime."

"Has he interviewed Evangelíne Vókos?"

"Yes, ma'am, and recorded it, he thinks."

"Good. Did he mention hearing from Roúla, Pandelís's sister?"

"No, he didn't."

Chrístos was able to confirm that Pandelís was on his list, which now comprised just eleven names. So were Foteinákis, the tree surgeon, Manólis Vernardákis and Márkos Papatónis.

"All the chainsaw owners," remarked Náni. "Hmmm. If you wanted a body cut up and you owned a chainsaw, wouldn't you just get on with it yourself, rather than risk everything by involving a stranger?"

She did not recognise any of the seven remaining names on the list.

"What about the foreigners, Borkowski and James?"

"Greek not good enough to write those cards, we reckoned," said Chrístos.

"And that old bastard, Antoníou?"

194

"Too short."

"Theodóris or Andréas Katzatákis?"

"Grigóris would have recognised his brothers, even silent and disguised, he said."

"What about the café owner, Alékos?"

"He's too frail, ma'am. This man's movements were more vigorous."

"All right. Have a seat, Christo. Sounds like you've been very thorough. Take me through what we know of the other seven names."

He went through them, one by one, relaying the small amount of information gleaned: approximate age and height, location in the village, family situation.

"You've not questioned any of these, as yet?"

"No, ma'am."

"Have you considered that Grigóris may have invented this hooded man to protect someone? That he knows who asked him to dispose of the body and this is all a charade?"

"Why not just refuse to say who it was?"

"Because that would be obstructing our investigation. With this farce, he appears to be doing his best to assist us in the hope of earning clemency."

"So, you think he knows who it was, ma'am?"

"I don't know. I'm asking the question. Does he have *other* family connections in the village? Have you checked?"

"I'll get on it, Sergeant."

"And I'll get two of the other constables over to Kardánes to check out these guys."

After the constable left, Náni put in another call to Roúla's number. It was her fifth. Once again it ran to voicemail.

*

Nick arrived at one thirty and went straight to Déspina's desk and asked her for the Medical Examiner's contact details.

"Is this something I can help you with, Nick?" she asked, handing him a scrap of paper.

195

"No, that's okay, it's just a quick question. Pánagou? Is that right? I thought she was Chaniá."

"She is, but she's having to cover both prefectures at the moment. Our regular lady is on maternity leave."

Náni had spotted him from her office and now waved him in, moving from behind the desk to join him at the table.

"We have a lot to catch up on," she said. "And I just had a call from forensics. They confirmed it was Lukas's blood at the base of the wall."

"That's good. So, Pandelís has some explaining to do."

"He has."

"I'd like you to listen to this as soon as you can," he said, placing his phone on the table.

"Can't you summarise it for me?"

"I could, but I'd prefer you to listen to it. I want to see if you draw the same inferences. It's less than fifty minutes."

"All right. I'll try, later."

"And I've just come from the Hedingers."

She looked at him angrily.

"You didn't tell me you were going there, Nick."

"I tried to. You were tied up with the judge. I left a message."

"Déspina said there was something you needed to do. You were vague. You didn't mention the Hedingers. I hope you haven't been upsetting them."

It was not the right thing to say, and Nick saw red.

"If anyone's upsetting them, it's *you*, Náni. They're disappointed you haven't kept them updated and they're concerned not enough effort is being put into finding their grandson's body parts. We have the people who did it in custody and a team of divers on hand, allegedly, so they don't understand why you haven't found more of him for them to take home."

"I'm not defending myself to *you*, Nick Fisher. You know we'll probably never find all those packages. What does it matter if the body is forty, sixty or eighty per cent complete? The young man is dead. We don't have the resources. Let them bury what they have."

"It really isn't your call, you know. I told them divers were out there, looking."

"I called them off after twenty-four hours. They found nothing. They're expensive, Nick, and the team leader was far from optimistic."

"Twenty-four hours? We owe the Hedingers more than that. It's not a pointless exercise to them, Náni. Far from it. And what about the tourists, for God's sake? Are you happy to have them swimming in your beautiful waters alongside decomposing body parts? How's it going to look if more bits start surfacing? You *have* to get the team back, Náni. Give it a full week at least. Maybe enlist a local diving club as well. There's one at Skinária. Offer a hundred euros for each package found. God knows the water's clear enough. How difficult can it be?"

"I'll think about it."

"I'm sorry, Náni. Not good enough. If you don't act on this, I'll have to take it to the Lieutenant."

"This is not your show, Nick Fisher, now back off. When I say I'll think about it, I mean just that – and I'll try to do it today. The diving club idea might be a help."

"All right. Let me know what you decide, please. And what about their updates? Why hasn't that been happening?"

"I have nothing to tell them, Nick. What's the point of calling them every day to say we're no further forward?"

Nick closed his eyes for a moment, frowning and shaking his head.

"The point is *doing what you said you'd do*. It's *so* important, Náni. In everything, actually. And it's not true you have nothing to tell them. We've apprehended and charged everyone involved with the disposal of the body and we're whittling down the list of possibles for the killer. It's just a matter of time now. We're going to get them, no question. And these poor people need to hear that."

There was a pause. Náni was looking down, eyes closed, holding her head at the temples.

"I just feel like I'm screwing up, Nick. I want somewhere to go and hide."

"You said 'I' three times there. This is where you're going wrong. It's not about you, Náni. It's about what happened to poor Lukas and finding the bastards who did it for the sake of the Hedingers and the world in general. *That's* what matters. Get angry about *that*. Get committed to putting *that* right. If you succeed, it will be great for your future, but you can't be thinking about your career now. If you do, it gets in the way."

"You make me sound like a self-centred bitch."

"Well, I'm sorry if it sounds like that. It was to be expected. Your boss should have seen it coming. You're a talented and ambitious young woman. You've found yourself in a situation where a missing person case has morphed into a complex, brutal murder. You have few resources and little support. Your abilities are under the spotlight, for better or worse, and you're terrified of messing up. Of course, you are. It's your big chance. It just came along too soon. Now you're concerned for yourself – understandably – but you need to be concerned for *others*. The career will take care of itself."

She looked at him steadily for several seconds, anger, fear and frustration fighting each other, tears not far away. Nick's tone softened.

"All right, Náni. Now tell me what you've been up to and then perhaps we can listen to this recording together," he said, and for once she allowed him to tell her what to do. It would be short-lived; he was sure about that.

It must have been about three pm, as she was talking Nick through Chrístos's list of suspects that Déspina interrupted them.

"Stéfanos is calling from Roussospíti, ma'am."

"Put him through." She turned to Nick: "I asked him to bring Pandelís in."

She switched the phone to loudspeaker.

"I'm outside the Fotákis house, ma'am. It looks like they've gone off somewhere. When I got no reply, I asked around. One of the neighbours saw them packing up the car, early Sunday morning. She said it looked like they were going on holiday. She doesn't know where."

"Was the old lady with them?"

"Just a minute, ma'am."

Náni heard muffled voices, uncertainty.

"She can't say for sure. She didn't see them drive off."

"Done a runner, do you think?" asked Nick after she ended the call.

"We need to check Eléni's house in Kardánes. She's a little old for impromptu holidays. Maybe they dropped her back first. Níkos is in the village. I'll see if I can catch him."

*

While the constable was checking on the old lady, Nick identified the estate agency where Pandelís worked. Their head office was within easy walking distance so, rather than calling, he strolled round to their office.

"Kalimérasas," he said to the receptionist. "I'd like to speak to Pandelís Fotákis."

"I'll just check his line for you, sir."

She listened intently and her face developed an apologetic look before she spoke again:

"I'm sorry, sir. O kýrios Fotákis is on leave for the next two weeks. Was there something else I could help you with?"

"I need to contact him urgently. Do you know where he's gone?"

"I don't, but one of the other partners may know. Have a seat, sir. I'll see who's available."

Nick did as he was told and sat on the end of a row of red-cushioned, tubular steel chairs. He was checking his phone just a couple of minutes later when he became aware of a woman standing over him.

"You are looking for Pandelís?"

Nick stood, grinned and introduced himself.

"He is not here, Mr Fisher."

"I gathered that. Perhaps you could tell me where he's gone?"

"He's on holiday. I'm sorry, I don't know where. Have you tried his mobile?"

"I don't have a number for him."

"All our business cards are on display in reception. You will find it there."

"It seems very sudden, this holiday."

"It's June, it's warm, and things are quiet. He was due a break, so why not?"

"When did he decide to go?"

"I am the managing partner, so he let me know Saturday evening."

"Very short notice for a fortnight's break."

"Pandelís has been with this firm for over twenty years, Mr Fisher, and a partner for twelve. I don't get to tell him how to organise his life."

"Did he give you any explanation?"

"He didn't have to."

"Is there somewhere he often goes – a favourite spot, a second home, perhaps?"

"Not that I know of. Now, if you don't mind …"

Nick thanked her and went back to reception to scribble down the mobile number. When he called, it was no surprise when it went straight to a voicemail message: *I'm sorry, Pandelís is unable to take your call as he will be on annual leave until the seventh of July.*

While he was out of the office, he took the slip of paper from his back pocket and called the number Déspina gave him. She remembered him well. That was good. And yes, she could find half an hour for him tomorrow.

*

When he got back, Náni was ensconced with Níkos and Stéfanos. As soon as she saw him, she waved him in, then raised her eyebrows.

"Waste of bloody time, I'm afraid. He's cleared off for two weeks at very short notice. He can get away with that because he's a partner. They've no idea where. I've got a number for him, but guess what? Voicemail."

"When did he tell them?"

"Later, the day we saw them: Saturday."

"What a coincidence. Stéfanos has found their vehicle details so we're putting out an alert across the island, ferry ports and airports. And Níkos says there's no-one at Eléni's house in Kardánes, so we must assume she is with them."

200

The young men looked up at him, glumly.

"Anything from Roúla?" asked Náni.

Nick shook his head.

"Me neither. She could have been away at the weekend, but I'd have expected to hear from her today. I think the whole family is trying to avoid us, Nick. What next?"

"Well, if you want my guess, I'd say Pandelís is still in Crete. He won't want to subject a ninety-two-year-old to a ferry ride or a flight and there are plenty of remote places to lie low here. If I were him, I'd drive somewhere overnight Saturday or early Sunday morning and then stay put."

"What's he hoping to achieve? Does he think we'll lose interest in him? Isn't he just signalling guilt by doing this?"

"Maybe he needs a little time to get his ducks in a row."

All three of them looked askance.

"To come up with a story, I mean," Nick explained.

"Ah."

"Roúla, on the other hand, would not find it so easy to cut and run. She's an immigration lawyer. In the thick of it. People rely on her day-to-day. She's ignoring our calls, perhaps hoping we'll go away, but she might still be there, at work or home."

"Do we know where?"

"Not yet. All I have is her name and a mobile number. I can make a couple of calls, though. There can't be many people in London called Fotákis."

*

Later that afternoon, Nick made the long trip to Chaniá. Pánagou welcomed him like an old friend. She was smoking again, he saw and spent the first few minutes bitching about the extra workload she'd been obliged to take on – for no more money, of course – then eulogising about her time in London, all those years ago. Finally, she gave him a chance to explain the long shot idea he wanted to explore, but soon interrupted him:

"This cannot be done with any certainty, Nick." And she went through the technical difficulties. "Are there other close relatives you can reach?"

They talked through what was possible. As he was leaving, she pressed three sealed envelopes into his hand.

"There are instructions inside. It's not so difficult."

"I've seen it done, Doctor."

"Okay, good, but you must be precise, or you will be wasting our time. When you get back to me, we'll see what can be done."

*

It was the call he dreaded having to make and he put it off until mid-evening. Early evening in the UK. He let a couple of beers soften him up until he reasoned it wasn't such an awful thing he was about to do. It would be okay. Still, his stomach tightened at the sound of his son's voice:

"Oh, hi Dad. It's great you called. I was going to text you. I've got those things you wanted: the chutney, the ketchup and the oriental sauces? I've got black bean, chilli and ginger and … what was it? Oh yeah, oyster and garlic. Hope I don't have to eat that one."

"Son …"

"I haven't got the chocolate yet, but I can pick some up at the airport. Did you want me to get some Scotch? Is it Talisker you like? I couldn't remember. Anyway, I'm just about to start pack—"

"Son."

"What, Dad?"

"I'm sorry, buddy. I have to come to London. Tomorrow. To interview a witness. I'm going to ask you to put your visit back a week."

"A week. Ah … er … okay … So, you're working again."

Nick heard his son's voice fall at the end of the sentence.

"Just helping out on this one case. I thought we'd get it wrapped up well before you got here, but it got complicated, so we're not quite there yet. It's a bugger, I know, but we'll still have a fortnight together, won't we?"

"Sure."

"If you can change your flight out, I'll cough up for whatever it costs. And buy you a slap-up meal into the bargain. In Réthymno. I know just the place."

"Must be an important case."

"I'll tell you all about it when you get here."

"I could meet you in London. We could travel to Crete together."

"I'll be with a colleague, mate. And I don't want our first proper chat for three and a half years to be fifteen minutes grabbed over a pie and a pint."

"Oh. Right."

"Sorry to spring this on you at the last minute, son."

This time there was no response. Only silence. Nick gripped the phone harder.

"Are you okay?"

"I was looking forward to seeing you, that's all."

"Me too. I feel crap about this, but I will make it up to you, I promise. We're going to have a brilliant time, just the two of us. Lots of stuff planned, don't worry."

"Right."

"You'll let me know on those flights? Only, I have to go now. Speak soon, okay?"

Nick ended the call and poured himself a rakí. He had hurt his son. Again. And he knew it. But his own need was too great. Perhaps Náni should not have asked, but when he went back with the addresses, it was a no-brainer. He should be the one to go. Find Roúla. Like an addict, he could not leave it alone. He had been a fool to take it on, perhaps, but now he must see it through. He did not even protest when she organised flights for him and Déspina. Relieved, if anything. *She* decided. *He* was given no choice. It was not his fault. Not this time.

It would be okay. The boy would come around, and they would still have two lovely weeks together. Plenty of time to put everything back where it belonged.

CHAPTER 22
A DATE TURNS SOUR

On Tuesday morning, Pandelís woke to Eléni's coughing again.

"I'm sorry, but this is driving me crazy," said his wife, who was already sitting up, playing Sudoku on her tablet, Pandelís saw. She tended to retreat into games when unhappy or stressed. It frustrated the hell out of him that she seemed to waste so much time.

"She can't help it," he said. "Anyway, this was all your idea, Giorgía. We should never have brought her here. The dry wind from the south, it gets to her."

He was up now and staring out of the hotel window at the tamarisk trees and the reedy brook beyond the hotel garden, where a woman with two spaniels was crossing the footbridge to the beach and the sea that stretched all the way to Libya. They would never find him there.

"Where was *your* great master plan, then?" she sneered. "We're only here because you didn't know what the hell to do next."

"I've been thinking, though. Why don't we just say he fell?"

"Because, if a young man happens to fall off your garden wall and kill himself, most people don't react by cutting the body into pieces and dumping it in the sea. That's why."

"It wasn't *me* who did that, though, was it? They must know by now."

"You gave him the body. You paid him the money, Pandelí."

"Yes, but I can say it was all a terrible misunderstanding. He wasn't supposed to do *that*. Anyway, this is futile. Mum's suffering, and it's only a matter of time before they find us; the hotel has our passport details. We'll go back home. It'll look much better if I go to them."

"It's not going to work."

"I've thought about it, Giorgía. Even if they don't believe me, they have to *prove* something else happened."

"Why even admit you saw him? You already said you didn't. If you admit you lied, they'll assume you're still lying."

"Because I think they *know* he was there. I heard they used a sniffer dog. There might be forensic evidence that places him there, witnesses even. Why else did they zero in on us, out in Roussospíti? There must be a firm connection to Mum's house."

She put down her tablet now and tucked her hands under the duvet. She stared back at him, lips compressed.

"And then there's Grigóris," he went on. "He could give us up at any time."

"He doesn't know it was you."

"He might have recognised me."

"Even if he did, he wouldn't tell. He's family."

"Your family, not mine."

"He has no reason to."

"Oh, don't be so naïve, woman. They'll be doing their damnedest to get the whole story out of him. Tell us who put you up to this and wipe three years off your sentence. That sort of shit. You *know* how it works. You've seen enough cop shows on television."

"He's a good lad. I don't think he'll fall for those tricks."

"*Good lad?* Your nephew is a nutter – a full-blown psychopath, I shouldn't wonder. I should never have listened to you."

"We're all in this together, remember? And he saved our arses."

"For money. And he'll surrender us just as readily, *for time*. Anyway, I've decided. I *have* to do this. Anything else is only delaying the inevitable and making things worse. So, get yourself out of bed and start packing. I'll tell Mum and explain at reception."

*

They took a taxi from Paddington station, after waiting in a queue for ten minutes. It was raining and Nick had mixed feelings about being back in the country of his birth. After more than two years, the frenetic pace and the stress on people's faces, the traffic, the pollution and the weather were all getting to him. And he was hungry. He was relieved when they were finally in the cab and the guy seemed to know where Furnival Street was.

"I'll 'ave to drop you in Holborn, guv'nor, otherwise I 'ave to go all the way around 'cause it's one-way, see? You'll only have 'alf a minute's walk, all right?"

"It's raining," complained Nick.

"It'll save you a few quid and it's just spitting now, mate."

*

It was a modern, pale orange, brick building in a narrow street of older, more elegant buildings, all of which were four or five stories high.

"Spitting, my arse!" cursed Nick as they arrived breathless in the porch of numbers thirty-six and thirty-seven. "Sixteen quid and a soaking, in both senses of the word. The great London taxi."

Déspina grinned back at him ruefully, stowing the remains of her tiny, red umbrella.

Nick pressed the button for Ogden, Cranfield and the front door buzzed, allowing them to escape the rain and enter the foyer. He checked his watch and found it was twelve thirty-five; two thirty-five Greek time. No wonder he was ravenous.

There was no reception on the ground floor, just a metal display board with business names and floor numbers. They took the lift to the third floor where a sign directed them left, to frosted glass doors embellished with the firm's name.

"And what time was your appointment, sir?" responded the receptionist.

"We don't have one," said Nick, "but I'm sure she'll find time to see us."

"Well, she's with clients at the moment. I'll let her know just as soon as she's free."

"Listen," said Nick. "We've just flown here from Greece to see her on an important, private matter. Perhaps you'd like to give her a note right away? Maybe she'll be able to slip out."

"I can ask her assistant to do that for you. I can't just up and leave reception, sir."

"Just make sure she knows it's me, Nick Fisher."

206

They sat in the little holding area where sober, blue seating for six was arranged in a right-angle around a glass table. Lawyer Monthly and The Law Society Gazette lay on the glass along with a brochure about Ogden, Cranfield. To one side, the pointy, green leaves of a dracaena were looking surprisingly healthy considering the nutrition-free gravel in the elegant pot and the icy wafts from the air-conditioning. Nick picked up the brochure and went straight to the pictures of *the team*.

"This is her, Déspina," he pointed. She was looking a few years younger and very smart. Below the picture, it said Roúla Fotákis, Solicitor Advocate.

Déspina lowered her chin and made big eyes like she was impressed.

"*Ogden, Cranfield*, what a joke," he said. "They just make up these posh-sounding English names. Good for business, I suppose."

"How do you know, Nick?"

"Can you see any Ogdens or Cranfields in the list? Any British names at all, in fact?"

"They're *immigration* lawyers, Nick."

"But they're all foreigners!"

"They are because it's good to have experience of going through the system. To be on the receiving end. Because this is what they do; they fight the system for their clients."

Nick looked at Déspina with fresh respect. And she was right. He read the mini-biographies. It seemed to be all about getting people off. Immigrants accused of serious crimes. Roúla's listed triumphs were all acquittals. Standing up to the British system that was trying to condemn them and winning. The system and the rules Nick used to enforce …

"Mr Fisher?"

He looked up to see a fresh-faced, bespectacled young man. He, at least, looked thoroughly British.

"I'm Lachlan. Assistant to Ms Fotákis. She's with clients now but there's a space between two thirty and four today. Would that suit you?"

"We'll take it, Lachlan, thank you."

"Just come back here at two thirty, then and Lily will buzz me."

"Tell me, is there a decent place for a pub lunch nearby?"

"There's Number Twenty-Six, further up Furnival Street, on the corner with Norwich Street. I like it, it's quite modern, or there's a Fuller's pub around the corner on Holborn. It's got a legal name of sorts …" He looked helplessly at Lily.

"The Inn of Court. Meant to be a pun, I think."

"Any good?"

"It's okay if you like that sort of thing."

*

One look at the menu and Nick understood why most of the country was overweight. He liked the sound of the curry until he discovered it was in a pie. In the end, he settled for the farm burger with chips, shocked to discover it would cost him over seventeen pounds. Déspina opted for the healthy choice, the chargrilled vegetable and pine nut salad, hoping to ruin it with a sticky toffee pudding if she got the chance. As soon as their drinks arrived, Nick took a generous swig of his London Pride.

"I hope she's going to be there, Nick."

"You think she might do a runner?"

"Her brother did."

"True, but I reckon she loves her job too much to run out on it, destroy her reputation. Anyway, we have her home address. We'll go straight there if she lets us down."

*

With Nick in London. Náni was able to forget about Roúla and focus on finding Pandelís. She did not know if either was guilty of anything, but she was desperate to interview them both. People do not run from the police or dodge calls for no reason. No trace of Pandelís showed up at the exit points so, unless he split from the others and was travelling on a false passport, he must still be on the island, she reckoned. But where? Would they head somewhere remote or lose themselves in one of the cities? And did they really have a ninety-two-year-old lady with them? She would restrict them. She stared at the map, hoping for inspiration, but it did not come. They could be anywhere. Eventually, she called the Lieutenant.

"Good morning, sir. I want to give Pandelís to the media, put together a press release with a photograph saying we need to speak to this man urgently in connection with the murder of Lukas Hedinger. I think we need the public's help if we are to find him quickly."

"Okay, Náni, but the last time you spoke with the Investigating Judge, she wouldn't grant you a search warrant for the man's house. She might not be too impressed if you suggest hounding him in the media instead."

"With respect, sir, I'm not hounding him. He's run out on us and I need to talk to him. I've left messages on his mobile and at his place of work, alerted the police in the other prefectures and on the mainland, ferries, airports and so on. I think he's hiding from us, hoping this will somehow blow over."

"Still, the press? You need to tread carefully, Náni. Tell you what. Get something drawn up and then *we'll* take it to the judge. Try to get her on-side. Maybe we can revisit the search warrant while we're at it."

*

Roúla looked at her watch again, more pointedly this time, but he pretended not to notice. The executive buffet was well-depleted, but he was still toying with a chocolate éclair and asking for a top-up of coffee. Even his aides were beginning to look uncomfortable. The man was one of her top clients and he fancied her; no doubt about it. Nothing was said directly. That was not the way these lascivious Englishmen operated. But she felt his eyes on her, listened to his treacly descriptions of her *incisive intellect*, her *extraordinary clarity of thought*, her *insightfulness*. He would be rich as Croesus, but well into his sixties and with a paunch like a bloated goat's udder. When her assistant came in with a second, blue Post-It note, it gave her all the excuse she needed.

"I'm so sorry, Crispin, but I'll have to excuse myself. My two o'clock is here. I'll draft up those revisions in the morning and get back to you. No, please don't rush. My assistant, Julia here, will stay with you

209

and see you out when you're ready. And she's *much* more interesting than me. When she's not skiing or scuba diving, she writes vegan cookbooks. I'm sure you'll have lots to talk about."

And, with that, she gave them the mischievous, winning smile, picked up her files and fled. She looked again at the little blue note. It made no mention of any two o'clock meeting. It said simply: *Thought you might need to escape about now.* Good old Julia.

Fifteen minutes later, Lachlan put his head around the office door: "Mr Fisher's back, Roúla. Shall I go and get them?"

"Them?"

"Sorry, didn't I say? He's with a young woman, foreign-looking."

"And did he say what this is all about?"

"Just that it was a personal matter. Perhaps it's a massive legacy from some long-lost great-aunt."

That sort of thing might happen in privileged families like yours, she thought. *Not mine.* His flippancy might earn him a rebuke later, but for now, she was more concerned with the fluttering of her heart and the pit of dread forming in her stomach.

"Better get them up here right away, then," she managed to say, with enough brightness for him to think she appreciated his little joke.

She heard the ping as the lift doors opened, then the suction as they came through the outer glass doors to the offices. And there was Lachlan again, manners perfect now, as he ushered the guests into the meeting room, took orders for tea or coffee and then withdrew. She took out her compact and checked her face. Her heart was beating at twice its normal speed. Would they see? Anyway, maybe it was not what it seemed. Maybe it *was* a legacy. Who knows? Then, she checked her eyes to see if they looked honest and open. *Perhaps inscrutable would be the better word*, she thought.

*

"Nick Fisher, what a nice surprise!" she said as she swirled into the room. "And who might this be?"

"I am Déspina Karagiánnis."

210

Roúla looked askance at Nick.

"I wish this were a social call, Roúla, but sadly it's not. It's a police matter. I've been working with the Greek police and Déspina is part of the team at Réthymno. We've come here to discuss the murder of Lukas Hedinger."

Roúla looked hurt, fleetingly, Nick thought, but her recovery was almost instantaneous.

"I didn't know you were a policeman."

"It was a while ago, here in London."

"I see. And Lukas Hedinger was the young Swiss man who went missing in Kardánes."

Nick and Déspina nodded.

"I'm not sure how—"

"We need to record this interview if that's okay?"

Roúla shrugged and Déspina removed the recording device from her bag and went through the preliminaries. Then she nodded to Nick.

"I believe you were staying at your *mother*'s house on Sunday evening, the eighth of June?"

"Yes, I'd been there a few days and I stayed until the following Thursday, the day you and I bumped into each other."

It was Nick's turn to be hurt. Her words made their meeting sound so inconsequential. Which, of course, it was. He needed to pull himself together.

"But Eléni's *not* your mother, is she?"

"No, not really. She's my mother's sister but we started calling her Mum after mother died. It's what she wanted, I think, and it just stuck, after a while."

"That's a little odd, wouldn't you say?"

"Odd things happen in families, Mr Fisher. It works for us. She lived with us right from when we were little. Suddenly, mother was not there anymore. But she was. It just happened."

"And this new *mother* of yours, what did you know about her?"

"What do you mean? I'd known her all my life."

"What did you know of her life, before you were born?"

"She rarely talked about it, but I heard she fought in the civil war when she was still very young. Something of a heroine."

"Did you look up to her, would you say, you and your brother?"

"What has this to do with your case, Mr Fisher?"

"I'm just trying to understand the relationship between you and your aunt, Roúla."

"I can see that. I just don't understand why. We love her, we respect her. She's an admirable woman."

"Even these days?"

"What the hell is that supposed to mean?"

"When I met her, she seemed a little barmy, to be frank."

Roúla's dark eyes were flashing, just as Nick intended.

"How dare you? She's ninety-two years old. She's entitled to be a little eccentric."

"I heard she has dementia."

"I don't know who put that idea in your head. She's as sane as you and me."

Any hopes of a relationship with this woman were being consumed by this anger, Nick saw. He was the enemy, but hopefully just for now.

"Going back to that Sunday evening, were you alone with Eléni all evening?"

"No. My brother came over later."

"Why was that?"

"To pick her up."

"What time?" asked Déspina.

"It would have been nine thirty or so, but he stayed a while. They would have driven back around eleven, in the end."

"Why did he stay so long?"

"It was a chance to catch up."

"What did you talk about?"

"This and that. Family stuff."

"And you were in Kardánes to see Eléni, as you are every few weeks."

"I come when I can."

"I'm struggling with a couple of things, Roúla. Why didn't you drop Eléni over to Roussospíti yourself? You were renting a car, weren't you?"

"No reason. Pandelís offered and, to be honest, if I can avoid driving in Crete at night, I will. Also, it's good to get time alone with him."

"Without Giorgía, you mean."

"Yes. Don't misunderstand me, she's a nice enough woman if a bit neurotic for my taste. It's just good to have my brother to myself, occasionally."

"The other thing that baffles me is why you would travel almost three thousand kilometres to see Eléni and then let the man who lives just thirty-five kilometres away steal her away from you with four days of your trip left. Four days you spent alone in Kardánes; I assume."

"He didn't *steal her away* at all. We spent a good stretch of time together but it's tiring for her and anyway, I needed to work. There are cases I'm involved with, people I'm trying to help. We all thought it was the best solution."

"And, going back to that Sunday evening, did you see or hear anything of Lukas Hedinger?"

Nick was staring at her now, watching her every move. She returned his stare, unblinking. The solicitor advocate at work.

"Not a thing, no."

The lightness of the chosen phrase plus the double negative were a giveaway, Nick felt sure. Coolly, and with great composure, she was lying to him.

"I find that surprising," he said, turning to Déspina and raising his eyebrows. She picked up the reins:

"We have evidence that Lukas came to your mother's house at around eight forty-five and made his way to the top of her garden wall to photograph the sunset. At its highest point, the wall is five metres. This also happens to be the best vantage point for such a photograph. We found blood near the base of the wall matching Lukas's DNA profile."

"So, the poor man fell off. I've heard that can happen, taking photographs. I remember someone telling me about this American investment banker—"

"All right. Let's assume he fell," interrupted Nick. "It was a hot evening. Your windows would be open, maybe the door, too. You were no more than twenty-five metres from where this happened and yet you heard nothing."

"I can't speak for my mother, but I heard nothing."

"I don't know about you, Roúla, but if I were falling off a high wall, perhaps to my death, I would make a noise. I'd yell. I might even scream, and then my body would make a noise as it hit the ground, my head as it hit the rock, my camera as it shattered. Violent death is a noisy business in my experience. And yet you heard nothing whatever. Just the silent night, maybe the cicadas, a very light breeze rustling the leaves …"

"We were talking, remember."

"Of course, you were."

Nick let his words float on the ether to give her a few moments to reflect on the ridiculous nature of her remark. Then he went on:

"So, let's go with your theory, shall we? The unfortunate Mr Hedinger falls silently to his death at around nine pm. Pandelís was not there at this point, so it was just you and Eléni talking. His death was presumably instantaneous as well as silent, or you would have heard him suffering. You then continue chatting away happily. Pandelís arrives after half an hour and the three of you chat for a further hour and a half. Am I right?"

"Eléni went to rest and pack at about ten, I think, but otherwise, yes, that's it."

"Did it get cold, as the evening wore on?"

She looked at him, not understanding, "No, it was a warm night, very still."

"So, the windows and door remained open."

"Yes."

"And did you hear anything else between nine and eleven? People moving around, vehicles?"

"Nothing I recall."

"Which is more surprising still, Roúla. So, your theory has the silent man's body just lying there dead, at the bottom of the wall, throughout two hours of family chit-chat."

"I suppose he must have been. Ghastly thought."

"Do you have the witness statement to hand by any chance, Déspina?"

She did, as he knew, and he nodded at her to read from it.

"After I walked up from the cemetery, I met the hooded man again at the sheep barn and I saw what looked like a body, wrapped in black plastic and leaning against the side of the barn. It would have been about twenty past ten."

"This is from the sworn statement of a man who helped dispose of Lukas's body," said Nick. "So now we have a body in two places – or two bodies. How do you explain that?"

"Well, I can't obviously. He must be lying about the timing or they must have been extremely quiet removing the man's body."

"Why do you say *they*?"

"I'd have thought it would take two, especially if it needed to be done quietly."

Nick looked at her for a long moment before continuing.

"So, to summarise, a fit young man falls from your wall for no apparent reason. He falls in silence and lands in silence, though the fall is severe enough to kill him outright. Then his body and all but one of the pieces of his shattered camera are removed by one or more persons unknown while you and your brother are chatting less than twenty-five metres away with windows and door open on what you described as a still night."

Nick threw a sceptical look at Déspina, who looked like there was a very bad taste in her mouth. He went on:

"Perhaps we could trouble young Lachlan for those refreshments? And then you might like to clear your remaining appointments for the day and try again, Roúla. Your story is a total fabrication and you know it."

Roúla gave him a look that said: *How dare you, you arrogant prick?* She seemed about to say something but then turned and flounced out of the meeting room.

"I didn't know the camera shattered," said Déspina. "Did we find some plastic shards or something?"

"Just a touch of artistic licence," said Nick with a smirk. "The camera is in its case at the bottom of the sea."

They found the toilets next to the lift, thanks to Lachlan, who was embarrassed at his failure to bring the promised tea and assured them this would be rectified forthwith. On the way back, Nick saw Roúla standing at her office window, facing away from him. She was holding a phone, her other hand gripping the desk. Even from six metres, he could see the bloodless white around her knuckles.

"We're a bit *off-piste* here," said Lachlan, finding Nick staring out of the window. He laid down the tray and came over. Nick bit his lip as he slipped the phone back into his pocket.

"We're not quite in Gray's Inn and we're not quite in Lincoln's Inn but handy for both and prices aren't quite so insane here," he said with a conspiratorial grin.

Nick was looking across the road at a substantial five-storey building in pale yellow brick with stone-framed windows and a pillared portico.

"It's a fine-looking building."

"Isn't it?"

"Must be magnificent inside," said Déspina.

"Er ... no. Not really. It's just serviced offices now. Very smart and modern, mind you. The building was gutted a while ago, but they kept the façade. Rents for squillions, no doubt. That's modern London for you."

Faintly disillusioned, they turned back to the table where Lachlan set out cups and saucers and a plate of expensive-looking biscuits, some wrapped in gold or silver foil.

"I've brought milk," he said, "but would you prefer lemon?"

Déspina smiled and shook her head.

"Milk's fine," said Nick, and Lachlan manoeuvred his way past them, almost colliding with Roúla on his way out. She closed the door from the outside and spoke with Lachlan for a couple of minutes before entering.

"Can I pour you some tea?" asked Nick.

"I won't, thank you," said Roúla.

The teaspoon clinked repeatedly as Nick stirred his tea. Seconds passed. He seemed to be enjoying the ritual. Déspina was about to speak when Nick's knee nudged her thigh. Finally, he laid down the spoon and unwrapped a chocolate biscuit.

"Well?" said Roúla.

"I'm sorry. We were waiting for you, Roúla."

"To do what, exactly?"

"To tell us the truth."

She blinked several times, then picked up a pencil and started drawing geometric shapes on a yellow, legal notepad. Finally, she looked up.

"I just spoke with my brother, Pandelís. He's checked in after a few days' break and discovered the police want to speak to him again. So, he's arranging to see Sergeant Samarákis in the morning."

"Good."

"I'd like to make a formal statement now, Mr Fisher. Would that be in order?"

"Sure. We can do that."

He nodded to Déspina and she took the recording device from her briefcase and laid it on the table, just as Nick's phone beeped. He cursed quietly and excused himself, left the meeting room and called the number back. He returned in less than two minutes.

"Sorry about that. Please go ahead, Roúla."

"I'm afraid I may have put a slant on things which is not wholly accurate," she said carefully.

"Putting a slant. Is that the same thing as telling a lie?"

"Perhaps I could just make the statement?"

Nick shrugged, then nodded at Déspina who activated the recording and went through the preamble before inviting Roúla to begin.

"Mum and I – I'm sorry, Aunt Eléni and I – were enjoying a glass of wine at her house in Kardánes and talking quietly. It was beginning to get dark, just before nine pm, I think, when we heard a noise. There was a scuffing sound and then someone cried out. We looked at each other and knew we must do something but, as you know, Mum's quite frai—"

"Shall we just call her Eléni?" said Nick.

"Sorry, Eléni is frail. So, I told her to stay there while I checked. The sound seemed to come from the garden wall, but I couldn't see anything. I was relieved, for a moment, but then I went through the gate and saw. A young man was lying at the base of the wall and I knew he must be dead right away. He wasn't moving, didn't seem to be breathing. His neck was at a very strange angle and it's rocky there. He must have hit his head, and the wall is high, at this point."

"Did you check his pulse, try first aid of any sort?"

"I didn't want to touch him. But I was sure it was pointless, anyway."

"Did you go for help, Roúla?"

"I was in a panic. And I couldn't think of anyone who *could* help. There's no doctor in the village, anyway."

"You could have called someone," said Nick.

"So, what *did* you do next?" asked Déspina.

"I told Eléni and right away she said, 'Call Pandelís. He'll know what to do'. She has more faith in him than me. It's like she sees him as the grown-up and me as the child. I don't know why. Perhaps it's a gender thing or because he has a family. Anyway, I was in no fit state to argue, so I made the call. He came right away and was with us inside half an hour."

"And no-one came down the alley, in the meantime?"

"I doubt it very much. It's not lit, and no-one ever comes down it at night. Hardly anyone outside the family ever uses it. I checked on the body a couple of times but there were no signs of life."

"You didn't try to move it?"

"Pandelís said not to touch anything till he got there."

"Why didn't you call the police instead of Pandelís?" asked Déspina.

"I honestly don't know. I was confused. The young man was clearly dead, anyway. We could call the police later. It would make no difference to anything."

"And then Pandelís arrived?"

"Yes, and right away he said: 'It's okay, I have a plan'. I remember Eléni looked at me knowingly, like her faith in him was fully justified, and I felt sick. Then he looked at the body and said: 'We have to get him moved, away from us, away from our land'. 'Why not just call the police?' I said. 'Are you mad?' he said. 'Just *think*, for a minute. This boy is obviously not Greek. So, a foreigner dies in suspicious circumstances on our land. There'll be police, forensics, the world's press, news cameras crawling all over the place for weeks. A nightmare. And, if there's anything wrong with the wall, we'll be liable, and you know it's falling down at the other end. We could find ourselves being sued by a big insurance company. It could wipe us out. And they'll be lifting stones, digging into our private lives. I don't know about you, but I don't want to see Mum put through all that. It could kill her. And what about you – your job, Roúla? This could get in the way, hold you back for months, even leave a stain on your character. Which you can't afford. It's not *our* fault he chose to trespass here and got himself killed. Why should *we* have to go through all that, *risk* all that? The boy's dead. He doesn't care. And I have a number. Someone who will come and take the body away.'

"'Who?' I asked. 'You don't need to know,' he said. 'It's someone nearby. Someone we can trust.' 'It needs to be,' I said, 'because we're laying ourselves wide open here'. Well, I don't think he'd thought of that angle, but he said: 'Whatever you're afraid of, it's not going to happen, Roúla; it's *family*'. 'How much will it cost?' I asked. 'Five thousand, I reckon. Half each?' 'Five thousand euros, to move a body a few hundred metres?' I said, 'and that's the *family* rate?' 'It might be a bit more involved than that and it's not *our* family, Roúla,' he said."

"What did you understand him to mean by that?" asked Déspina.

"That it was *her* family. Giorgía's. She's from the village too, originally. Pandelís married his childhood sweetheart. And her brother – he's dead now – married Aléxia."

"Aléxia?"

"Katzatákis."

Nick raised a hand to his forehead.

"Hold on, let me get this clear. Giorgía is your brother Pandelís's wife. *Her* brother is – or rather *was* – the missing father in the Katzatákis clan, so he would have been the father of Andréas, Theo and Grigóris …"

"Meaning those guys are Giorgía's nephews," finished Déspina.

"Jesus, these bloody families!" said Nick.

"Makes sense, though," said Déspina. "She put forward someone to sort out the problem. Someone she knew very well and thought she could trust *because* he was family."

"Trust, at a price. All right, we'll go with it. Please go on, Roúla."

"I'm not a dishonest person, Mr Fisher, so I wasn't comfortable with this. Nor am I a wealthy one. My particular branch of the law is not highly paid and my living expenses here are high, so two thousand, five hundred euros is a significant amount of money to me – and I was afraid the final bill would be more, knowing Pandelís. But he made a good argument. What would it matter to the dead man – or indeed anyone else – if the body were found in a different place? And we'd be off the hook then. So, I agreed."

"Off the hook," said Nick. "An interesting choice of phrase."

"I meant, we'd be able to avoid involvement, attention, litigation. All those points Pandelís made so forcefully."

"So, what happened next?"

"He just took charge. Everything happened very quickly. He texted this person, then disappeared for a while. Perhaps fifteen minutes later, he went off to meet him. At least, I assume it was a him. After a while, he was back, alone. He made sure Eléni was shut inside, then asked for my help. He reversed the car down the alley. We wrapped the body in black plastic bin bags and put it in the back of the car along with his stuff – there was a man bag and a camera bag and the camera itself. It wasn't shattered, Mr Fisher. You have that wrong, though I suppose it might have been chipped, I didn't notice. Then we drove up to the top road and carried the body and the two bags over to a concrete building with a corrugated iron door. After that, he drove us back around the corner and told me to wait."

"What was he doing?"

"I imagine he was going back to strike a deal with this person."

"What was he wearing?"

"I have no idea. Usual stuff – jeans and a top of some sort, I should think."

"Nothing different."

"Not that I recall."

"Was he carrying anything?"

"I do remember a shoulder bag."

"What size bag?"

She made a frame with her hands.

"About so, maybe forty or fifty centimetres by thirty or forty. Like a satchel."

"Had you seen the bag before?"

"I don't think so, apart from earlier. He had it when he went to meet this person."

"Did you see what was inside at any point or did he tell you what was inside?"

"No. I assumed it was the money."

"He didn't ask you for money?"

"We'd agreed to share the cost, but he came up with the cash. When he confirmed that it cost him five thousand, I transferred half to his account."

"His normal bank account?"

"I assumed so. He just gave me the codes."

"Did it surprise you that he could come up with that sort of money, in cash, at the drop of a hat?"

"Not really. He often uses cash in his business."

"As an estate agent?"

"Yes. When he's negotiating to buy plots of land. It oils the wheels, he says."

"And reduces the tax due?"

"I didn't say that."

"So, how long before he returned to the car?"

"Less than fifteen minutes, I think."

"And then what?"

"That was it. We drove home, he checked the garden and the lane with a torch in case we'd missed anything, then hosed down where the body had been. Then we shared a rakí before he took Eléni back to Roussospíti."

"Was Eléni aware of what was going on?"

"Absolutely not. I said a young man was hurt, but he'd be okay. We'd taken him to the clinic at Spíli."

"And then you enjoyed a celebratory drink and went to bed, knowing your little problem was solved," said Nick, with a sneer.

"The drink was to settle our nerves, Mr Fisher. It was a very stressful experience."

"What did you imagine was going to happen to the body?"

"I left it to Pandelís. I assumed it would be moved again, but not too far. Somewhere not connected with us where it could soon be found."

"Do you know what actually happened?"

"Pandelís told me it was found at sea. That's all I know."

"There's rather more to it than that, I'm afraid. Lukas's body was cut into ten pieces with a chainsaw, then placed in rubble sacks inside six black, plastic bags, each of which was dumped in a different location in the sea, off Triópetra. One of the bags was ripped, enabling the headless, limbless torso to escape and be found by a young couple snorkelling on the first day of their holiday; a ghastly image that will haunt them forever. His family cannot begin to understand who could do this to their gentle, sweet-natured boy, or why. This torments them every living minute and will forever blight their lives. You can add that to your two thousand, five hundred euros, Roúla. That was the true price of avoiding inconvenience."

Her mouth was slightly open, her eyes wide, a great weight slowly settling on her shoulders. Then she closed her eyes as if trying to shut out the picture of the mutilated body.

"I didn't know. I had no idea that would happen, I swear. I am so, so sorry."

Nick signalled to Déspina and she ended the recording:
He stood and went to the window.

"You're a lawyer, Roúla. You know you can't just lie to the police if it's convenient to do so. There are consequences, be it for wasting police time or perverting the course of justice. I'm not sure what Greek law says on this, but, in the UK, you can be sent to prison for up to six months. I wouldn't be surprised if Greek penalties are worse."

He moved across the room and leaned over her, hands on the table.

"Wouldn't look so good on the CV, would it? And six months or more in a Greek jail would *not* be a pleasant experience for a sensitive, educated woman such as yourself, Roúla. They're not your kind of people in there.

"We're going to leave you to reflect overnight. I'm not convinced you've told us the whole truth, so be in no doubt. If that proves to be the case, the police will use the harshest penalties available to them.

"You might be thinking of calling your brother this evening. Don't bother. He'll have been taken into custody by now. It'll be interesting to see how his version of the story compares to yours. We might need to compare notes in the morning. Nine o'clock sharp. I suggest you clear your diary for a further half-day, at least."

He placed his card on the table.

"In the meantime, if your memory comes flooding back, feel free to call me.

"Great biscuits, by the way," he added, grabbing another of the foil-coated ones as they gathered the recording device with their papers and left.

*

When they hit the street, Nick suggested they have a quick drink and sort out a hotel for the night. They found a more modern bar where Nick bought a vodka Martini for Déspina and an American IPA for himself.

"Tell me, Nick," said Déspina, once they were seated, "do you think she was lying back there? She seemed genuine to me."

"She's a skilled solicitor advocate, Déspina. She always seems genuine."

"But why would she lie now?"

"I haven't made it past nine pm that night, to be honest. How can a fit, young man just fall off a wall and be so unlucky as to kill himself outright?"

"He was tipsy. We know this from the Polish couple. And he was taking a photograph. It happens, sometimes. And it's a five-metre drop to a rocky path …"

"I know it's *possible*, Déspina. It's just not terribly *likely*, is it?"

"But neither of them has a motive for murdering a stranger."

"No, they don't, on the face of it. But why the extreme methods to dispose of the body? Why not drive it a couple of hundred metres, leave it by the side of the top road somewhere? She claims they just wanted to get the thing off their land, away from any responsibility for it. If that were true, nothing more was needed."

"A misunderstanding between Pandelís and Grigóris?"

"Misunderstanding? I don't think so. If Grigóris was telling the truth about what was written on those cards. Remember? *It must never be identified. It must never be found!* Doing what Grigóris did was a logical response to such demands."

"*If* the cards weren't a figment of Grigóris's imagination, and *if* those were the words written on the cards."

"And those," said Nick, raising his glass to her, "are the key questions, Constable. Because, if they were, we have to ask ourselves why Pandelís felt it necessary to go to those lengths for a bloke that just fell off a wall in his aunt's garden. Now let's get some rooms sorted and then I can get showered and shaved and buy you dinner."

CHAPTER 23
A REWARDING SEARCH

It was almost six pm and the meeting with the Investigating Judge was entering its third hour, but Náni felt they were getting somewhere, at last. Then her phone beeped. It was a text from Nick marked urgent. She apologised and left the Lieutenant to press their arguments further. Within five minutes, she was back.

"That was Nick Fisher. He wants us to bring Fotákis in for questioning as soon as possible."

"We would if we knew where he was," said Stávros.

"He's back home, apparently."

"Good, so we can forget about the media. Do you still want that search warrant, Lieutenant?"

"It would be helpful, judge, if we could search while he's being questioned."

"I'll give you one, against my better judgment. But you will proceed with care, Lieutenant. Fotákis has been a respected businessman in Réthymno for many years. By all accounts, a stable family man. You will *ask* him to accompany you to the police station, you will *ask* his permission to search. No arrests. And you will show this document only if he refuses. Understood?"

"Yes, ma'am. Thank you."

"And thank you both for taking the time to keep me informed. I appreciate it."

Outside, Stávros put a hand on Náni's arm.

"Look, Náni, I couldn't afford to spend over two hours in there. You don't need me for this, do you? Just grab a couple of burly constables and get on over there."

He handed her the search warrant.

"Keep it in your back pocket or handbag or whatever. I doubt you'll need it."

And with that, he was gone. He drove home ten minutes afterwards, she heard later. By then she was already in the car with Chrístos and Stéfanos, taking the winding road up and out of Réthymno, heading for Roussospíti.

*

They managed to find a relatively inexpensive, ultra-modern hotel on Fleet Street. The restaurant was a short walk, back up Chancery Lane. The place was light and airy with high ceilings and giant rubber plants. It was about half full when they arrived, garlic wafting pleasantly around the place despite a massive, stainless-steel, extractor hood in the open kitchen at the back, where chefs formed part of the entertainment, cheers going up for every flambé. They took a table at the end of a row of striped, banquette seating.

"I hope this is okay for you," said Nick. "The cooking's from the south of France."

Nick went for the comté cheese ravioli followed by roasted cod, Déspina the cauliflower velouté and the grilled duck magret. They drank viognier and pinot noir. They swapped tales of youthful ambition and gritty experience, compared Réthymno and London, talked about Náni and Stávros, even touched on each other's private lives a little. The coffee arrived just as Nick's phone started ringing.

"Damn. Should have turned the bloody thing off. Excuse me," he said, waving an arm in apology to Déspina and other nearby diners and heading out to the darkening street where a light summer rain was falling.

"Nick, it's Náni. We have Pandelís in custody. Picked him up just before seven, Greek time. Was that quick enough for you?"

"That's good. We were still with Roúla then. Have you started questioning him?"

"He's just following the same line as Roúla. A terrible accident, then they panicked. Horrified at what crazy Grigóris did."

"Predictable."

"Yes, but there's something he doesn't know yet, and neither do you."

226

"Go on."

"We asked his permission to search the house and he readily agreed. Said there was nothing to hide. Well, we didn't find any prompt cards or sacking hoods. Everything was squeaky clean, just like he said. We were coming to the end of the search when Stéfanos found it."

"Found what?"

"He was going through the clothes in Pandelís's wardrobe. He'd already done it once, but, like a good copper, he did it again. And this time he found it. It was nestling in the back pocket of a pair of jeans, right in the corner. He'd shaken them before, but this time it fell out."

"Found *what*, for Christ's sake, Náni?"

"A SIM card."

"Bingo! Well done, Stéfi! That'll be the one he took from Grigóris's phone, right?"

"We'll check with the phone company. Perhaps we can recover their text messages, too."

"If he has a proper account, that should be possible, but it's less important than finding that link to Grigóris. So, Pandelís was our hooded man."

"If there *was* a hooded man, it was Pandelís," she corrected. "Whatever, if this checks out, Pandelís has to be the guy who instructed Grigóri."

"Hmmm. Tricky. We need to know what he said – or wrote – to demolish this story of theirs. Or it's just his word against Grigóris's. The word of a fine, upstanding citizen against a gipsy ruffian with a violent record."

"Why do we care, Nick? Surely, we have him now, either way."

"We have him for paying Grigóri to lose a body that could possibly have died in an accident. But I'd much rather have him for murder and giving explicit instructions that the body should be *never identified* and *never found*. Wouldn't you, Náni?"

"I would. All right, I'll see what I can do, but I wish you were here for this, Nick. One other thing. The ME asked forensics to share the DNA samples from Roussospíti. They checked with me first."

"What did you say?"

"I saw no reason not to, in confidence, but was that you? Are you up to something?"

"Just a long shot. You'll be the first to know if it leads to anything, I promise."

"I'd better be, Nick. And stay close to your phone for the rest of the evening, please. I may need to touch base with you."

"I will. Good luck."

Back at the table, they ordered another coffee and Nick brought Déspina up to speed.

"So," she said, "now we know Pandelís instructed Grigóri, but we don't know *what* his instructions were."

"Well, Grigóris's version was quite explicit and justified his subsequent actions. Think about the alternative, for a moment. If Pandelís asked him simply to lose a body so it wasn't found on their property or connected to them, why wouldn't Grigóris just drive it a short way and dump it? Job done. It would be a psychotic reaction to chop it into bits and dump it in the sea, don't you think? And it's work. A lot of very unpleasant work. Work you don't need to do. And risk, involving the cousins and the boat. Risk you don't need to take, not to mention giving away fifteen hundred euros of the money."

Déspina was stirring her coffee, nodding slowly. He went on:

"And, talking of money, five grand is a huge amount to pay someone in Grigóris's position just to drive a body down the road and dump it, don't you think? I reckon he'd do it for five hundred, maybe less."

"Pandelís is not short of money, Nick."

"No, but people like him don't get where they are by splashing money around needlessly. I suppose you could argue that he needed to buy the guy's silence, to some extent."

"Does he need to? Grigóris is his wife's nephew, remember."

"I do remember, Déspina, but *Grigóris doesn't know it's Pandelís*, does he? In this scenario, Grigóris doesn't know who the hell he's dealing with. I think he *still* doesn't know – other than it might be one of the eleven names on that list of his."

"Unless Giorgía told him."

"I don't think she would make contact. She just gave Pandelís his number."

"Hang on. Didn't Pandelís tell Roúla it was okay, nothing bad would happen *because it was family*? That wouldn't work unless both parties knew who was involved."

"An excellent point, Déspina. But I think they were talking about the risk of being blackmailed, after the event. The family relationship could be revealed *then* to stamp on it. But, in the absence of that, they were desperate to be invisible, unconnected. To stop anything unpleasant getting back to spoil their lives."

"So, you're starting to believe all this stuff about sackcloth hoods and prompt cards?"

"I am. I know it sounds far-fetched, but there's been a murder. You're desperate not to be identified by a fellow villager, who also happens to be related to your wife. And you've only a few minutes to think of something, so why not?"

"So, you think Pandelís killed Lukas."

"It's very possible, but all I feel sure about right now is that *someone* killed Lukas and Pandelís took it on himself to cover it up."

"So, it could have been Roúla, even."

"This is possible, too."

"I still can't see how either of them would have a motive."

"People can do anything, Déspina, if they feel it's the only option. Now have a little more coffee and let me run something by you …"

CHAPTER 24
THE INNERMOST DOLL

It was eleven pm before they finished questioning Pandelís. He stuck to his guns in the most irritating fashion. There was a terrible accident, his sister called him, he drove over. They made the ill-judged decision to get the man's body removed from their property and then Grigóris must have completely misunderstood what was asked of him. And no, of course, he had not dressed up in a sack and mimed with cards.

When Náni pointed out that a transfer of two thousand, five hundred euros was credited to his wife's bank account on Wednesday, the eleventh of June, he denied any knowledge of it. When she claimed he destroyed Grigóris's phone, he denied it. When she suggested that he murdered Lukas and gave explicit instructions to Grigóri on what to do with the body, his lawyer intervened and called her bluff, demanding she charge her client or let him go.

"I'm not yet required to do either, as you know," she responded. "O kýrios Fotákis will remain in custody for now, pending further enquiries. We will resume in the morning."

She kept the finding of the SIM card to herself until ownership was confirmed. Before leaving, she gave Nick another call. By then, he was back at the hotel with Déspina. They swapped notes and agreed their respective strategies for the morning, promising to remain in close touch.

*

Roúla was looking tired and strained, thought Nick, as Lachlan ushered them into the same meeting room the next morning.

"Help yourselves to coffee," she said, without enthusiasm, "and there are more biscuits for you, Mr Fisher."

"How kind."

Déspina went through the preamble and set the recording in motion.

"There have been developments, since we last met," said Nick. "We now know it *was* your brother who gave instructions on the disposal of Lukas's body, though Grigóris may not have known who was instructing him."

"How do you know?"

"Our search unearthed a SIM card in his possession. The phone company has since confirmed this came from Grigóris's phone, which Pandelís is alleged to have destroyed."

"If you're right, how could Grigóris not have known it was him?"

"Pandelís was hooded and avoided speaking."

"So, how did he communicate, by text?"

"To begin with, yes, but then he brought handwritten prompt cards with him when they met."

"What?"

"Instead of speaking, he showed cards, one by one. *It must never be identified,* and *It must never be found.* That's what Grigóris said was written on the cards. We're taking that as an instruction to do pretty much what he did. Wouldn't you?"

"That's not what we said, though. We agreed it would be moved off the property and put somewhere not far away, where it could be found. That's what Pandelís set out to tell him."

"But that's not what happened, is it? And I'll tell you why, Roúla. It's because someone *murdered* Lukas Hedinger and Pandelís needed to hush it up. Make it so it never happened. That's the only plausible reason for him giving instructions like that to Grigóri. And, if that's correct, then you've continued to lie to us. You told us Lukas was killed outright sometime before your brother arrived. So, with your brother's behaviour telling us it was murder, and not an accident, we must conclude that either you or your ninety-two-year-old aunt murdered Lukas. And I know which of those a jury would think more likely, don't you?"

"Now, wait a minute, Mr Fisher. Nobody murdered anybody. All right?"

"Then let's have the whole truth – for the third time of asking."

"I did leave out some of the story. It's true. But it makes no difference to anything. I only did it because I was so ashamed of myself."

"Go on."

"As I said, when I found him, there was no doubt in my mind that he was dead. But I couldn't bring myself to touch him. I didn't check his pulse. I didn't try heart massage. I didn't get help. I did nothing, Mr Fisher. I was frozen to the spot. It's something I will regret for the rest of my life.

"I checked on him a couple of times, as I said, but nothing changed. When Pandelís arrived, we were standing near the body, wondering what to do, when it groaned. I swear there was no movement for the forty minutes up to then, but now, suddenly, he was crying out. It was getting louder, more insistent. We were terrified the villagers would hear and find us in this compromising position. Then Pandelís asked for my headscarf and we tried to gag him with it. We were struggling and only partly successful but then he stopped. For an awful moment, I thought we'd killed him, but we checked his pulse and it was still pounding away. He'd just passed out and seemed stable. Then I heard Eléni call out, so I went to check on her. She'd been unwell earlier, and I was concerned, but now she seemed fine. I was only a few minutes but, when I got back, Pandelís was standing there, looking bereft. 'What happened?' I asked. 'It's all over,' he said, 'must have been an embolism or something. His eyes opened wide. He looked startled, then he made a gargling sound and died. Just like that.'"

"How very convenient," said Nick. "But let me go back a moment. A young man has fallen from your wall in a terrible accident. You're at the scene with your brother, wondering what to do, when the guy comes round and starts making a noise. Explain to me why you feel it's such a compromising situation that you rush to gag the poor fellow when, from your earlier description, he might have a broken neck!"

"Dead, or alive but severely injured, the same arguments applied."

"You didn't want to get involved and you didn't want to get sued," he said in a flat voice.

"If you like."

Nick slapped the table hard with the flat of his hand.

"I don't like, as it happens. I don't like at all. There was some excuse when it was just a dead body, but now a man's life is at stake and all you can think about is your own risk and inconvenience."

"He wasn't going to survive, Mr Fisher."

"I'm sorry, Roúla, I didn't realise you were a lawyer *and* a doctor."

"I'm not, of course, but anyone could see. He wasn't going to make it."

"Someone made damned sure of that."

"What are you suggesting?"

"If you didn't finish him off, then your brother did."

"As I said, Mr Fisher, nobody murdered anybody."

"I beg to differ, but let's have a ten-minute break and grab some coffee. Then I'd like to take us further back."

*

Nick put in a quick call to Náni and was surprised to be put straight through.

"Thought you'd be locked up with Pandelís," he said.

"We were with him for an hour and a half. Waste of time. He's taking his lawyer's advice now and refusing to answer questions. The lawyer reckons it's down to us to prove we have a case that can be prosecuted successfully. And you know what, Nick? We might struggle to do that. In the absence of a clear motive and with the family obfuscating the facts, it's going to be tough."

"Tough, but not impossible. Look, I'm mid-session with Roúla here. I'm going to push her harder now and I'm going to try to bring her back to Crete with us."

"Has she involved a lawyer, yet?"

"No. She *is* a lawyer of sorts, so perhaps she saw no need, thus far."

"Then you might be lucky."

"You think a lawyer would encourage her to stay here?"

"Very likely. Force us to seek a European Arrest Warrant from the Brits."

"Do they still work, after Brexit?"

"Good point. I don't know, Nick."

"I'll try to convince her to come back for a few days to try and clear herself of this."

"That would certainly help, Nick. I'm not sure where we go from here."

"We might need to think about interviewing Eléni again. Maybe she can shed some light on that evening?"

"I don't see how. Sounds like they kept her in the dark. Anyway, I'm not sure we could trust her answers to make much sense, do you?"

"Bear it in mind, anyway. I'll get back in touch when we're finished here."

*

Back in the meeting room, the three of them assembled. Nick was flipping back through his notes.

"I'd like to revisit a couple of things, Roúla. Twice you said, *nobody murdered anybody* but you also said, after your botched attempt to gag Lukas, that his pulse was *still pounding away*. Forgive me, but that doesn't sound like a young man who is about to give up the ghost five minutes later."

"No. And I was surprised when he died. My brother's explanation of an embolism seemed to fit though. If the fall caused a blood clot that worked its way round to his brain, death would have been delayed, but then instantaneous. Or perhaps there was bleeding into his brain the whole time. However, as you pointed out, I'm not a doctor."

"And neither is your brother, but he might know just enough to convince you after he murdered Lukas."

"I don't believe he would do such a thing."

"Oh, come on, Roúla. The young man survives a five-metre fall and forty minutes or more of unconsciousness. Then, despite being assaulted by two people intent on shutting him up, he still has a strong pulse – and yet he dies very shortly afterwards, at *precisely* the time you are absent from the scene. Then, within the hour, the only person who *was* there – your brother – is handing five thousand euros to a man with a violent past with extreme instructions on what to do with the body and he does this disguising his appearance and without using his voice.

"Any jury will regard that as an open and shut case of murder. A murder of convenience, I suppose they'd call it or is there rather more to it, I wonder? You also said Eléni *was unwell earlier*. What did you mean by that, Roúla?"

"Oh, it was just a few minutes. As I said, she was fine, later."

"Please tell us what happened."

"She was scaring me, to be honest. Pandelís and Giorgía have been saying for some time that she has spells, but I thought that was Giorgía exaggerating again. I'd never seen one."

"What sort of spells?"

"She looks at you like she doesn't know who you are. Says stuff that doesn't make sense. This was the first time I'd seen it."

"What happened, exactly?"

"I took a walk around the top of the village, just for half an hour, at most. I don't like to leave her for much longer than that, these days. It was getting dark when I got back, but I noticed the washing dragging on the ground, so I opened the door and yelled out: 'Mum, my nice clean washing's getting ruined. Didn't you see, for Heaven's sake?' but she didn't reply. When I found her, she was sitting on one of the dining-room chairs in the middle of the room, not by the table, which was odd. And she was sitting backwards on the chair in an ungainly, gawky manner, legs askew, and she was grinning at me, but there was no warmth, no humour in that grin. And there was an intensity in her eyes but without focus, if that makes sense. I wasn't sure what to do, so I said the same thing again, only more softly: 'My washing's getting dirty, Mum. Didn't you see?' And she turned to me, as if seeing me for the first time, and said: 'Hello, Kiki. So, you've come back, too. Missed all the fun, as usual.' I said: 'Why are you calling me Kiki, Mum? It's Roúla.' But it didn't seem to make any difference what I said, she just carried on this rather childish, one-sided conversation. I don't remember all of it, but the gist was: *You were right, Kiki, and I was wrong. So wrong. I was the stupid one, I was blind, but it's all right now. Everything is all right. It's all over now.* She said these things many, many times."

"Did the name Kiki mean anything to you?"

"Kiki was my mother, Mr Fisher, my *real* mother. Eléni's sister. She died in 1978."

"And the washing. Why was it dragging on the ground?"

"The prop fell over. It does that sometimes."

"On windy days?"

"Windy days, yes."

Nick walked to the window and stood, staring at the building opposite for a good two minutes. No-one spoke. Eventually, he turned to Roúla.

"It's almost lunchtime on Wednesday, June the twenty-fifth. I think there's a chance – just a chance – that you can save yourself, Roúla. Save what you have here: your life, your job, your reputation. You need to trust me on this, and you need to help me. Because, despite all the misleading statements you've made, I think we're finally getting close to the truth and I believe you're innocent of murder. I want you to come back to Crete with us today. If you do that, I'm hopeful of wrapping up this case by the weekend. You could be flying back to resume your life here by the start of July."

"I hear what you say, but it sounds like you're looking for me to help convict my brother. Pandelís is not a murderer, Mr Fisher."

"I just want you to tell the truth, Roúla. The whole truth. That's all I ever wanted."

CHAPTER 25
BACK HOME

Nick was in the window seat and there was a stranger between him and the other two, who were cross-aisle from one another. The engine noise did not allow for easy conversation and talking across the stranger was awkward. They soon stopped trying and this gave him plenty of time to think, for once. By the time they were crossing the Italian Alps, his thoughts were distilled. When they reached the islands off Croatia, Nick thought he knew the answer.

The young man's injuries occurred before Pandelís arrived. That was clear. They brought him in to deal with a problem. *The cleaner*. It was a dangerous situation, a dead body to be disposed of, but somehow, it would be worse still if the man survived. Why? Nick racked his brains but could come up with only one reason. Because then Lukas could point a finger at the person who hurt him, left him brain-damaged, wheelchair-bound or whatever. It would not be murder; it would be attempted murder or grievous bodily harm. But it would be enough. Enough to bring about the very things Pandelís feared. And so, he needed the man to die, the body to be made unidentifiable and lost forever. Then nobody would be pointing a finger at anybody. Only the family would know.

Darkness came quickly as they raced east. By the time they crossed the bay in front of Iráklio, the white lights of the city were glowing bright and steady against the dark mountains. Nick felt an overwhelming sense of coming home. Home, to this island three thousand kilometres from the country of his birth. This place with one-hundredth of the population, extremes of geography, climate and emotion, a place he both loved and hated, day by day. A place where his new life might be beginning to take shape.

Náni had organised a police car to pick them up from the airport and a hotel in Réthymno for the night. They would need a good sleep, she said. Further questioning was to commence at ten am sharp. When he checked in and went to his room, Nick was relieved to see an envelope on his bed, containing the Jeep keys. *Good lad,* Níko, he thought.

*

The next morning, he checked out early. It was a classic, Cretan morning; warm with a strong breeze. He would just have time to get there and back before ten. The Jeep was in the police parking area, looking unusually smart with its newly sprayed bonnet and a very comfortable looking, if slightly incongruous, new driving seat. He gripped the corner of the windscreen and the top of the driver's door and rocked it gently.

"Good to have you back, buddy," he muttered.

As he filled up with petrol in Arméni, he called ahead to get them up. They were waiting for him when he knocked on the door of room number three.

"Perhaps you could explain again why you need this, Nick?" said Heinrich.

"The Medical Examiner has asked for it and I live nearby, as you know. They need more DNA from the family for their sample analysis work."

"Can't they take it from the body?"

"No longer suitable, apparently. But you two are the next best thing. As paternal grandparents, together you make up fifty percent of Lukas's DNA and your *Y* chromosome, Heinrich, is identical to his. It's a straightforward procedure and would be a big help to the investigation but listen, if you're uncomfortable, we can call the ME. No problem at all. She'll explain much better than me."

"That won't be necessary, Nick. Just tell us what we have to do."

"Well, if you could sign these consent forms for me and then rinse your mouths out with some fresh water, we can make a start."

*

Náni was looking strained, he thought, but she managed a smile when she saw him.

"Welcome back, Nick. Come on in."

"The others will be here in a few minutes, I guess. Any change with Pandelís?"

"He's still here, in custody. We haven't questioned him again. Not yet."

"We need to interview Eléni again."

"On what grounds?"

"Roúla went for a walk that evening and, when she got back, Eléni was behaving oddly. I want to explore that half hour with her, and I want her take on the rest of the evening. See if we can find any anomalies."

"It will be traumatic for her, Nick."

"I expect it to be. We need a family member present, preferably Roúla, and a doctor or nurse, I would suggest."

"The family will still object."

"I know. Because the last thing they want is for us to talk to her. We're going to have to override those objections."

"I think I should take this to the Investigating Judge, Nick. I'll be in deep shit if the old lady keels over."

"Just keep her in the loop. Send her a text or something. We don't have time to check our every move with her, Náni. The Lieutenant wouldn't do that, would he?"

It was a low blow, implying that, as the new kid in town or just because she was a woman, she didn't have the confidence to make her own decisions, but it produced the desired effect.

"All right, then. Let's just do it. We can interview Roúla later. I'll call Giorgía."

"Let's just roll up with Roúla, unannounced. We don't want her running away again."

Before they set off, Nick had a quiet word with Déspina. She agreed to have his little package couriered to Chaniá as a matter of urgency. It's a private matter, he explained, pressing fifty euros into her hand. He should pay for it himself.

*

At the front door, Giorgía said: "Is Pandelís with you?" looking over their shoulders. And then, spotting her for the first time, "What are *you* doing here, Roúla?"

"Your husband remains in custody, kyría Fotáki," said Náni. "We

239

have until Saturday to decide whether to charge him with murder. We are here to interview Eléni and we'd prefer you not to be present. Roúla is here to ensure the old lady is treated with due consideration, and a qualified dementia nurse is waiting in the car over there. We'd like her to attend as well, in case of any medical issues."

"I can't allow it. It will be too much for her."

"If you refuse, then we will have no alternative but to take Eléni down to police headquarters which will be more distressing and potentially more dangerous for her. We don't want to do that, and I don't think your husband would want that, do you?"

"Why are you trying to exclude me?"

"Several reasons. I want Eléni to speak freely about certain past matters and I don't want her to feel constrained by your presence. Some of our concerns relate to an evening in Kardánes when you were here, not there, and, frankly, I don't need to waste your time. I'm sure you have better things to do."

"I'll allow it only if I am present."

"No, I'm not having that unless Eléni herself requests it. I will ask her if you wish."

There was a doorstep impasse for several more seconds, then Roúla spoke.

"Come on, Giorgía, you don't want Mum dragged off to Réthymno. If anything significant comes out of this, I'll be happy to share it with you, afterwards."

"It's a bit rich, to be told where I can and can't go, in my own house."

She was on the verge of tears, it seemed to Nick.

"I understand how you feel," said Náni, "but it's only happening in your house because that's where Eléni is and because she's so frail. You wouldn't expect to be invited to an interview at the police station unless the police needed you there, would you?"

"As her carer, of course, I would."

"Yes, but we have Roúla and the nurse for that."

Little by little, the door was opening. The woman looked sick with worry or even dread, Nick thought, but, at last, she let it fall back in resignation.

"You give me no choice. Give me a minute to make sure she's okay with this."

Náni signalled to the waiting nurse and then the four of them followed Giorgía through the hall and into the front room to wait. It was several minutes before she reappeared:

"I've set things up in the dining room. It's easier for her there, with the table."

"Would you two like to go in first?" Náni said to Roúla and the nurse. "Let us know when we're good to go."

"You're wasting your time, anyway," said Giorgía, when the three of them were alone. "She's losing it fast now. Half the time she doesn't recognise people or thinks they're different people. Sometimes she talks nonsense. It's all very sad, for someone so strong, someone who made us so proud."

"Is it Alzheimer's?"

"The doctor thinks so, but she manages to seem quite *compos mentis* on his visits. Loves a bit of attention, she does. Seems to perk her up, for a while."

Her patronising tone was grating with Nick and he was relieved when he heard Roúla call: "We're ready for you."

Náni said a pointed: "We appreciate this very much, kyría Fotáki," as they left her, eyes flitting, a handkerchief twisting in her hands.

The nurse took them to one side as they entered the room and ran through the basic checks she had carried out and would monitor. She asked them to be slow and clear with their questions and have frequent breaks. Then Nick and Náni went up to the table where the old lady was sitting, looking bright and wary.

"May we call you Eléni?" asked Náni.

"Please do, dear. It's my name, after all."

"And we will record the interview if that's all right."

"For posterity?"

"To save making notes and to be sure we remember it right if we're honest," said Nick.

"Do whatever you have to do. I won't make a fuss about little things. Never have. Never will."

"Giorgía is not in the room with us. We don't need her here, but if you'd rather she attended?" Náni asked.

"Lord, no. Five's quite enough, I think. I can't remember when I was last in a room with four other people. Last Christmas, perhaps. Anyway, Giorgía and I see quite enough of each other, day to day. And we'll need someone to bring the tea."

She finished with a mischievous look that brought a small chuckle from everyone and cleared the way for things to begin in earnest.

Nick saw Náni slip the recording device onto the table and the red light come on before she listed time, location and those present. Then she went on:

"Eléni, I'd like to take you back two and a half weeks to Sunday, the eighth of June. You were at home in Kardánes, with Roúla. It was the last time you and Roúla were together. Do you remember?"

"Was this the day the young man hurt himself?"

"That's right. Lukas Hedinger."

"Oh, I never knew who he was, but the others were rushing about, trying to help him."

"Do you remember what happened?"

"He fell from the wall. Quite a fall, that would be. I remember climbing it when I was a girl. We were told off for that. It's a long way down."

"Do you remember a little earlier that evening? Roúla went out for a walk, left you alone."

"Did you, dear?"

"Yes, Mum. Only for half an hour."

"It was beginning to get dark. There was a glorious sunset. Do you remember?" Náni went on.

"Oh, we get a lot of those here."

"Only, when Roúla got back, she says you were acting strangely."

"Was I, dear?"

"She says you spoke to her like she was your sister, you called her Kiki, and you said: 'You've come back, too'. Why did you say that, Eléni?"

"Sometimes I say odd things, these days. I get confused."

But, as she said those words, it was as if she had summoned up a cloud that crossed in front of the sun, somewhere in her head. Her eyes grew larger, her mouth wider. Imperceptible, almost, but a change was happening. Nick saw it and he pounced on it:

"I think you said *too* because she wasn't the only person who came back from your past that evening. Who else came to you, Eléni?"

Her face was contorted into a caricature of concentration now but there was anger there, too. Was it anger at herself, at her failing abilities, or something else? Her hands were gripping each other, nails digging into the palms, her shoulders hunched with tension.

Nick slipped the wartime photograph from his pocket and placed it on the table.

"Did this man come back to you, Eléni?"

He slid the photograph across until it was almost touching her wringing hands.

When she looked up, the anger and the madness broke through. Her face was distorted by an unfocused fury. Nick sensed rather than saw the nurse hurry across the room to sit at her side.

"How *dare* he? How *dare* he come back?" Eléni said.

"You're sure it was him?"

"You think I could forget that face? After what the evil man did? It's haunted me all my life, his face. Every day of my life. How *dare* he?"

"What did he do to you, Eléni?"

She leaned forward, her tongue protruded from her mouth and a brownish gob of spit fell onto the photograph. She turned eyes filled with hate on Nick. Then she felt for the photo and tore it in half, and then again, scattering the pieces from the table with a sweep of her arm.

Nick was about to ask the question again when he felt a hand on his shoulder. Roúla's eyes were boring into his and she was shaking her head.

He nodded slightly and turned back to the old lady.

"What did you do then, when you saw him, Eléni?"

"Well, I couldn't believe it. The bare-faced audacity of the man! He was just outside but he didn't see me, so I went outside and chased around the house after him. By then he was on the wall, right in the corner, looking away from me. Framed by the sunset."

"And then what?"

"Well, I was wild now. I wasn't going to let the bastard get away. Not again. So, I grabbed the prop and I charged him with it, like a lance. Got him right in the middle of the back and over he went. In the dream, I was still able to run, you see. And then I was sitting on a chair in the dining-room with Kiki and we were teenagers again and I was able to tell her it was over. That we were free of him. At last. Free to live our lives."

"Why do you say *we*, Eléni?"

The old lady said nothing.

"You said we. You *and* Kiki were free of him."

"He did things to Kiki. Dirty things. I found out later after he'd gone. She was so damaged. A broken child. The rest of her life, a broken child."

"You're saying this man molested your eleven-year-old sister?" asked Náni.

"Ten. She was ten, then."

Nick heard a small gasp from Roúla, followed by a suppressed sob, but he pressed on:

"You tried to kill him then, Eléni. With good reason. Did you succeed?"

"It was a dream, Mr Fisher. I know he's dead. He died a long time ago. Kiki, too."

"And what did you think later, when they said a boy was hurt, falling from the wall?"

"I thought my dream must have been a premonition. I should have done something to stop what happened to him. But I didn't understand, you see."

"No, I see that."

The nurse laid a hand on Nick's.

"I think that's enough for now, Mr Fisher," she said.

Outside, in the neat but uninteresting garden, Náni turned to Nick. There was resentment in her eyes again.

"You might have told me Franz and Lukas were lookalikes, doppelgänger."

"I wasn't sure it was relevant, till today."

"Since when do *you* get to decide what's relevant to *my* case?"

Nick held up his hands in submission.

"You're right. Sorry, Náni."

"And this *dream* of hers – it really happened?"

"In her head, Lukas was Franz and Roúla was Kiki, so yes, I think it did."

"But she believes it was all a dream."

"Yes, she does. Perhaps her subconscious is trying to protect her, somehow, absolve her from responsibility. It wants there to be no connection between her demented actions and the injured man, so it invents a dream for her. In the dream, she avenges herself on this man who brought so much hurt to their lives, but, in reality, she tried to kill poor Lukas."

Roúla was approaching them now.

"I'm sorry you had to hear that about your mum," said Nick.

"It's unbelievable. And I never knew. It would explain a lot about my poor mother, though."

"Are you all right to talk some more?"

"Eléni is sleeping now," she said. "The nurse wants her to rest until after lunch and she's going to stay with her. So yes, let's get it over with."

"And Giorgía?"

"Just nipped out for groceries, I think."

The three of them made their way back to the same dining-room table to discover plates of sandwiches, pies and fruit, jugs of freshly squeezed orange juice and sparkling water with ice and lemon. It was all prepared with great care and attention to detail.

"Gosh. This is very welcome," said Nick.

"It was Giorgía."

"How kind. Quite unexpected."

"We Greeks are always hospitable in our homes, Mr Fisher, even to unwelcome guests."

They helped themselves, then sat. Náni set up the recording device away from the food and then nodded in Nick's direction.

"We know something about Eléni's romance with a German soldier," he said, "but it would be very helpful if you could tell us everything *you* know, Roúla."

"Okay. Some of what I know comes from my mother, more than forty years ago. Eléni never spoke of these things: not the soldier, not the war, not the civil war. None of it. Except this one time, three or four years ago. An old friend of hers died that day. She was sad and needed to talk, I think. He was a German, too. They'd corresponded ever since the war. After his wife died, she thought he might come to Crete, even propose to her, but he never did. Too old by then, probably. Or got cold feet, in the end. Who knows?"

"Was this Werner?" asked Nick.

"Werner, yes. How do you know?"

"Someone in the village mentioned him."

"Anyway, that day, we sat drinking wine together and she talked for hours and hours. Things I knew nothing about. It was magical for me, but also very sad. I can tell you what I remember.

"She said the Germans came to our village a few weeks after the invasion and suddenly the place was full of young soldiers. Of all the German boys, this one young man stood out for her. He was taller and his hair was white-blond. He was very good-looking, I believe, and he was a Gefreiter, a corporal."

"Do you know his name?" asked Nick.

"Eléni never said. And I was curious about that, but I figured, if she didn't want to tell me, that was her business. So, I didn't ask."

"And your mother Kiki never mentioned it?"

"If she did, I've forgotten. Sorry."

"That's okay. Please go on."

"It wasn't long before this man started paying particular attention to Eléni. She was young and pretty then. She tried hard to be dutiful, to ignore him, but he made her laugh with his antics and he seemed kind, helped her, brought her little gifts.

"By the summer of 1943, they were seeing each other. Clandestine meetings outside the village. Exploring each other, falling in love. He would even come to the house on some pretext when he knew the parents weren't there. My mother Kiki was younger, but she knew what was going on, and she was terrified of them being discovered.

"By late summer, Eléni was in a quandary. She knew the church said it was wrong, she knew the villagers would condemn her for it, but she so wanted to make love with him. Their love was beautiful, she thought, and it was only natural to consummate it. It felt like the right thing to do. Surely God would not condemn her? Their love must be a God-given thing, after all. And yet …

"Half of her wanted to give herself to him, seize the moment – which is what you had to do in wartime, after all – but the other half wanted to be the dutiful girl she'd been brought up to be, save herself for the man she would marry, be honourable, truthful and open in the community.

"Every time they met, they would get a little closer to the act, but then Eléni would push him away gently, saying: 'Not yet, my love. Not yet'. And he was always careful to respect her wishes."

"While taking his frustration out on Kiki whenever he got the chance," said Náni.

"Well, Eléni knew nothing of that then, if it's true."

"You're not sure it is?"

"I can't be. It has a *ring* of truth because of how my mother was, later, but I never heard anything until today. Not from anyone. Not from my mother, not from Eléni, before. And honestly? What opportunities were there for him to do such things? Eléni would have been at his side whenever they could be together, surely."

"You think Eléni would make up something like that?"

"No, Sergeant. But maybe she's losing sight of what is and isn't real. She's not well and she is *utterly* poisoned against this man."

247

"Go on with your story then, Roúla," urged Nick.

"So, we get to one day in September. He was particularly sweet that day, she said. Funny, romantic. They talked of a future together, after the war. He said she wouldn't have to leave Greece. He loved it there and would leave the ruins of his country to be with her in her country – even then, he could see that Hitler would be defeated, in the end. It was a beautiful thing for her to hear, that he would put his love for her before the fatherland and she held him close. But, when they kissed, things became intense. He was excited, desperate. He wanted her – and this time he was pushing hard for that. She wanted him, too, but she was trying to resist, trying to tell him *No*, only this time he wasn't listening. Perhaps, in the back of her mind, she wanted him to resolve her dilemma for her. Anyway, he forced himself on her and her resistance collapsed. She said she cried, the whole time they were making love."

"I'm sorry, but that sounds like rape to me," said Náni. "A fifteen-year-old says *No* and a tall, strong, twenty-year-old forces himself on her."

Nick was nodding, but he didn't see things in quite the same way:

"If that's exactly what happened, I'd agree."

"Don't give me that, Nick. Rape is rape. And he raped her."

He held up his hands in self-defence.

"Maybe he did, but we don't know for sure, do we? All I'm saying is, if *you'd* got yourself pregnant with the man you loved – a forbidden, *consensual* relationship with a Nazi – it might just save your life to *say* it was rape."

"*Got yourself* pregnant? Just listen to yourself, Nick. *He* got her pregnant by raping her. The man she *thought* she loved was a Nazi rapist."

But Nick was losing patience with Náni's black and white view of the world.

"Let's just get on with the story, shall we?"

Roúla's eyes flipped between the two of them until she felt it was safe to proceed.

"After the sex, they were lying there, I imagine, and it was coming up to the time he needed to head back to the barracks. Then he told her. He'd been posted to Italy and was leaving in the morning. She couldn't believe it. 'You *knew*, and you said nothing? You forced yourself on me, knowing you were leaving me?' She was devastated, and furious. He tried to talk again about being together when the war ended but she was not interested. The last thing he said was that he would come back for her. One day, he would be back, he promised. And then he was gone.

"When she missed her next period, she knew. She was carrying his child. She tried various stupid things, hoping to miscarry, but nothing worked. When the morning sickness started, it became obvious to the family. There was a session around the kitchen table where she confessed to everything. They knew they must get her out of the village before it started to show, otherwise there would be reprisals, but they didn't know where to turn.

"Then Eléni spoke to Werner. He had become a secret friend. A quiet, kind German who was a bit older. He had an inkling of what happened. He was a little in love with Eléni himself, of course, but she saw him only as a friend. But what a friend he proved to be. His sister worked as a doctor in the German hospital at Thessaloníki and he was able to arrange for Eléni to have her baby there when the time came. It helped that the father was a German soldier, I think. They wanted to tidy up after themselves, I suppose. So, in late November, Eléni was sent to the mainland, to an aunt in Kavála, a lovely place on the coast, east of Thessaloníki, where she spent the months while the baby grew.

"When it was time, she went to the hospital and was able to check in without papers. She said they were lost in an attack on her village and she gave a false name. I think this sister of Werner's must have been very kind to her. Anyway, they let her in and took care of her. It was a long, difficult birth. She was sixteen hours in active labour, an hour for every year of her age, she said. At last, the nurses said: 'You have a beautiful baby boy! Wouldn't you like to see him, hold him?' But she was firm in her resolve and refused to see him, fearful of forming any bond with the child she was to give up. The baby was taken for adoption later. She never saw him."

There was a pause. Roúla seemed to have finished.

"What a dreadful start to a young woman's life. You never get over something like that," said Náni.

"Can I take us back to the night Lukas died?" said Nick. "And shall I tell you what I think happened?"

He had their attention.

"Eléni tried to kill Lukas. In her dementia, she believed him to be Franz Engel. But, instead, she injured him, badly. Your brother worked out Eléni was to blame, knew this would bring disgrace to the family and a secure mental hospital for her. He wasn't ready to accept either of those outcomes. When you went to check on your aunt, he took his chance and smothered the man. And this is—"

"Wait! Wait, Nick, please. It's my brother you're talking about! I don't believe Pandelís is *capable* of murder."

"You'd be amazed what people will do when they're in a corner, trying to save their families or themselves. And look at what he's built up over thirty years in this city: a solid reputation in the business community, a beautiful house and family, a comfortable lifestyle – it's a hell of a lot to lose, Roúla, and he wasn't about to surrender it."

"But he's not *like* that, Nick. He cares about Eléni, of course. Adores her. But he doesn't care about those things. That's *Giorgía*. All their lives, it's been *Giorgía* pushing for wealth, status, reputation. Her family were much poorer. She pushed him hard to get her away from all that."

"That's all very interesting, Roúla, but Giorgía wasn't even there that night."

Another pause, longer this time.

"You lied about this, too?" said Nick softly, almost sorrowfully.

"Pandelís asked me to keep her out of it. He said she'd been through enough looking after Mum for us and it wouldn't be fair to put her through all this as well when it wasn't her problem. It seemed reasonable to me at the time. Remember, I thought we were dealing with a young man who had an accident in our garden. Nothing more."

"Let's dispense with that fiction as well, shall we, Roúla? You knew – or at least you *must* have suspected – that Eléni was responsible. You found your washing dragging, the prop on the ground on a windless night and your aunt in a demented state. You *must* have put two and two together. The cry you claimed you heard later was a fiction, too. Because you went to look right away. You're a human being, after all. And you found the man, dead. Or so you thought. Then you rang Pandelís."

"All right, Nick. Enough. I *wondered*. Naturally, I did. I'd never seen her like that before, but to attack a total stranger? Just forty minutes earlier, I was sitting with her chatting, like always, over a glass of wine – and now this."

She reached for a tissue from the pack Náni offered. There were real tears now, but only a superficial crack in the dam. After a few dabs, she went on:

"Okay, Nick. I admit it. I am guilty of trying to protect my aunt. I'm sorry for what happened to the young man. He didn't deserve it. But then Eléni didn't deserve what happened to her, either. It destroyed her life."

"And the son must pay for the sins of the forefather?"

"No. I don't mean that. We didn't know who he was, remember, and I'm not condoning what she did for a moment. And anyway, it was the dementia, not her. But it wouldn't be right if anything bad happened to Eléni, ever again. I feel that so strongly and so does Pandelís. And to think of her spending the rest of her life in some ghastly, secure mental hospital or in prison? It's just unbearable, after how she suffered, after she gave her life to fighting for us, caring for us. The huge sacrifices she made."

"So, you tried to cover it up."

"I took the washing in, put the prop away and called Pandelís. He brought Giorgía along. He usually does when he collects Mum, so there's someone to look after her during the drive back."

"So, you weren't surprised to see her."

"No. But, as I said, Pandelís took charge when he got here. You know the rest."

"Not quite," said Náni. "We don't know who murdered Lukas. And now we have four candidates, as far as I can see. Either he was killed by the fall and, despite your story, he never revived. In this case, your aunt is the murderer and your stories were an attempt to obfuscate the fact. Or he did revive, only to be killed by you or Pandelís – or now Giorgía."

"Or he just died, as Pandelís said, from the embolism or whatever."

"No, Roúla. Whether this is a medical possibility or not, that it should happen at precisely the time of your brief absence makes it too convenient to be believable, not to mention Pandelís's subsequent behaviour."

"But can you prove otherwise? And what would a jury think? I am not your murderer, if there is one, Mr Fisher, and I don't believe my brother is."

"So, you're saying it was Giorgía."

"No, I'm not. But I can see that the threat to her status and reputation would mean *everything* to Giorgía. And I'm asking myself now: why was my brother so keen for us to leave her out of things, pretend she wasn't there. Aren't you?"

Nick exchanged glances with Náni.

"Meaning he knew," he said. He glanced at his watch. "What time did she go out?"

"Er … it would have been around noon, I think."

"It's ten minutes to three. How long does it take to get a few groceries when you're fifteen minutes from the city?"

"Not this long."

"I think we'd better find her."

Náni called into the station and mobilised the available constables to alert airports and ferry ports. The registration plate of her car was circulated throughout the emergency services. Nick visited Pandelís in custody to ask him where she might have gone: her friends, relatives, favourite haunts.

"There's no-one, Mr Fisher. She's with me or she's at home. This is her life these days. The boys and their families are too far away for a casual visit."

He grabbed Nick's arm and turned his eyes up to his.

"She doesn't do this sort of thing. I'm scared, Mr Fisher. Please find her."

"Was it her, Pandelí? Did she smother Lukas?"

"Just find her. Please."

CHAPTER 26
ATONEMENT

At eight fifty the next morning, Nick received an email from Pánagou. It said: *Record time and I think you'll be pleased with the results! Call if you need me to explain further.* Two charts were attached, but they were too small to see clearly on his phone. He asked Déspina to print them out for him and then studied them for several minutes. He did not fully understand the forty-odd coloured bar charts but then he didn't need to. He saw the word *conclusive* on the first sheet and the label *100% match* on the second sheet, as expected. Moments later, he was at Náni's office door.

As he went in, he said: "You're not going to believe this, Náni."

*

The owner of the Pélagos Taverna at Triópetra was walking his Cretan hounds along the beach that morning when he spotted a small, blue car, perched on top of the sandy cliffs above the beach. It was not unusual for cars to be left overnight or even for the odd tourist to sleep in a car, so he thought nothing of it, at first. Then, as he climbed up, he saw it was steamed up and a woman of about sixty was asleep inside. It was not until he reached the other side that he saw the pipe. The engine was not running, but red and amber lights were glowing inside. He let the dogs run free, covered his mouth by pulling up his sweatshirt and opened the unlocked passenger door. Then, as he reached across to turn off the ignition, he saw the fuel gauge was below zero. He wondered how long the engine had kept going before the fuel ran out. *Long enough.* Long enough for a damp, grey film to have formed on the inside of the car, he saw. *And the inside of the woman*, he thought.

He looked at her face then. It was pale pink with bright, cherry lips. *That must be good*, he thought. Not the blue or grey he might have expected. He felt her wrist. It was cold but not yet lifeless. There was the faintest of pulses. He tapped her face, called out: "Yeiá sas. Hello lady." But there was no reaction. Then he let her be, opened both car doors and the hatchback and reached for his phone.

*

Déspina interrupted them at nine fifty-eight. She said the ambulance service just rang with details of a call received a few minutes earlier and she passed on what she had heard. Náni grabbed Nick and they raced to the scene. She drove fast. They made it from Réthymno in thirty-seven minutes.

They found the car perched sixty metres above a windswept part of the beach, just a few metres from a rocky cliff edge. They stepped out of the police car and gazed over the beach, sensing her desperation, the depth of her sadness. *She must have watched the red sun slipping into the sea by the White Mountains,* thought Nick. *She waited till the last tongue of fire disappeared below the horizon. Then she turned the ignition key and reclined the driver's seat for the long night ahead and the darkness that would never end.*

Some six hundred metres to the east, wild waves were slapping the eponymous rock towers, spray shooting high into the sky. Closer at hand, Nick saw the medical team unloading a stretcher and emergency oxygen.

"How is she?" Náni yelled against the wind, pointing her police identification card at them.

The older man stood as they came over to him.

"She's unconscious and very poorly. But she has a chance," he said. "Not much of one, I'm afraid. We'll do everything we can."

"Is it carbon monoxide poisoning?"

"Yes. Did you see how bright her lips are? I'd guess the engine was running most of the night. She was a determined woman. You have to be, these days."

"What's that supposed to mean?"

"Catalytic converters. They've reduced the carbon monoxide

content. It's not the easiest way to kill yourself, nowadays. Takes a long time. There's an envelope on the passenger seat, by the way. We figured that was your territory."

Nick slipped on a forensic glove and reached inside. He looked at the plump but still pretty face, the smart clothes. He wondered if she knew when she chose those clothes. Did she opt for something comfortable to spend fifteen hours in a car or something smart in which to be found? Keeping up appearances, even now. Did she know, when she prepared that exquisite lunch for them; her parting gift? At what point did she conclude this was the only route left open to her? And how did she hide her desperation so well? Or had they just failed to read the signs?

Just as he withdrew, something caught the corner of his eye. Was there a movement? Was it a fly or an eyelid flicker? He stood motionless for several moments, staring at her face, but whatever it was, did not recur. He stepped back from the car and found Náni talking to the medics.

"Just open it, Nick," she said.

The envelope was not sealed so he was able to slip out the note and unfold it.

"Read it aloud," she said.

"It's in Greek, Náni, and handwritten. I'm not quite up to that, yet."

She gave him a sharp look and reached for the letter.

"Then I will read it to you, in English. It's not addressed to anyone. It says:

Do not look for anyone else in connection with the death of Lukas Hedinger. I am responsible. I was trying to save our family. And I thought it would be a merciful release for him too, given the severity of his injuries. But that decision was not mine to make. I see that now. I made a terrible error of judgment and find that I cannot live with the consequences. I am so sorry – for his family and for mine, who I have always loved, heart and soul. Please forgive me.

"It's not signed either, but I'm sure Pandelís will confirm Giorgía's handwriting."

"My God, Náni. Just when we thought this case couldn't get more tragic. Now, this."

As he finished the sentence, he caught a faint, but familiar sound. For a second, he could not quite place it. Then it was there again, and he knew, from before. Tyres on sand. He and Náni stared at each other in a simultaneous dawning, just as one of the medics gave a desperate cry. They turned to see the little, blue Honda rolling steadily, almost silently, for the cliff edge.

Náni seemed rooted to the spot in horror. The younger medic was running now but he was too far away. He wasn't going to make it. Nick sprinted a few paces and made a desperate lunge but fell half a metre short as the car slipped away from him. The tyres found purchase on gravel at the cliff edge, the suspension creaked. In slow motion, they saw the car tip up. The open doors fell forward as if it were trying to take flight on hopelessly inadequate wings, and then there was just space where it had been. And silence. A dangerous, deceitful silence unmasked moments later by the sickening crunch of metal on rock, a shattering of glass and then the screams of tortured steel as the car lurched, rolled and bumped, blow-by-blow, down the escarpment to the waiting rocks.

At the edge, they saw. The car lay upside down on rocks, sixty metres below, wheels spinning to a halt, like the death throes of some stricken insect. It must have dropped twenty-five metres through the air to smash into a massive rock, now bruised and littered with windscreen shards, where the passenger door lay, ripped from its hinges. Then, it would have tumbled and cartwheeled a further thirty metres down the side of the cliff.

"Quick," called the younger medic. "Let's get down there before it blows!"

"Not going to happen," yelled Nick, pursuing him down the side path. "The ignition's off and there's no petrol left, anyway."

"She might have survived. We have to hurry!"

The younger man got further ahead and, thirty metres from the car, Nick slowed, then came to a breathless stop. She had not survived.

No-one could have survived. The roof was flattened by the boulder on which it landed. He saw blood. An arm stretching out from the mangled metal. And then he saw the medic turning towards him, lips compressed, shaking his head.

CHAPTER 27
THE RIGHT THING

"I suppose it was a need to atone," said Nick as they climbed the precipitous mountain road out of Triópetra. The Paximádia islands and the headland round to Mátala and beyond were blurring in a heat haze over the glittering sea behind them.

"You mean her suicide?" said Náni.

"There has to be some significance to doing it here, maybe starting at sunset."

"You think so?"

"Why else would she drive forty kilometres to the place where his body was found? That's not just coincidence."

"Who knows? Perhaps it was a special place for her. There was nothing in her note to suggest any more than that."

As they finally reached the top, the views inland opened up. A fertile plain stretched out briefly below them before the mountains of Kédros and, further back, Psilorítis rose up in barren magnificence. It never ceased to amaze Nick that a small island could feel so massive. His own village, Saktoúria perched sun-baked and defiant on the mountainside, away to their right. *I should be there right now, organising a trip to the beach with my son*, he thought.

They dropped steadily down to Acoúmia and then picked up the Réthymno road, heading north-west.

"Do you want to grab some lunch?" said Nick.

"I don't know how you can think of food at a time like this, Nick Fisher."

"Simple, Náni. I'm hungry. Must be the sea air."

"Do you know somewhere?"

"Turn right in a couple of kilometres," said Nick. "There's a sign on a bend to Kendrochóri."

∗

A large, smiling man with a dark moustache hooted a welcome and then grabbed Nick in a sweaty bear hug. His wife beamed at them from behind the counter. *They think Náni is the new woman in my life*, thought Nick, *God forbid*.

Only a couple of tables were occupied on the large terrace, so they were able to find a private spot to enjoy the stunning view of the mountain. A small carafe of rakí arrived almost immediately, along with a large jug of iced water.

"Rakí *before* lunch?" queried Náni.

"Before and after, here," said Nick. "It's traditional."

"It must be traditional to be a drunk in Kendrochóri then."

"I think we need a tot after that experience," said Nick, pouring.

"Hmmm. It *is* a rather good one," acknowledged Náni, wetting her lips.

When the owner reappeared, Nick handed back the menus.

"You choose what's good, Agamémno. No snails, no lambs' testicles. Okay? And not too much to eat."

He grinned and nodded. "Lígo, lígo, né. Krasí? Aspró, kókkino?"

"Red, I think. Half a litre should be enough for lunch."

Náni raised her eyebrows and Agamémnon departed.

"The red is better than the white," said Nick.

"You might be drinking that," said Náni. "I'm driving, remember?"

"I'm sure you can manage a glass."

"Is he really Agamémnon?"

"Not only that, but he named his son Krónos."

"The one who ate his children. Are you quite sure about this menu, Nick?"

"You'll be fine," he said.

Dish after dish began to arrive: yellow, mashed fava beans with raw onion and olive oil; loukánika – spiced local sausages; oyster mushrooms dunked in seasoned flour and fried crisp; hórta – bitter, wild greens cooked with lemon; fried red peppers; beetroot slices in vinegar; fresh sardines; tzatzíki. After a few minutes, as their appetites slowed, Náni said:

"I feel guilty enjoying this. It doesn't seem right, somehow, after this morning's tragedy and now, knowing what we know …"

"The body has to be fed, Náni, and it was only a two-kilometre diversion. Don't feel bad because the food is so good."

"It's not that. It's knowing about Giorgía when Pandelís doesn't. Especially when I feel to blame."

"You were told she was unconscious."

"I should have realised she might do that and got her out of the car right away."

"You're a police officer, not a clairvoyant, and you are not to blame, Náni."

"Let's hope the inquiry comes to the same conclusion."

"There won't be an inquiry because no-one will demand one. And, even if there were, they would conclude that we acted reasonably. You have to put it out of your mind, Náni."

Nick was thinking, *If anyone was to blame, it was me,* but he said nothing further.

"I have something else to own up to," said Náni.

"What's that?"

"I had a visitor."

"Go on."

"You'll work it out. She was in Réthymno for the shopping, she said. Thought she'd pop in and say hello, put my mind at rest …"

Nick was ruffling the hair on the back of his head, forehead crinkled.

"… after visiting her husband earlier, in Kardánes. They hadn't seen each other for quite a while."

"Ha! Not buried in the garden, then."

"No. But, to be honest, Nick, I could understand if she were. Bit of a smug bitch, I'm sorry to say. Still, I must admit, I got Papatónis dead wrong."

"You might have to cut him a bit of slack now. He is a slimeball, though. I could see where you were coming from. Anyway. Good-oh. Another loose end ties itself up."

"I have one more. Whatever happened to Lukas's passport?"

"Who knows, Náni, but I do have a theory."

"Go on, then."

"Grigóris kept it."

"Why, though?"

"A little insurance. Just in case the hooded man came calling. Or, if he found out who it was, he could turn his hand to a spot of blackmail."

"Until he discovered it was Uncle Pandelís. Hmmm. You could be right. Anyway, I can live with that answer."

"That just leaves the matter of my vandalised Jeep."

"I thought we'd sorted that out for you."

"You did, and generously, thank you. Except for the culprits."

"Right. Well, good luck with that, Nick. It'll be Andréou or someone connected with him, I imagine. Some little man with big ideas and potatoes on his back, as Varvára put it. Please don't ask me to waste police resources on it. And now, we must thank the excellent Agamémnon and head back. Are you up to interviewing Pandelís with me?"

"Never better," said Nick, leaving the last half glass of wine on the table.

*

On the drive back, Nick said:

"I assume you're clear in your head about who to charge with what now?"

"I think so. I'll need to talk to the Investigating Judge about Eléni, see how she wants to handle her, given the dementia. With Giorgía the eventual killer, the others are all accessories, to varying degrees."

"Pandelís could be an accomplice."

"True. We might need to explore that."

"I assume you'll let Roúla get on with her life now."

"Why would you think that?"

"I know she hid the truth from us on a few occasions, but she was in a difficult position and it was all to protect her family."

"She lied repeatedly, Nick, and you know it. If she had helped Lukas when she found him, he might be alive today. If she had admitted

262

earlier that Giorgía was there that night, so might she. And then it was Pandelís *and* Roúla who moved the body to the barn. That makes her an accessory. No question."

"She agreed to come back with us, Náni. That must count for something."

"Her lawyer can use that to make a case for leniency, sure."

"But any charge will mean the end of her career, everything she has worked for. It seems harsh."

"She's a lawyer, Nick. She knew exactly what she was doing and now she must face the consequences. I can see you admire the woman, but if you led her to believe she could get off scot-free, you were way out of line."

Nick started to speak again but Náni wasn't having it. The discussion was over.

*

Náni told Pandelís what had happened straight away. She kept it short, the bare facts were indisputable. His wife was dead. It was enough. It would only cause further upset to mention that four members of the emergency services were present when the car went over.

She then placed the suicide note in its forensic wallet on the table. As he read it, Pandelís turned ashen, but there were no tears yet.

"How courageous," he said. "It crossed my mind she might do something like this. Find something heroic out of this bloody mess. I didn't know she was brave enough, frankly. She would think it was the right thing to do. To atone. A life for a life."

"Atone for what, exactly?" asked Náni, gently.

There was a long moment. Pandelís was staring at the empty ashtray, but then he nodded slowly, several times, perhaps concluding there was little point in suppressing the truth anymore.

"That night, she'd brought out a cushion earlier, placed it under the young man's head, despite the blood. I was touched by the kindness of the gesture. When I came back from the toilet, I saw she was doing it again. Inserting the cushion under his head – again. I said, 'What

263

are you doing?' and right away I saw the guilt on her face. I rushed to feel the man's pulse. Nothing. I said, 'What the hell have you done, Giorgía?' And then she said, 'It's for the best, Pandelí. He would have died anyway. Or spent his life brain-damaged, in a wheelchair. We'll tell Roúla he just upped and died. Then you can text that number. Problem solved.' I was stunned by the heartless pragmatism in those two little words: *Problem solved*."

"How did you feel about what she'd done?"

"A mixture of horror and relief, to be honest. I was horrified that she'd done it – it was not something I wanted or expected her to do at all. But, by doing so, she'd given us a chance, the whole family, to be untouched by this. To keep Mum out of the asylum, preserve our lives, our hard-won prosperity, our reputations. And, when Roúla came out, I could see she was relieved too when I told her that he had died."

"*That* he'd died, but not the truth about *how*."

"No. Roúla doesn't know."

There was a pause, then Náni said:

"We'll let you have a minute, Pandelí," and raised her eyebrows at Nick. He followed her out of the room and found her waiting when he shut the door.

"Look, Nick. I'm going to be tied up here for ages now. I have to bring the Lieutenant and the judge up to speed, there are all the charges to draw up, evidence to be assembled, statements to check. You know how it is. I wonder, would you be able to handle the Hedingers? It's a tough call, given all that you have to tell them, but you've developed a good relationship with Heinrich. And it's going to be particularly hard on him, obviously. Maybe take Déspina as my representative. She has the soft touch."

She checked her watch. It was seven thirty-five pm.

"There's nothing that won't keep till morning, though, apart from Roúla."

"What about her?"

"We should be bringing her in, too."

"She's not going anywhere, Náni. There's no way she'd leave Eléni on her own and she's here of her own volition, remember. Let me talk to her tomorrow after I've seen the Hedingers. If necessary, we can bring her in after that."

"It *will* be necessary, Nick, but okay, we'll organise that tomorrow."

When he got into the Jeep, he sat for a long minute, thinking. There might not be a chance tomorrow and Roúla needed to know. It would help her understand. And it was only a few kilometres. He would go to Roussospíti now, on the way home.

CHAPTER 28
A DESPERATE INHERITANCE

The terrace outside their suite was featureless but pleasant enough and private.

"We will be able to sit out here for an hour, but then it will get far too hot," explained Ilse, as Heinrich helped her raise the parasol. Déspina busied herself pouring iced water with lemon from a giant jug into four glasses. When they were all seated, Nick said:

"Sergeant Samarákis sends her apologies and wishes you both well. We are here to give you a full update on what's been discovered."

He scanned their faces. Apprehension. An expectation of further, prolonged pain.

He spoke for ten minutes without interruption, starting in 1943 and finishing with the sad events of the previous day. The old couple listened attentively, without questions, nodding here, wincing or gasping with astonishment there. Finally, Nick took two sheets of paper from a folder and placed them on the table face down.

"After you were kind enough to provide your swabs the other day, I had an idea. The Medical Examiner agreed to run some tests for me."

He turned over the first sheet.

"I'm not sure how much you know about DNA, but the twenty-third chromosome pairing determines gender. It's xy for boys and xx for girls. A boy's y chromosome comes entirely from his father and his, in turn, from his father, and so on. This chart compares your y chromosome with Lukas's. Unsurprisingly, they are identical, proving that you are, indeed, Lukas's paternal grandfather."

"Why would you doubt that?" asked Heinrich.

"I didn't. But I needed to be certain. When I saw that photograph of Franz on the laptop, you'll remember how struck I was by his close resemblance to Lukas. Having learned about Eléni's wartime affair with a German soldier, I asked the ME to run another test."

He turned over the second sheet.

"This is a comparison of all the chromosome pairings in your DNA, Heinrich, with those of Eléni. As you can see, in the assessor's opinion, it's a conclusive match. That means the child she had to give up for adoption was you. Eléni is your birth mother, Heinrich, and of course, Franz Engel was the father."

Finally, Nick took a drink of water and sat back. The old man looked crushed and grey, but he was the first to respond:

"As you were telling the story, I began to suspect as much, but that doesn't reduce the shock of seeing it proved."

The old man stood and went to the window.

"So, Nick, what you have told us is that our grandson was attacked by his great-grandmother – the mother I've never met – whose dementia led her to believe Lukas was my dead father, Franz."

Heinrich turned to look but Nick just compressed his lips and raised his eyebrows slightly.

"And, when she failed in her bid to kill Lukas, this Giorgía woman – her nephew's wife – then smothered the boy while he was unconscious, ostensibly to save her family. This woman then killed herself yesterday from remorse or perhaps to atone, somehow."

"A lucid summary, Heinrich."

"And what I have learned along the way is that my father was a Nazi rapist and possible child molester, and my mother was a wartime-collaborator-turned-communist-killer who eventually lost her mind and tried to kill her great-grandson."

The old man's voice cracked in the final sentence and he sat down again. He seemed bitter and distressed, close to tears.

"I think most of us would use more sympathetic language, Heinrich," said Nick, as Déspina placed a hand on the old man's arm.

"And those terrible things they did to Lukas's body," said Ilse. "Was that just a bungled attempt to prevent identification?"

"Yes. A horrible thing, but I believe it was done without malice."

"Without malice …" she echoed faintly, staring hard at her water glass.

"How the woman must have suffered," said Heinrich, "to store so much hatred for so long – the length of my life, in fact. Does she understand now what she did?"

"We don't know, Heinrich. She has a memory of pushing a young man off a wall but in a dream. There's a parallel universe in her mind, somehow. She knows Franz is long dead, in her more lucid moments, and she believes another young man hurt himself but was nursed back to health. No harm done. We haven't tried to correct her, nor have we told her what happened to Giorgía."

"I want to meet my mother, Nick."

Ilse's hand moved to cover Heinrich's. As Nick hesitated, Déspina cut in:

"Not such a great idea, Herr Hedinger. Either she won't understand who you are, which you'll find very upsetting, or she will, and that might force her to face the terrible thing she did. The shock could be too much."

"I think I have a right to meet my own mother. Do you have any idea what it's like to live almost sixty years without knowing who the hell your mother was? I have a right, Nick Fisher. I have a goddamn right."

The old man was quivering with rage now. Ilse looked at Nick, pleading.

"Listen, Heinrich. I hear you, but I have to say, I agree with Déspina. It's dangerous for you both. Let me talk to Roúla, though. I'll call her right now."

*

In the police car, he explained from the passenger seat, while Déspina drove.

"Roúla will *not* allow you to meet or confront the old lady, I'm afraid. But you will be able to observe her from a distance. Roúla will spend time with you, talking about Eléni, the past, what she knows of your father. There are photographs she will share with you. She will not tell Eléni who you are, and you must not either, for now. I expect her to undergo a psychiatric assessment leading to a period in a secure mental facility. It may not be that long a period. Who knows? There may come a time …"

"If we are both alive, and if I can get back to Crete."

"I'm sorry it's so limited, Heinrich. Roúla is genuinely sympathetic, just very scared."

"I'll take it, Nick. It's all I have. And it feels like a lifeline."

*

Roúla had set up a table in the garden for her aunt with a giant blue and white striped parasol and a comfortable outdoor chair. On the table were: a jug of water, a small carafe of honey rakí and a pack of cigarettes. The old lady was reading when the others arrived, and everything seemed normal except that she took no notice of them whatsoever.

"It's okay," said Roúla. "I said I needed to spend time with friends this morning. She'll be fine. She's quite self-contained."

"Won't she be too warm out there?" said Ilse.

"She'll be fine," she repeated, watching Heinrich as he stared at Eléni. "Now, come inside. We can see her better from there."

"The constable and I will wait here, give you some privacy," called Nick, as his phone beeped. Roúla shot him a grateful smile as they filed into the house. The pang of regret it triggered surprised him in its power.

Nick checked his watch. It was just after twelve. He saw from Náni's text that there was still a little time.

*

At one fifteen, Nick re-entered the house and tapped on the door to the kitchen before entering. He saw a table scattered with sepia photographs and coffee cups. Ilse was alone at the table and Nick followed her eyes to the garden to see Roúla helping the old man back towards the house. He was in tears.

"The old lady fell asleep," said Ilse. "Roúla took Heinrich to see her up close. That's all. It's been very difficult for him, all this, but Roúla has been very kind. She's devastated about what happened and says she'll stay in touch, try to get the two of them together at some point."

"I'm glad to hear that," said Nick.

As the others approached, he reached out with both arms and the old man seized them. Nick had seen, as if for the first time, the stoop, the hesitancy in the once-proud walk and he knew Heinrich would never get back to this island.

The old man lifted his head so the red-rimmed, blue eyes bore into Nick's.

"I am so grateful for this, Nick," he said. "Now I understand a little, and I feel proud to be the son of this courageous woman. We will take our grandson home now. It's time to let the world remember him."

Déspina appeared with perfect timing and they walked the old couple to the police car together while Roúla tended to Eléni. At the car, Heinrich gave Nick a fierce hug and Ilse leaned her head on Nick's shoulder, but there was nothing more to be said.

Back inside, Nick saw the garden chair was empty. He was scanning the photographs when Roúla reappeared.

"I took Eléni in for a nap. She was getting too warm out there. Oh, and by the way, Nick. Thanks so much for dropping in last night. I needed that time to absorb what you told me before meeting them. And what a fine, old couple they are. So disciplined and courteous – and so much in love! But I have to say, I'm glad that's over. Now," she said, gathering up the photographs, "do you have time to join me for lunch?"

"That would be lovely, Roúla, but first we need to talk."

"Sounds ominous."

"Please. Let's just sit for a minute."

She finished tidying the photos and sat opposite him at the table. Her eyes shone with intelligence and there was still some warmth there, he felt.

"Roúla." He looked steadily at her and put his hand on hers for the first time. "I think you know I have feelings for you, so this is not easy, believe me."

"Just tell me, Nick."

"A medical team will be here at two thirty. They will take Eléni with them under police supervision. She will undergo various tests and a psychiatric assessment. When the results are available, there will be a meeting between the Investigating Judge, the police and the medics to decide what course of action to take."

"What do you think will happen, Nick?"

"Worst case, they find nothing wrong with her and she is charged with attempted murder. I don't think that's likely, but it *is* possible. However, if the assessment confirms she is delusional and the judge is convinced she acted while in a deluded state, then a period of detention in a secure hospital would be the more probable outcome. If there were no further violent episodes, then Eléni could be released in due course. But the judge will be conscious of her duty to provide the Hedingers with justice for their grandson – retribution – and to protect the public at large."

"Are the Hedingers looking for retribution? I doubt it, somehow. Not now."

"Maybe not, but there's an aspect of justice being *seen to be done*, irrespective."

"*In due course* could be years, though! She could die in there, Nick."

"She could."

"What on earth is the point, Nick? Why can't we just keep her safely here?"

"The judge has to punish crimes and keep the public safe. You know this. To her, this is a potentially dangerous old lady who knows how to kill and has recently tried to kill someone."

"But that's such nonsense, Nick."

"Perhaps. But it's the law, Roúla. You know how the law works."

"Can I at least go with her?"

"No."

"Why the hell not?"

"Because the police will take you into custody at the same time."

"I thought we had a deal, Nick."

"A discussion is needed, at the very least, Roúla. For which you'll need a good lawyer."

She was silent now, pondering her position.

"No-one is going to charge you with murder or attempted murder," Nick went on, "not after Giorgía's suicide note. But the police are angry with you. Your actions were not those of a good citizen, to say the least. You lied to them several times and you were still lying when we came back here after talking in London."

"Everything I did was to protect my family."

"Your lawyer can stress that."

"If I'm charged with *anything*, my career will be over."

"You'll find something. Life goes on."

"I trusted you and you let me down, Nick."

She said nothing further. After a minute, she gave him a bleak look, stood and left the room. He assumed she was preparing Eléni for her ordeal, maybe putting together overnight bags for them both. He felt suddenly empty. Older and wearier. When the clock finally clawed its way to two thirty and the ambulance and the two police cars pulled up, Náni took one look at him and walked him to the side of the garden.

"We'll take it from here, Nick. You look tired. Go get some rest. Then give that son of yours a call."

"You know what, Náni? I think I will."

"And Nick?"

He looked up to see her smiling and extending her hand.

"It hasn't been easy, has it? But well done. And thank you. I'll tell Christodoulákis you were a great help – and mean it. And I hope we'll meet again, one of these days. Now, Níkos is waiting. He'll drop you back to your Jeep when you're ready."

But Nick didn't go right away. As he watched, two medics helped the bewildered, old lady into the ambulance while Roúla looked on. Then he saw her lock the front door of her brother's house. Náni took her elbow gently but firmly and led her to the police car. She did not look in Nick's direction. Not then. As the police car pulled away, Nick was still watching. He knew she would sense his eyes on her, and he knew with increasing certainty that she was not going to turn her pretty head and smile. As the car slowly disappeared down the hill, he knew for sure. It had never really begun, but now it was over.

CHAPTER 29
THE HEALING POWER OF RAKÍ

He pulled over on the drive back and ordered a large lunch in the busy village of Arméni. He sought comfort in food, and this was a good restaurant he knew quite well. Their meat and side dishes were excellent, fish absent. He chewed his way through a beef stifádo, aided by half a litre of good, red wine. But this was no celebration. He was relieved to get free of it all. There had been mistakes. It was a sad, bloody mess most of the time. But at least he survived that marathon swim, against the odds. And now it was over. He finished the wine just as the waiter arrived with watermelon chunks and a carafe of rakí. As he sat there, drinking it, he remembered how difficult it is to get drunk when you want to. *There must be some inborn defence mechanism*, he mused.

The phone beside him beeped for some reason. He picked it up listlessly and saw there were two messages on voicemail.

The first was Leo. After a sign-off call with Náni, he wanted to thank Nick for his help and say well done, once again. He promised to help him spend some of that hard-earned pay on a slap-up dinner, very soon.

Second up was Jason. The boy sounded breathless, super-energised, self-absorbed:

"Hi Dad, it's Jace. Listen, you remember Lenny, my mate from school? Well, he called me the day after you rang and I had no idea how long you'd be tied up with everything, so I said: 'Yes, why the hell not?' And now I'm in Bangkok with him and two other guys! It's brilliant. We're here for a few days then it's off on the night train to Chiang Mai for a five-day trek through the jungle. Then some paradise beach on the east coast. I figured coming here would take the pressure off and let you focus on your case without having to worry about me. Good luck with that, by the way. Anyway, I can come out in

September or something, if that works for you. Might be just a week, though. Hope that's okay. Bye."

Nick groaned and slumped forward with his head in his hands. He sat like that for a full minute until the waiter approached him, concerned, but then his shoulders started to shake. When he looked up, he was still chuckling. Then he shook his head and a rueful smile spread across his face and the waiter smiled with him. Perhaps the boy was a chip off the old block after all. The selfish, little sod.

He stood then, tucked a twenty euro note under the empty carafe and waved thank you as he stumbled out of the restaurant. Outside, he breathed a huge sigh of relief. It was still warm, and it was wonderful to feel the wind in his hair again as he drove his beloved Jeep up the hill, past the artificial football pitch on the left, the stoneworks on the right. Over the brow, amongst rolling, silver-green hills with the timeless peaks of Psilorítis rising in the distance, he broke into a weary smile. It had worked out after all, as it always did. They'd solved a difficult case. Apart from Lukas, no-one died who didn't choose to. All the guilty parties were nailed, with any luck.

There was still one beer in the fridge if he remembered right. When he got home, he would put on that Dexter Gordon album, take the beer to the roof terrace and watch another glorious sunset unfold. The sky would streak with magenta, the face of Kédros would turn a dusty pink and the horizon would melt in an orange and crimson blaze. But he would save the first sip for that magical moment when the horizon eclipsed the last of the sun. And he would remember. As he would always remember, now.

And then this unstoppable planet would roll round to another day. Maybe it would be a brighter, easier one.

THE END

LEAVING A REVIEW

If you have enjoyed reading my book, it would be wonderful if you could find a minute to complete a short review of *Beneath the Stone* on your chosen retailer's website. Thank you!

Alex

THANK YOU

One person made a significant contribution to this novel. Together, we devised the original plot outline for *Beneath the Stone* and the character and back story for *Nick Fisher*. She also provided a detailed critique of the final draft of this novel and came up with ideas and changes, most of which I adopted. She is my very good friend Leonie Carter McMahon and she has my sincere thanks and gratitude for her continuing help and support. I hope that she will be publishing her own novel before too long.

I would also like to thank my brave beta readers, including George Schrijver, Sarah Toonen, Terri Jones, Dr David Tune, Christine and Bob Hoare, Kathrina Valters, Peter and Denise Simon. Your feedback and support made all the difference to me and, without doubt, helped me improve the quality of the book.

Thanks also to my newsletter subscribers and all those who have been kind enough to leave reviews or make comments on Amazon, Facebook, Goodreads, or anywhere else. It's challenging for a new author without the marketing muscle of a major publisher to achieve any kind of visibility in today's fiercely competitive marketplace and letting the world know that you enjoyed my books is extremely helpful and important to me. I read every comment and review and am very grateful to those who have taken the trouble to do this.

And lastly, but by no means least, thank you for buying and reading this novel. I hope you enjoyed it and will seek out more Nick Fisher novels and perhaps also give my short stories a try. You can see all my published writing at www.alexdunlevy.com

ABOUT THE AUTHOR

Alex abandoned a career in finance at the age of forty-nine and spent a few years staring at the Mediterranean, contemplating life and loss. Finally, he accepted what his heart had always known. So, he joined a local writing group and he began to write.

He has now completed two novels in a series of intelligent crime thrillers set on the island of Crete and featuring British protagonist Nick Fisher. *The Unforgiving Stone* was the well-received debut, awarded 5 stars by 65% of its Amazon reviewers (overall average 4.6) and earning a B.R.A.G medallion in the USA. *Beneath the Stone* is the second in this series.

Alex has also published a collection of short stories, *The Late Shift Specialist*. These are quite different from his crime writing. Uniquely personal – and quirky, funny or sad – they are written straight from the heart.

Simultaneously, he has been working on other ideas including a black comedy set in the world of corporate finance and a bitter-sweet, coming-of-age story set in the 1960s.

Born in Derbyshire, Alex now divides his time between Wiltshire, England and Crete, Greece, where he has an old, stone house in the central south of the island, between the Amari Valley and the Libyan Sea.

CONTACT

If you would like to get in touch with Alex, please visit his website: www.alexdunlevy.com where you can register for his newsletters, if you wish, listen to him read, and find out more about his writing. Alternatively, just drop an email to: alexdunlevyauthor@gmail.com

He can also be found on Facebook and Twitter.

ALSO BY ALEX DUNLEVY

The Unforgiving Stone
(the first novel in the Nick Fisher series)

The Late Shift Specialist
(a collection of short stories)

Printed in Great Britain
by Amazon

18060093R00164